DAWNING GOLD

An evocation of rural Kent in the 1950s...

When, fresh from a boys-only public school, 16-year-old Graham opts to become a novice farmer, he is quickly plunged into a world of completely new experiences. Shy and knowing nothing of girls, he encounters the friendly banter and innuendo of his co-workers who, in the course of showing him the ropes, also set him up for his first sexual experience. Flattened by a herd of bullocks on his first morning, he quickly learns how to fork potatoes, cut cabbages and feed the cattle – in all weathers. Graham's story takes you straight into the sights and smells of the 1950s farming world.

DAWNING GOLD

DAWNING GOLD

by

Graham Davis-Cooke

Magna Large Print Books
Long Preston, North Yorkshire,
BD23 4ND, England.

British Library Cataloguing in Publication Data.

Davis-Cooke, Graham
    Dawning gold.

        A catalogue record of this book is
        available from the British Library

        ISBN   978-0-7505-3332-4

First published in Great Britain in 2008 by The Book Guild Ltd.

Cover illustration by arrangement with Book Guild Publishing

The right of Graham Davis-Cooke to be identified as the author
of this work has been asserted by him in accordance with the
Copyright, Designs and Patents Act, 1988

Published in Large Print 2011 by arrangement with
Book Guild Publishing

Magna Large Print is an imprint of Library Magna Books Ltd.

Printed and bound in Great Britain by
T.J. (International) Ltd., Cornwall, PL28 8RW

Dedication

Firstly, to Joan, my wife. Without her constant support and encouragement this book would never have been written.

Secondly, to all the women that worked on market garden farms in the 50s and 60s everywhere, but especially in Kent.

They were the salt of the earth and my heart and thanks go out to them.

Their earthy humour and fantastic endurance was the spur that got me through my early days on the farm and set me on a way of life I have loved all my life.

I thank you all.

Chapter 1

The 4th of January 1954 – this date is frozen into my memory. It was on this day that my working life and career in farming began.

I was sixteen and a half years old, fresh from the insular and cloistered life of a boys-only public school and bursting with enthusiasm and the boundless energy that teenagers have. I lived with my parents. My Dad was the owner of a ship repairing business by the side of the Thames and my Mum ran the firm's office. We lived in a detached house on the outskirts of a small village in Kent. I had a brother, Barry, who was seven years older than me and was an engineer on tankers in the Merchant Navy, so he was away at sea for long spells.

I disliked school, I really do not know why. It could be that it was so far from home. I had a three-mile bike ride to the railway station and a 15-minute train ride plus a mile walk the other end. The whole lot to do again to get home, so it was a long day. I enjoyed the Junior Training Corps and sport. I was a reasonable Rugby player and represented the school at Colts level.

My decision to go into farming was

motivated by this dislike of school and was a way of persuading my parents to let me leave. They, of course, wanted me to stay on and take all those exams, go to college and on to a life as an accountant or some other 'posh' type job. I had other ideas.

'I want to farm,' I told them. 'What good will a load of exams and a college degree do me out in the middle of a ploughed field.' The logic of youth!

I don't think it was really this argument that persuaded them so much as the knowledge that I would not put any more effort into my studies. They finally agreed that I could leave at the end of Autumn term 1953.

I had, after all, been born in the country. I had always been an 'outdoor' child, running around in the fields and woods, making bows and arrows and enjoying the unlimited freedom that the countryside offered. There was no way I could ever settle for an 'indoor' job.

The cottage I grew up in and where I lived until the age of eleven had no mains electricity and no mains water. We had oil lamps to see by and us kids had a regular evening chore pumping up water to the roof tank for the next day's use. It took about an hour depending on previous day's usage. To many this may sound an idyllic life but it did mean that I met very few people outside the family and, as a consequence, grew up with a chronic shyness that led to what was almost a fear of new contacts. I would blush easily and had difficulty with conversation. School had improved this a little but there was still an area that I had big problems with: girls.

My contact with the opposite sex up to this point had been zero. I regarded them as soft boys, and had no knowledge, apart from school textbooks, of the difference between the sexes. There would be the odd smuggled picture of a topless female circulating around school but nothing more. I was about as unprepared as it is possible to be to enter the life I had chosen.

My father knew, by reputation, of a good farmer in the next village about four miles away. His name was John Willis, and Dad asked him if he would consider taking me on as farm apprentice. He said he would, subject to me going for an interview and to let him 'look me over'.

This was duly arranged for a day in the week before Christmas. I was more and more nervous as the day approached and began to wonder if I had, in fact, done the right thing. I thought it might have been better to stay on at school after all. The night before, I tossed and turned in bed and found sleep impossible but somehow managed to wash and dress in the morning. I couldn't face breakfast. After a lot of pacing up and down I set off on my bike for the 10.30 appointment.

Right on time I cycled up the tarred drive to Manor Farm house. It was a rather gaunt, square type of property, the walls pebble dashed, the paintwork green and peeling in places. I lent my bike against the wall and, with great trepidation, knocked on the front door. The house was right next to the yard and the smell of hay and cattle was clear on the air. A tractor was moving about and I could hear the sound of men's voices. It seemed a busy place.

My knock had produced no reply (it was later that I found that no one ever called at the front door of a farmhouse) so I followed a concrete path round the side of the house to a well-trodden paved one that led to the back door. This door proved to be unlatched and my knock opened it a few inches. Like magic a Jack Russell terrier shot out through the gap barking and set about trying to grab my trouser leg. It eventually succeeded and started to shake it enthusiastically. The dog was followed a very short time later by a middle-aged lady who was wiping her hands on a tea towel.

'Get away, Smudge, you little devil,' she shouted at the dog at the same time aiming a kick at it. The dog avoided the kick with ease but in doing so let go of my trouser leg and retreated down the path.

'I'm so sorry,' the lady said looking upset. 'I'm Mrs Willis and you must be Graham, come to see my husband.'

'That's right, please don't worry about the dog, there's no harm done,' I replied.

She held out her hand. 'I'm very pleased to meet you,' she was smiling now, 'do come inside.'

I shook her hand and followed her down a cream-painted passage to a brown doorway, leading off. The smell of newly baked bread wafted in the air and I regretted my missed breakfast. I had noticed that Mrs Willis was wearing a pinafore and had a smear of flour on one cheek.

'This is John's office,' she said. 'He won't be long. He's just gone to talk to Bert. Take a seat.' She moved some copies of *Farmers Weekly* and *Farmer and Stockbreeder* from an upright chair and held out a hand towards it.

'Would you like a cup of tea?' she asked.

'No, I'm fine thanks,' I replied.

'I'll get on then.' She smiled again and left the room and I heard her call in the terrier and scold it.

I looked around the room. A large leather-topped desk stood against the wall, beside the door I had entered by. It was the type that has got lots of little drawers in front of the writing area. It was cluttered with invoices, seed catalogues, shooting magazines and one or two odd-shaped bits of machinery, some of which were obviously broken. A number of 12-bore shotgun cartridges were laid among the other odds and ends. A solid-looking chair with a leather seat stood in front of it. The wall behind me was one long floor-to-ceiling cupboard, the top half glass fronted and behind the glass a row of shotguns and rifles gleaming in the light. The bottom section was all drawers. One was partly open, revealing assorted boxes of ammunition.

I was keen on shooting and had a .410 shotgun of my own so was more than impressed with this array of guns, of which there must have been about a dozen. Hanging on the back of the door was an assortment of wet-weather gear, a couple of well-worn caps and in the corner a collection of sticks, some with carved bone handles. The only window, on the right of the desk, looked out over the yard. The back wall had a sort of sideboard with two cupboard doors. The top covered with instruction books for various bits of machinery, a check tweed jacket, more catalogues and magazines and in the middle of it all a black and white cat was sleeping. It was a man's room without doubt.

A couple of minutes later I heard voices

from the direction of the back door and in a few seconds Mr Willis entered the study. He was well over 6ft in height, broad-shouldered, not stout but heavily built. His dark hair was greying at the temples and he had the weather-beaten face of an outdoor person. Crow's feet around his eyes gave him a friendly appearance.

He was wearing corduroy trousers and a tweed-type jacket over a check shirt and a pale brown tie and was in his socks. (This was something else I soon learned: one arrived at the door in gum boots, slipped them off and walked around indoors in socks, all ready to slip straight into the boots and be off again outdoors.)

If you had seen Mr Willis in the street you would know beyond doubt that he was a farmer. He couldn't have been anything else.

I stood up as he entered. 'Hello,' he said smiling at me and offered me a hand to shake that I could hardly span. It felt hard and rough.

'Good morning Mr Willis,' I started nervously, blushing 'it's good of you to see me. You must be very busy.'

'So you want to learn how to farm, do you?' His voice was warm and friendly and I started to feel more at ease. I nodded.

'It's a hard life to choose,' he went on, sitting down in front of the desk. 'Do you

17

think you will stick at it? The hours are long at times and it can be wet and cold.'

'It's what I want to do,' I told him. 'I'm keen to learn, I've always lived in the countryside and I like being outdoors.'

He asked me my exact age and a few other details, then he sat back and looked at me.

'All right,' he said, 'I'll give you a chance to see what you are made of.' He looked at the calendar on the wall beside the desk, the date section under pictures of prize cattle, and lifted it to reveal next year's underneath.

'You can start on January the fourth,' he said without turning round.

He turned back to me and went on: 'The hours are seven a.m. to five p.m. Monday to Friday and seven to twelve on Saturday.' He thought for a moment. 'I'll put you with Tom, he's our stockman, for the first day. He'll show you the ropes around the yard. You meet up with Tom here in the yard on the fourth.'

He made some notes in a new shiny desk diary and, without looking up, said: 'Bring some grub and tea with you. We have a break for half an hour at nine in the morning and lunch from one to two. Tom will introduce you to anyone who's about. We have got nine men and six women full time at the moment but that can go up and down.'

He put down his pen and looked at me

again. 'Is there anything you want to know, any questions?' he asked.

'No,' I said, 'thank you for taking me on. I'll do the best I can.'

He got up, put on his cap, and ushered me outside. The terrier poked its head around a door further down the passage, but when it saw who I was with it made no sound and bobbed back inside. Mr Willis slipped into his gum boots at the back door, and showed me out.

Outside he held out his hand again and as we shook said: 'You'll have to do what you're told, mind – no messing around.' With that we parted, he to the yard and me round to the front of the house to collect my bike.

I jumped on and pedalled down the drive (which looked as if it was hardly ever used) and back up the lane towards home.

I was so excited at the prospect of starting work that I had a job to contain myself until my parents got home and I was able to tell them the news. Mum was pleased I had the position but, as usual, very worried about me being outdoors in all weather and wanting to take up such a 'hard life' as she put it.

'You'll have to go to town with your father,' she said, 'and get some warm work clothes and some boots.'

The weekend duly found me in the local

town's Army Surplus Store, there being kitted out with a green, waterproof, three-quarter-length coat, blue beret, leather gloves, thick check shirts and some short fur-lined boots; also a haversack – all bought for me by my father ready for the big day.

'You'll be able to pay for things like this yourself soon,' he said as he settled the bill. It was only then that I realised that I had not asked Mr Willis what the pay would be.

When I arrived back home I went to my bedroom and tried on all my new gear. On reflection I shudder to think what the rest of the staff at Manor Farm thought. They must have been hard put to keep a straight face as the usual farm wear, I later found, was the roughest garb one could lay hands on, tied round the middle with a piece of baler twine.

Chapter 2

Christmas passed and the New Year opened brightly. The weekend before Monday 4 January I busied myself around the garden helping Dad with odd jobs, clearing leaves and tidying up. I was trying to take my mind off the approaching day. I remember thinking what an awful time 6.15 was as I set my alarm for the morning. I was then unable to sleep, my mind in a turmoil thinking about the people I would have to meet and talk to. I must have dozed off eventually, only to be startled by the alarm in the darkness of the bedroom.

I dragged myself from my warm bed and dressed with shaking fingers. On arriving downstairs I found Dad with breakfast cooked and tea ready to pour. Meal over, I packed tea-break snack and lunch sandwiches into my haversack, slung it over my shoulder and was ready to go.

'Well, good luck,' Dad said, 'tell us all about it tonight.'

'Thanks for everything,' I called, 'see you later.'

I collected my bike from the garage and pedalled away into the darkness, my eyes watering in the chill January air. I arrived at the farm flushed and breathless at 6.55. My eyes now accustomed to the gloom. I picked out an open-fronted implement shed to the right of the gateway so I pushed my bike into there and walked back out into the yard. There was not a sign of anyone. I could hear the rustling sound of animals moving around in straw and now and then one would give a low moo or cough. The wind moaned around the buildings and I was cooling rapidly after my ride.

I pulled my nice new coat tighter around me and retreated back into the shed. At least it gave some protection from the wind. I got steadily colder and anxious and was mightily relieved when, at around 7.25, as the sky was beginning to show signs of light, I heard the sound of footsteps coming down the yard.

A large figure loomed out of the darkness so I moved out from the shed.

'Hello, yew must be t'new lad?' a soft voice asked.

'That's right,' I replied, 'my name's Graham.'

'I'm Tom. Boss said yew'd be 'ere s'marnin. Come wit I an us'll gowan see ta lay bullocks.' I followed his outline through the gaining light to a building at the top of the yard.

There was more activity now. Voices behind me called good morning to each other.

A cock had started crowing, to be answered by another somewhere beyond where we were and a crow over the lane began calling to its mate.

'Bide 'ere a mo,' came Tom's voice. 'I'll gowan put us some lights on.'

He vanished into the building and seconds later lights came on, illuminating where I stood and floodlighting the cattle yard but turning everywhere else jet black again. This was broken by some lights coming on in the shed where I had left my bike.

Tom returned, to be revealed in the light as a tall lean man, grey hair showing round his cap, wearing glasses and bib and brace-type overalls under an old, unbuttoned, army-greatcoat. In all the time I was to know him, in all weathers, I never once saw it buttoned up.

He came over to me and held out his hand. As we shook I could see him looking over my new attire but he made no comment.

'Yew see that door at t'end of the yard there?' He pointed to a tarred board door in the end of a big barn.

The end of the barn formed part of the wall of the yard. I could now see where the rustling I had heard was coming from. There were around thirty bullocks looking expectantly towards us. Dotted among them were round wooden troughs on legs.

'Pop in thar an' grab two bales of 'ay for each crib in t'yard while I give they their barley and spuds.' He walked off. One or two of the bullocks started to moo at the prospect of their approaching breakfast.

I opened the gate and entered the yard, being careful to close it behind me. The bullocks eyed me with some suspicion as I was a stranger and many of them stopped chewing the cud to appraise me fully.

They watched me carefully as I made my way to the door Tom had indicated. It opened inwards into the barn and allowance had been made when filling it with bales. It was also a lot taller than a normal door, to allow for the rise in the depth of muck in the yard.

I pulled out the retaining pin, which was on the end of a piece of light chain, and pushed open the door.

The sweet smell of hay was almost over-powering. I went in and it was like entering a bale cave, the stack towered up into darkness in steps where some had been used. Every one I tried to shift seemed to have another pinning it down. Eventually I wrestled one free and staggered out into the yard. God, it's heavy, I thought, as I lugged it to the nearest crib, the strings hurting my fingers, and set it down beside. There was no way I could have lifted it in.

The bullocks were now in a line down the opposite side of the yard, their heads in a long trough that stretched for two-thirds of that side. The trough was under a lean-to-type building with a tiled roof, the front supported by heavy, tarred wooden pillars. Tom emerged from the end of the line, an empty sack under his arm.

'Have yew got a knife?' he called to me. When I told him I hadn't, he came over and held out a pocket knife with a bone handle and a large curved blade.

'Don't 'e lose un, mind, twill pay 'e ta git one o' thy own, lame allus 'andy.' While he was talking he took the knife from me, flicked it open, picked up the bale with one hand and swung it into the crib cutting the strings as he did so.

'That's the idea, two o' lay in each crib.' He handed back the knife, picked up the sack from where he had laid it and walked off towards the gate.

I returned to the barn and, as I did so, noticed that the darkness had eased and streaks of light were beginning to appear in the eastern sky among the dark clouds.

Back in the barn I once again started to heave and tug at the bales but to no avail. I was unable to free any of them. I'll have to get Tom to give me a hand I thought, so leaving the barn I made my way to the gate. Some of the bullocks had now finished their breakfast and were starting to back away from the long trough.

They began to spread out into the yard in search of their hay that I had not yet provided. I opened and carefully closed and latched the gate and went in search of Tom. I found him just round the corner of the building climbing a flight of stone steps, a sack on his shoulder.

'Finished already?' he called.

'No,' I called back. 'I need a hand to pull out the bales.'

''Ang on,' he held the sack with one hand and opened the green-painted door at the top of the steps.

He went inside and I heard a thump as he dropped the sack off his shoulder. He reappeared at once and trotted down the steps to join me.

'Can be a job ta git they bales out when barn be full,' he said. 'I reckon we'll 'av ta chuck a few down from top else whole lot'll fall in a bury some poor bugger.'

We made our way back into the yard and across to the barn door ... which I had not shut. The bullocks had decided that self-service was the order of the day and were jammed into the entrance, one or two right inside.

Tom went down the side of them shouting at them to come out while I started smacking their rumps to try and make them move. Like most animals they knew they were in the wrong and reversed rapidly out at Tom's shouts. That was fine except for the fact that I was right behind them. The first one knocked me flat and most of the rest trampled over me. Fortunately the muck was soft so I escaped with a few bruises. Tom held out his hand and pulled me from the mire, my nice new kit now very much the worse for wear.

I looked at Tom who was laughing so much the tears were streaking his face.

'I reckon that be lesson number one yew,' he said still chuckling, 'never stand behind they cus they wun't care if youm in their way, they do jist keep a'comin.'

I certainly looked more the part now with dirty trousers and a stained coat and my face streaked with muck. The bullocks were now standing in a half circle round us, swishing their tails, coughing and sticking their tongues up their noses still waiting for their hay.

Tom went into the barn telling me to stop outside and keep 'they buggers' out. Looking in I saw him start to climb up the stepped face of the stack and soon, amid a cloud of dust, a number of bales came tumbling down from above. In a trice he was back down and, swinging one bale on his back and, picking up another in his other hand, set off for the farthest crib.

'Follow I round and cut they strings, we'll be done in no time,' he instructed. 'Be sure to cut 'em at t'knots, yew'll find out why when thy go's cabbage cuttin'.'

'Bring the string and my knife t'ware yew found I jest now.' He left me to it and I couldn't help but be amazed at his strength and dexterity.

He had all the cribs filled before I had cut the strings in the third. The bullocks were pushing and shoving round each one and pulling out hay regardless of any string. I wondered as I worked if I would ever be able to lift two bales at once and throw them around as Tom had just done. I managed to complete the task in spite of being jostled and having my feet trodden on and, cut strings in one hand and Tom's knife in the other, went in search of him.

The sky had now lightened to the colour of lead and dark clouds were scudding across it, chased by the freshening wind. I was quite warm from my close encounters with the bullocks and from turning the bales in the cribs to get at the knots, which was where Tom had said they had to be cut, so the conditions did not bother me. I found Tom in an open-fronted shed that contained what was obviously a grinding mill for corn.

To one side was a beet chopper with a long handle and beneath it a freshly cut pile. Tom had been busy. I gave him his knife and the bundle of string which he hung over a wire, like a washing line, that was stretched across the back of the shed. There was already lots hanging there and I wondered what it would be used for.

The yard in front of the shed where I had left my bike was now quite busy; a tractor had started up and gone and several people were moving around. I noticed some of them were women in headscarves and long coats. Some of them had sacks draped around their shoulders for extra protection.

I followed Tom as he went about what were obviously his daily chores. We mixed rolled barley, from bags by the mill, with the chopped beet. It was just mixed on the floor like cement and Tom showed me the right way to hold a bag so that it could be easily shovelled into. Having got one lot bagged up, we went off with a wheelbarrow, to the clamp that was alongside the yard wall and fetched more fodder beet. I threw them into the chopper while Tom turned the big handle. It was now daylight and I could see the big tythe barn that was the centre of the yard and a green-painted corrugated iron implement shed, its front open, its back to the lane.

'Tis quicker wid two,' Tom said. 'I might not 'ave yew wid I tomarry.'

Having chopped up the barrow load Tom declared that: 'Tis time for us brekfas'.'

'If yew goes roun' t'other side of the big

barn there,' he pointed to where there was a track from the yard, 'yew'll find the rest of they roun thar wit a fire an yew can 'av a warm up and eat.'

With that he went off towards the farm house (I found out later that he was a cousin of Mr Willis and had his breaks in the house).

The farmyard was now deserted, all having gone for their break. I could hear laughter and voices coming from where Tom had indicated. I collected my haversack from my bike but shyness and embarrassment prevented me from going round to join the others by their fire. Instead I headed for the big barn. There was a big sliding door in the long wall facing the yard which I pushed open enough to slip inside. There was just enough light to enable me to climb onto the hay bales where I made myself comfortable and had a cup of tea from my flask. I left early to replace my haversack, not wishing to meet any one else, and walked back up to the cattle yard. Tom was coming towards me.

'Bide 'ere a mo,' he said. 'Boss'll pick 'e up int Land-Rover an tak 'e fer a ride aroun' farm and show 'e where 'tis all to.'

Even as he spoke a Land-Rover came from the direction of the house and stopped beside us. Tom opened the door and Mr Willis called for me to get in.

'How's it going?' he asked. 'Tom tells me you were looking a bit downtrodden' – this said with a wide grin on his face.

'He's larnt 'is first lesson,' Tom said over my shoulder. He shut the door and walked off.

'Did those bullocks do you any harm, you know, cuts or bruises?' Mr Willis asked as he drove out of the yard and down the lane.

'No, well a few bruises, nothing serious,' I told him.

'Well, you won't make that mistake again,' he was smiling again. 'Looks like you've christened that new kit your wearing.'

He turned off the lane onto a muddy land-way that went between two fields and then round the side of a wood. As we drove he told me about the farm. It was 400 acres and, because of its proximity to London, just 25 miles, specialised in market garden crops. He said that they also grew around 100 acres of corn and 60 acres of peas for the new freezing works. He gave me a sort of running commentary about what was in, or going in, each field along with its name and acreage.

We drove to the high point of his land and he pointed out the boundary. It seemed an enormous area. Driving on he talked about farming in general and pointed out items of interest, stopping now and again to look at a crop or just to walk on a field prodding it with his stick. Every time he got out the three dogs in the back piled out. There were two Labradors, one black, one golden plus Smudge.

'What are the dogs' names?' I asked.

'Black one's Harry, wonderful gun dog but he's getting a bit past it. The other one's Gertie, she's a young dog belonged to a friend of mine who died recently, so I took her in. Missus tells me you've met Smudge.'

I never heard him call the dogs but they were always in the back when we drove off. We came out of the landway on to another lane and, a short way on, he turned into another farmyard. There was a sizeable barn, a Dutch barn and an assortment of open-fronted implement sheds. I could see a threshing machine backed into one of the bays in the largest of these. He stopped in the middle of the yard and got out and I joined him.

'I bought this farm about six years ago,' he said. 'Previous owner drank himself half to death and never looked after it. Went bust in the end. These buildings and the land all were on our boundary so now they all come inside our ring fence. We contract out the threshing machine all round the area. In fact it's due out this week. A lot of farmers will be threshing their stacks now that Christmas is over.'

The sound of hammering came from the direction of the thresher. We walked over and up alongside the machine.

'Ted,' Mr Willis called. The hammering stopped and a short, thin, wiry man emerged

32

from the back. He was wearing a boiler suit and the most greasy cap I had ever seen. I would say he was in his forties.

'Marnin Boss,' he grinned showing yellow tobacco-stained teeth. 'Didn't 'ear yew drive in.'

Mr Willis turned to me. 'Ted, this is Graham. He's sort of farm apprentice at the moment.' Ted and I shook hands.

'All ready for Wednesday?' Mr Willis asked.

'Jest got to put a couple more rivets in that walker and she's ready to go,' Ted replied, taking roll-up material out of his overall pocket and starting to fashion a cigarette.

'Good man. Walter will come with you as usual.'

Ted finished his roll up and lit up, dragging the smoke deep down into his lungs.

'Shouldn't tak us too long over at Baxters,' he said, the smoke reappearing with every word.

'Right, we'll let you get on,' Mr Willis turned away. Ted lifted his hand to me.

'See you about I 'spect,' he called.

'That place is called Hills Ley,' Mr Willis said as we turned out and drove up the lane, 'and this is Oldbarn Lane.'

'Oh, this comes out on the lane I come down to Manor Farm. I've never been this far along it,' I told him.

He turned along another landway and

pulled up alongside some sheep that were penned behind wire netting. The netting was tied to light wooden stakes, and Tom was there rolling out more to put up another fence. Mr Willis explained that the sheep did not belong to him but were brought in by a neighbouring farmer whenever there were the remnants of market crops to be eaten off.

'Helps him because he can carry more stock and helps me because the sheep do the land a power of good. They are on what's left of the Christmas cabbage that we cut,' he said.

Where Tom was putting up his fence the field was covered in stalks, leaves and old 'blowy' cabbages not fit for market. The area where the sheep were penned was eaten bare, so it was easy to see the logic of what Mr Willis was telling me.

We alighted from the Land-Rover, the dogs being told to stay, and walked over to Tom. There was a strong smell of rotting cabbages and sheep. I looked around the open fields around us, my eyes watering in the chill wind. I wouldn't want to be a sheep I thought. They were baaing loudly because they knew that soon they would be let into a new area to eat off.

'Everything OK, Tom,' Mr Willis said as we arrived with him.

'Ah, lame lookin' good yew,' Tom replied, pausing in his work.

I discovered after a while that lots of Kentish country folk finished a sentence with the word 'you' or 'yew' as they pronounced it.

Mr Willis was looking round the sky that was still leaden with black clouds building up.

'I reckon there could be some snow around, it's cold enough,' he observed.

'They bin forecastin' it for tonight, we could do without un,' Tom replied.

Mr Willis walked off to look at the sheep and I watched as Tom worked along the unrolled netting, stopping at each stake to make a hole with a pointed iron bar. A 'pitcher' it was called, Tom told me. The pitcher was about 5ft long and the top of it where his hands slid up and down as he made the holes was polished like a piece of stainless steel. I wondered how many holes, days and months it took to polish an ordinary steel bar like that, just by use.

Mr Willis returned and we said goodbye to Tom and made our way back to the Land-Rover. The dogs had not got out but were hanging as far as possible over the tailgate watching to see where we were. Their tails were going like mad as they saw us returning. Driving off, I looked back and could see Tom lifting the wire netting and dropping the stakes into the holes he had made. He gave each one a couple of thumps with the pitcher just to firm it in. The sheep would soon be happy in a new pen and Tom could roll up the one they were in now, ready to repeat the process all over again tomorrow.

Chapter 3

Arriving back at the yard, Mr Willis drove round the end of the big barn, the way Tom had indicated I should go to breakfast, and into a second yard. This was formed by the back wall of the big barn, another implement shed across the end, and a six-bay Dutch barn on the other side. A small black shed stood alone on the way in. I later found this was the fuel shed with pumps for petrol and tvo/paraffin.

The Dutch barn appeared to have the further four bays full of baled straw. In the next bay I could see full sacks were stacked neatly, two high. In the first bay the back of a red combine was visible with the words 'Massey Harris' on either side, and there were also some sheaves of straw.

'The girls are riddling spuds here,' Mr Willis said. 'I'll put you with Bert, he's our foreman, he'll show you what goes on and sort you out for the rest of the day.'

My heart gave a lurch and my mouth went dry at the prospect of meeting all these new people. He stopped by the bay with the sacks and walked inside with me following nervously behind. I was amazed to find that the straw bales were only a wall, as was the other side, and the whole four bays were a huge potato store. Two and a half bays had already been emptied. Drawn up to the face of the heap was the riddle. A motor-driven tube around 3ft in diameter made of heavy mesh was revolving, on the heap end of which was a heavy wire hopper into which a woman was shovelling the spuds. The tube sloped away from the heap so the crop was passed through it by the rotation. This allowed any soil or small potatoes, 'chats', to fall through and down chutes into boxes. The good, 'ware', potatoes, were then spilled on to a wooden-slatted elevator that allowed any soil still remaining to fall through. Two women on either side checked for cut ones or stones. The elevator ended with a wooden box with a flap-over bottom. This had hooks underneath to take two sacks. When one was full the flap was swung over and that sack could be changed without stopping the flow. The 1cwt jute sacks were then tied and stacked two high awaiting collection. A man and a woman were looking after that end of the operation.

It was gloomy between the bale walls. The riddling operation was illuminated by two bare light bulbs hanging from lengths of baler twine. The bulbs lit the work area but increased the darkness around and gave the whole scene a Dickensian feel, especially as the women were in rough coats and head-scarves and wore tatty mittens. They glanced up briefly as we entered.

Mr Willis called out 'Good morning all', and was greeted in return by a chorus of 'Marnin Boss' with no pause in the work.

He introduced me to the man bagging off.

'Graham this is Bert, our foreman.' We shook hands. Bert was, I would say late thirties, dark hair showing round his cap, with an easy smile that crinkled the sides of his pale blue eyes. I liked him at once and we always got on well from then on. He was a jolly, easy-going man and had a ready wit. He ruled the farm women and got the very best out of them, but was always ready to laugh with them even when the joke was on him.

Mr Willis then turned to the woman whom he introduced as Katie. She was quite small – around 5ft 5in – and a lot younger than the others, probably early twenties I thought. She was the only one not wearing a head-scarf but had her hair tied back with a coloured bandanna. It was shoulder length, almost black, and hung in waves and ringlets and this combined with the bandanna, gave her a gypsy appearance. She held out her hand and it was then I noticed her impish eyes that seemed to have a sparkle of their own. She held my hand for longer than a normal handshake and I could feel those eyes appraising me. Looking at them caused stirrings I had not had through female contact before and when she finally released my hand, I felt a red blush spread over my face and inwardly cursed it.

Mr Willis called out again: 'This is Graham, he's the new 'prentice so you will see him around.'

They all waved and called hello.

'End of today us'll 'av enough bagged fur they two loads youm bin on about,' Bert said to Mr Willis. 'That'll leave us clear ta start cuttin they January Kings.'

'Good going, Bert,' Mr Willis replied. He walked over and looked into the hopper where the bags were being filled. In a slightly raised voice that could be heard by the women sorting beside the conveyor he said.

'I hope there are not too many stones or cuts going in here.' This with a bit of a grin on his face.

In a trice one of the women, I found later was called Anna, turned to him and flared up.

'No thar fuckin' ain't in spite of yew keepin' on push, push to git yar bleedin' loads out. If yew ain't got nuffin' better to do, fuck off back tew your office an let us git on.'

Mr Willis put his head back and roared with laughter. Bert leaned towards me and said: 'Boss loves stirrin' up old Anna, she allus bites.'

Mr Willis came over still smiling. 'Stay here with Bert, you can help clear away the boxes of dirt and chats, and don't get stirring up the girls. They are a hard crew.' He walked off chuckling to himself.

When he had left, Anna looked up with a big smile on her wrinkled, weather-beaten face.

'That's made 'is day,' she chortled. 'He allus like to wind I up, so I lets rip to keep 'im 'appy.'

Her outburst had amazed me. It was certainly the first time I had ever heard a woman use language like that.

Bert showed me how to change over the boxes of dirt and chats and as they took a while to fill up, I was able to walk around and see how everything worked.

Bert was lifting the full sacks off the riddle straight on to a weighing machine where Katie was correcting the weight by putting some in or taking some out. She then tied the sack by making a small cut through the sides of the sack in the middle. Then, folding a piece of baler twine in half, she passed the loop through the two cuts, the ends then went through the loop and were pulled tight. This secured the middle of the sack. The two long ends of twine then went out to the sides where the two corners were twisted into ears, the string was then tied round the base of the ears and the ends trimmed off.

The finished job was a 1cwt sack tied up tight and easy to move with the two ears on the top. Bert and Katie used a stick to move the full sacks to the heap. The stick was placed nearly at the bottom and with one hand lifting the stick and the other holding an ear they had no problem in carrying and stacking the sacks.

While I watched this operation it was not possible to miss the fact that Katie was a very attractive woman and every so often her eyes would catch mine and she would open them wide and pass her tongue over her lips.

I had no idea what was going on but decided to enjoy it what ever it was!

Moving down to the front of the riddle and to the impressive heap of spuds that were being sorted, I found a lone woman feeding in the crop with a wide fork. This fork had raised sides and each tine had a ball on the end like a marble, which prevented any damage to the spuds as they were shovelled in.

'Hello, I'm Ruth,' she smiled. 'I 'spect you're at a loss trying to remember all the names.'

'Well I've not actually met all that many yet,' I replied blushing because I thought it sounded a bit posh.

'You'll soon git to know everyone, an a right ole mob they are. 'Ere, do yew want to 'av a go with the fork?'

'Well I'll give it a go,' I said taking it from her.

The first thing I found was that a forkful of spuds is very heavy and I had to tip a few off in order to swing the load into the machine. The next problem was accuracy. I found half the forkful going in the riddle and the rest bouncing down the sides of the rotating mesh.

After a while, however, I got the hang of it. It was a knack which involved having the fork at a sharp angle to the hopper and stopping it with a jerk so that all the spuds flew into the opening.

Ruth watched for a while, then moved to the other end, stopping to talk to the women at the conveyor. Now and again they would glance in my direction so I guessed I was being discussed. She stooped to move the boxes I was supposed to be looking after, so I carried on shovelling.

I continued to feed the riddle for around half an hour when Bert gave a loud whistle, and when I looked he held up his hand for me to stop. After a few moments the last of the potatoes in the machine fed through and up the conveyor. Once it was empty Bert went to the motor, flipped over a lever, and everything coasted to a standstill.

The women with Anna moved away and stretched themselves, moving their shoulders and getting the stiffness out of their joints.

'Christ, me effin back's locked solid,' said one bending forward with her hands on her knees.

'Make sure yew know where Bert is afore yew stan aroun' like that,' Anna cackled. 'He's like a bleedin' ferret, into a 'ole as quick as a flash.' They all shrieked with laughter and I noticed Bert was joining in.

'Let's go an' get some grub,' he called.

This time there was no hiding place so I had to go along. We trooped round to our bikes to collect grub bags, a couple of the women riding off. I assumed they lived close by and were going home to lunch.

On returning the way we had come, the women showed me a building I had not noticed on my first glance round. It was a lean-to on the end of the Dutch barn, four bays wide. The nearest bay had been set aside as a lunch place and Bert was putting old boxwood into a 5-gallon grease bucket with holes punched in it.

He poured a generous amount of tvo over it, lit a match, and in seconds a good blaze started.

There were boxes placed in a circle around the fire and an old tatty armchair into which Bert lowered himself. Two other men had turned up and Bert introduced me and told me their names were Percy and Walter. Both were wearing long torn coats tied with string, greasy caps and tatty gloves that would seem to do little to keep their hands warm. The day was still bitterly cold but had warmed a degree or two since dawn.

I found a space and sat down, the heat from the drum starting to drive out the cold. I was asked a few questions about where I lived and if I thought I would stick the life. I answered as best I could and noticed the smiles at my new attire even though it was now a bit stained here and there.

'What youm on today then?' Bert asked the two men as he rolled a smoke.

'Weem a edge brushin' just yon in Dollys,' Percy replied. ''Tis well due. The edge be 'alfways out in't field.' As he spoke he sliced off a large chunk of raw onion with his pocket knife and mated it with an equal size piece of cheese. Placing both on the corner of an inch-thick slice of bread he took a giant-sized bite and started munching happily.

I glanced down at my tiny sarnies, cut into quarters, and noted that two together would not match Percys for width. I tried to hide them with the lid of my lunch box and then noticed that all the others had brought their meal wrapped in a coloured cloth, the corners tied together. I felt I was the odd one out.

'Weem 'avin to cut a lot of un wid a bow saw yew,' Percy continued between chews.

'Still weem gatun a good fire goin', we only come around ere to stop 'e tarmentin they girls, we didn't know as 'ow you 'ad a chappyrone terday,' he nodded his head in my direction.

Bert laughed. 'The only one needin' a chappyrone is young Graham there, these girls go fer a bit of young dick.'

Katie, sitting next to him swiped his arm. 'Shut up, Bert, can't you see you're embarrassing the chap?' she admonished.

I noticed she didn't have the strong Kentish brogue of the others and there was a pleasant huskiness in her voice. She looked at me, once again her eyes held mine and again caused that unexpected stirring in my nether regions. I looked away on the pretext of getting my flask but knew she had noticed my blushing again and I felt she was aware of the effect she was having on me.

The meal continued in a like vein with a lot of banter between the men and the women, much of it laden with sexual innuendo. The hour passed all too quickly, a lot of it spent laughing.

With the time at 2 p.m. Bert heaved himself out of the armchair and picked up a 5-

gallon drum from the side of the shed and poured water over the hot brazier. There was rush of steam and a whoosh and the comforting warmth died away. Coats were pulled around and bits of string retied. It seemed colder than ever having just moved away from the fire. We walked once again to the front shed to hang bags back on to our bikes, as we did so the staff that had gone home to dinner arrived back. Among them was a young chap not much older than me who came over and held out his hand.

'I'm Neil,' he said as we shook. 'Boss said to get you to help me move the boxes of chats and dirt from the riddle. If you go on round I'll get the tractor and trailer.'

'Nice to meet you,' I replied, 'see you there.'

I walked off towards the riddle and Neil headed for a grey Ferguson tractor in the implement shed. As I turned the corner I heard the whirr of a starter and the tractor firing up.

Walking on to the corner of the big barn I stopped dead in my tracks at the sight of Bert and Katie in a clinch just outside the entrance to the riddle. Their kiss was long and lingering and when they broke apart they moved on to the entrance hand in hand. Katie stopped there and Bert went in alone, she following half a minute later. I then heard the sound of the riddle motor starting up. I carried on walking towards the barn as Neil came round behind me with a wooden flat-bed trailer in tow. He drove past the entrance, stopped and reversed the trailer inside. Stopping, he swung a leg over the steering wheel, dismounted and we walked into the barn together.

'Look out girls the charm department has come to get us, don't all rush to be first,' Katie called to the rest, a wide smile on her face.

Neil laughed. 'Don't matter about the rest of you, it's just Anna I'm after.'

Anna never even looked up but her wrinkled face split into a grin.

'Young Neil, you bugger, when yewm big enough yewl be too old. If yew tried it now yewd better had yourm name writ on the soles of yourn boots,' she went off into her cackling laugh, joined by the others.

'Fucking hell,' Neil replied, 'what a way to go.' He turned to me and said.

'I reckon we had better get on before this lot get out of hand.'

We carried the full boxes to the trailer and stacked them on, keeping chats and soil separate, as Neil said they had to go to different places. This involved turning sideways to get past the scales where Katie was weighing and a couple of times I felt something brush across my backside, but as soon as I turned to see what it was Katie was busy with her work.

With all the full boxes loaded Neil drove round to the string shed where we unloaded the chats for Tom to cut and mix for the bullocks. The soil we took into the cattle yard and as Neil drove around I emptied them off the back of the trailer into the straw.

'It'll get picked up with the dung and finish up back on the fields when we clear out the yard,' Neil explained.

'How long have you worked here?' I asked.

'Bout a year and a half, since I left school,' he answered. 'I'm just doing it until I can get in the RAF,' he went on. 'What about you? Are you going to stay in farming or go on to something else?'

'I want to stay in farming,' I told him. 'I enjoy the outdoor life.'

'I'm not sure you will once you've had a go at cabbage cutting,' he laughed. 'It's a right bastard this weather, freeze your fucking bollocks off no problem.'

Neil went off to park the tractor as Tom turned up for the afternoon feed so I stayed and helped as best I could. I climbed the hay cliff and rolled down enough bales to fill the cribs, came down and carried them out leaving Tom to throw them in and cut the strings.

I noticed at this point that the light was fading and the dark clouds were getting even darker. It was just 4.15.

Tom came over. 'Yew mighten as well push off 'ome,' he said. 'Thar wuzzent be time to start nuffin' else.'

'Don't 'e getten 'ere til 'tis startin' to git light in ta mornin', no point in pokin' bout in pitch dark.'

He looked up at the dark clouds. 'I dasn't like the look of the weather, anyways I'll see yew tomarrar. Boss'll might 'av summat else for 'e then.'

I collected my bike and pedalled off homewards, up the lane, in the gathering gloom. My first day's farming was behind me.

Looking back over the day as I rode there was one single memory that kept coming back, the vision of some sparkling eyes that, even in memory, disturbed me and it was not my exertions on the pedals that was causing a shortness of breath!

Chapter 4

The next morning, having stayed in bed for an extra quarter of an hour, I arrived downstairs for breakfast.

'Have you looked out the window?' my father asked.

I pulled back the curtain and in the light, shining from indoors, I could see it had been snowing. Leaving the house I went for my bike, the snow scrunching underfoot. It was around two inches deep and fine powdery stuff was falling, blown by an icy east wind.

Arriving at the farm I parked the bike and stamped around swinging my arms trying the get warm. Several of the others arrived, their good mornings accompanied by clouds of vapour from their warm breath.

I started to make my way to the cattle yard where lights had come on, indicating that Tom was about to start feeding. I had only gone a short way when I met Mr Willis coming from the house. He had obviously been about early because the wheel marks of his Land-Rover led out and back from the yard.

'Got another job for you today,' he said after our good mornings. 'Come with me and I'll see Bert. You can go with his crew.'

He arrived amid the group of women waiting with Bert and morning greetings were exchanged.

'Bert, I've had a look at Longcroft and we could be in luck, the wind is keeping the snow off a bit. I want to try and get 180 bags of cabbage for market tonight. Now it won't be much fun getting 'em, your girls can be off home as soon as they have finished and I'll pay 'em for the day. Take Graham with you, he'll make one extra so you'll be finished in no time.' This with a smile at me and some derisive calls from the women.

Neil climbed on the Fergy and started up, backed out and over to the trailer and hitched on. He then drove up to the string shed. I followed on with Bert. In the corner of the shed was a pile of jute bags printed with a salesman's name and under that appeared 'Boro and Brentford Market'. Bert picked up a pile and placed them on the trailer along with a large skein of the cut bale strings. From a cupboard in the corner he produced a bundle of wooden-handled knives like small machetes; they also went on.

Neil then drove back to the women and called 'All aboard.' Several of them had brought out boxes to make boarding the trailer easier and, after they were on, Bert put the boxes on also so they would have something to sit on. The wind had strengthened and was whipping the snow across the yard and sending swirls from the roofs of the buildings. The temperature out of the wind was well below freezing, in the wind...!

Neil called 'Hold tight.' I climbed on to the back of the tractor with Bert and we set off. Progress had to be fairly slow because of the snow flying off the rear tyres of the tractor – too much speed and it flew all over the women. We went about a quarter of a mile up the lane, sheltered for a while by the banks on either side, then turned up a cut way leading up on to a field. There the full force of the gale was unbroken and there were no hedges or banks to give us cover. The rows of cabbages were visible above the snow, leading out into the greyness of the day. The other side of the field was not visible in the swirling whiteness.

Neil pulled up on the headland and stopped the motor, the noise of the wind becoming clearer and louder and the blown icy snow rattling against the cabbage leaves.

The women climbed off the trailer, collected a knife each from Bert and spread along the edge of the field.

'Leave lay two outside rows,' he told them. 'I'll git Katie to put young Graham to rights, lay can work late two together.'

Katie showed me how to give each cabbage a bit of a kick to knock the snow off, to see if it was fit to cut. If it was OK, then it was pushed to one side to expose the stalk and one swift chop with the knife, just below the first row of open leaves, severed it. It was then thrown to the front, to the middle of eight rows, so a heap built up. As each heap was reached so another was started in front. In this manner we proceeded across the field, each taking two rows, except Katie and me. It was backbreaking work and the cold seeped in, dulling the senses. Gloves soon became soaked and all but useless.

Although we were only cutting one row each, the others started to draw in front.

'The only way to keep warm is to work at a crazy pace,' Katie explained. 'Try to beat everyone else because they will be trying to beat you.' She demonstrated and told me to keep up with her.

It was non-stop across the field working like things demented and we soon caught up the others and arrived at the far headland well ahead.

Standing up was painful and we were both flushed and breathless but at least most of me was warm except my hands. They were dead and frozen and towards the end of the row I was having trouble holding the knife. I swung them against my shoulders and suffered the agony of returning blood supply.

'How come you don't get cold hands?' I asked.

'They just seem to stay warm,' she replied,

her face pink and glowing and her breath smoking away in the wind. 'Here, feel,' she held them out to me.

I had dropped my gloves on the ground as I was swinging my arms so I reached out and took hold of her hands, sure enough they felt much warmer than mine. When I went to release them she held on and gripped mine for a moment or two and, glancing at her, noticed that her eyes were shining and a little smile was playing on her lips. Yet again I experienced feelings I wasn't at all sure of and the redness of my face wasn't all caused by the wind's icy blast.

The rest of the gang were now arriving at the headland. Nearest to us was Anna, who seemed to have the knack of bending across the hips and not across the back and had no problem standing up.

'Ain't youse two got nuffin' better to do than stan' aroun 'olding bleedin' 'ands?' she called. 'You'll 'av to watch 'e, Katie, 'e might be a young ferret taking after ol' Bert.' The usual shriek of laughter followed, bringing a cloud of vapour round her head.

Katie looked at me and smiled, and turning to Anna called: 'I was just letting him know my hands were warm in case he needed any relief ... from the cold.' Anna laughed again at that. Katie turned back to me and, looking at me through her eyelashes, her head lowered, she added so that

55

Anna could not hear, 'or at any time.'

I was completely flustered, so much so that I had no idea what to say or do, so turned and bent down to pick up my gloves as a good way of hiding my confusion.

Everyone was now on the headland so we lined out again for the return trip. This time I was cutting two rows and soon found I was being left behind, so I redoubled my effort. Katie was cutting the two rows next to mine and I started to find some of my rows had been cut before I got to them, so with her help I managed to keep up and arrived with the rest. Amazingly I felt quite warm, even my hands.

We arrived back with Bert, who had not been cutting but had been rolling down the bags and dividing them up in equal piles, putting each pile in a bag for us.

It was now morning tea time so we re-embarked on the tractor and trailer and headed back to the yard.

The blaze was soon started in the drum and we all huddled round steaming, hands round tea mugs or held out to the fire. The feeling slowly returned to toes and ears.

'Thanks for helping me out,' I said to Katie. 'I would never have kept up.'

'You were doing OK, I didn't do many. Next time you'll be keeping up with no problem.' She flashed a smile that did as much to warm me as the brazier.

The half hour went all too quickly and it was soon time to extinguish our haven of warmth and head back out to the trailer. The snow had got deeper, still mainly fine powdery stuff that whipped up in the wind. The tyre tracks from our inward journey were now almost obliterated. Driving back to the field we had our faces shielded behind coat collars to protect against the snow being thrown up by the front wheels. It was not a pleasant ride and we arrived back at the field snowy and chilled to the bone.

'Right, let's'us git baggin',' Bert called. 'Bag up wot 'tis cut and see how many we got.'

We took a stiff and frozen bag each, into which Bert had placed the rolled down ones, plus a bundle of string which we hung round our waists.

Katie was again on hand to show me what to do. It turned out not to be a case of throwing the cabbages in the bags until they were full. The first two had to go in the corners and the next two alongside them to push the sides out. The bag was unrolled a few inches and the next four pushed into the hollows between the first row and so it went on. If there was a smaller one it was fitted in the middle. The whole idea was to keep the filled bag as tight as possible. The last row which were right on the top and actually sticking out were reversed so that the stalks were showing. Cuts were made at intervals round the neck of the bag and the whole thing laced up with the string. Some of the bags that had been used before already had the cuts in, which saved us some time. When laced up and finished the bag could be picked up like a tight tube and not even bend in the middle.

It was impossible to wear gloves because of tying up so we worked bare-handed picking up the snow-covered, frozen crop, jamming the bags full, lacing up and moving on to the next. The pace was manic, it was the only way not to freeze. After watching Katie do a couple I had a go and soon got the knack of it. I also found I was starting to get quite warm.

Arriving again at the far side of the field it was satisfying to be able to stand up in what could only be described as a Siberian landscape and to feel reasonably comfortable. To this day I still enjoy beating the cold in this manner, working really hard at something, being outdoors in appalling conditions and yet feeling warm.

'You were really going for it there. I can almost see you steaming,' Katie said. She had been working bare-headed except for her usual bandanna and the powdery snow had coated her hair.

''Ow many empties we got left?' Bert

called. He had counted out 180 bags before he started rolling down.

We had a quick tally and found we needed 21 more. With half the crew cutting and the others bagging the order was soon completed.

It was now just over half an hour to lunch so the girls, who were now knocking off as agreed with Mr Willis, said they would walk back to the yard and leave Bert, Neil and me to load up the bags.

There were too many for one load so we put on about half and headed off. To one side of the yard was a specially built loading dock the same height as a lorry deck. We unloaded the bags from the trailer on to the dock ready for reloading on to the farm lorry for the journey to London that evening. The cabbages would be on sale in shops and greengrocers tomorrow morning.

Before returning for the rest of the bags we stopped for lunch and were soon huddled round the fire again.

'Well, watse reckon to a bit of cabbagin' then, young un?' Bert asked. 'Yew done well ta stick it out thar today, that fair freeze yer gizzard an' no mistake.'

'It sure was cold,' I agreed, 'how often do we cut?' I hoped he would say once a week.

'Us'll be at un every day all the time this 'ere snow do 'ang about an' as long as we can see to cut 'em.'

He held his hands to the fire, his face red from the icy wind and the remains of his roll-up stuck on his bottom lip.

'See thar's probly farms aroun' that's got more snow than weem or field is lying in oller so wind is fillin' in rather than clearin' it off. They can't git out to cut so market do git shart.'

Neil looked up and blurted, 'It's only fucking idiots like us that will go out and cut 'em. What are we, bleedin' nuts?'

Bert laughed, a puff of smoke coming from his mouth even though there were only the smallest shreds of cigarette left.

'Graham 'ere were a keeping warm, 'e were stood on 'eadland 'oldin' 'ands wid Katie.' Bert's pale blue eyes crinkled at the corners with mirth.

'Twas too fucking cold for her to have been holding anything else,' Neil retorted.

We all laughed and I was glad my face was already red from the wind.

Lunch over, it was back into the cold and up to the field for the balance of the bags. Returning loaded, we found a green lorry alongside the dock so we pulled up on the side of it. A chap around forty wearing a brown sleeveless leather jerkin over his coat was loading the bags we had fetched before lunch.

'Artnoon Harry,' Bert called. 'This young

gennelman is Graham. Come 'ere to larn 'ow to farm.'

I shook hands with Harry. He was round-faced and thickset and I found him to be a lively, talkative person and we got on well.

'You'll meet me Dad aroun'. He's off at present, he drives the County crawler. Only problem his name's Harry as well,' he told me.

'Do you go to market every night?' I asked him.

'Just about,' he replied. 'There's nearly allus summat to go. You'll have to come with I one night. It'll be an eye opener for 'e.'

'Thanks for that, I'd like to,' I said.

'Wait til this crap 'as melted an' driving is easier, then we can fix it up. I'll 'av a word with the Boss an git 'im to give you the marnin' off the next day, he won't mind.'

We stopped and helped Harry load all the bags. I went with Neil and we dropped off the trailer and parked the Fergy.

Walking back across the yard I came across Bert and Mr Willis in conversation so, as it was nearly feeding time, I headed towards the cattle yard. However, Mr Willis called me over.

'Bert tells me you did well out there today,' he said. 'It's a real sod of a day and I don't like asking people to go out cutting cabbages on a day like this.'

Bert's eyes were shining and the laughter

lines were deepening.

'I bet yew was really worried 'bout us while yew was toastin' yer toes in front of sitting room fire,' he chuckled.

Mr Willis laughed out loud and cuffed Bert on the shoulder.

I was surprised at the easy familiarity between boss and employee but it became clear later when I found that Bert had worked for Mr Willis's father. That meant that he had worked alongside his present employer for many years as a staff mate before John took over the running of the farm.

'You might as well push off home,' Mr Willis said.

'No, I'm OK, I'll go and give Tom a hand feeding,' I told him and headed towards the cattle yard.

Tom was bagging the afternoon feed, holding the bag in one hand and the shovel in the other.

'Thart you'd bin orf 'ome like lay girls,' he greeted me.

'No, I knew you would never manage without me,' I grinned at him.

'Blimy an hexpert already,' he laughed. 'Still a bit o' 'elp is wort a lot o' pity they do say.' He swung a bag on to his shoulder and headed for the trough while I made my way to the hay barn.

Feeding over, I finally headed for my bike with the daylight fading. The wind, if anything, had increased still more. It had started to push the snow into small drifts around the exposed corners of buildings, and a more bleak outlook would be hard to find. Looking out from the lee of the shed it was hard to believe I had been out in it for most of the day, especially in the middle of an exposed field. I had a little shiver at the memory.

Starting my ride home, as I scrunched along the lane, Bert's words were hanging on my mind: 'Us'll be on every day if this snow do 'ang aroun'.' Was I really going to be able to get up and do it all again tomorrow, I asked myself? Then I thought of Katie and the other women to whom this was just another working day. Probably better than most because they had gone off early and been paid for the whole day.

My admiration for them was boundless. What a tough bunch they are, out in all weathers, day in day out, and still with a house, husband and children to look after. I knew nothing. I was to find out from stories around the lunch fire just how tough they really were.

Well, I told myself, if a bunch of women can do it then I'm damn sure I can. With these thoughts in mind I continued riding into the gloom. Perhaps my readers can now understand why the date is frozen in my memory. One other thought from the day crept in concerning a certain attractive lady with snow powdering her hair and four little words, 'or at any time'. What was that leading to, I wondered?

Chapter 5

It snowed on and off for the next ten days with the temperature not getting above freezing day or night.

Each day as I rode down the lane to the farm I knew what was in store and what the day would be like. I could now more than hold my own cutting and bagging and seem to have been accepted as one of the crew. That fact alone made the atrocious working conditions slightly more bearable. I was showing signs of the extreme temperature, the tops of my ears were frostbitten and my hands had started to get cracks in the skin. I took to wearing a scarf over my head and ears and plasters over the cracks in my fingers and battled on. Katie and the girls helped by maintaining their sense of humour and gave me every encouragement.

We went over the field and cut all the first-grade cabbages, then started over again cutting second grade. By the end of the week, with the markets crying out for anything green, we finished up cutting the leaves left behind after the crown of the cabbage had been cut.

Two things happened that week that stick in my mind. I drove a tractor for the first time. We were loading full bags on to the trailer and had just put on the last ones from one spot and were ready to move to the next. I happened to be nearest the tractor so Bert called out, 'Move er up, Graham.' I had learned how to drive the family car around the byways and lanes so hopped on the Fergy and drove to the next pile of bags.

Since that day I have spent thousands of hours driving tractors of all sizes, sometimes cold, sometimes wet, sometimes both, often covered in dust or worse – but that first 50-yard drive will stick with me always. It was a proud moment.

The second thing was that on Friday I received my first ever wages amounting to four pounds and two shillings. It seemed a fortune, I had never had that much money of my own before.

Saturday afternoon saw me in the local town where I purchased (with my own money) firstly a cap. It was corduroy in a nice dark brown colour. Next a good pair of gum boots. The fur-lined boots I had started out with were woefully inadequate for the job and I was finishing every day with wet feet. I also got some long thick socks that I could tuck my trousers in before putting on the gum boots. That stopped the annoyance of socks working down and coming off inside the boots. My last purchase was a pocket knife with a rather neat bone handle.

My entrance to the farmyard on Monday was greeted with whistles and catcalls and a lot of good-natured banter.

'Fuckin 'ell,' said Anna. 'Yew ain't bought out the bleedin' place ower tha' weekend 'av 'e?'

'No,' I was laughing along with them. 'I got paid so much money for a week's work I just had to go and spend some of it.'

More shouts of derision greeted this and Bert piped up.

'No, 'e's right, I've got a drawer full of un-opened pay packets at 'ome. Boss keeps give 'em me an' I don't know what ta do wi 'em.'

There were howls of laughter at this and Bert wiped his eyes, his shoulders shaking with mirth.

The weekend had also seen a change in the weather. A slow thaw had started and later on Monday it started to rain, washing away the last of the ice and snow. The farms that had more snow than us were able now to cut their cabbages, but in the meantime we had cleaned up and sold the entire crop, leaves and all, at a premium price. Another year the boot might be on the other foot and it would be us that suffered.

My daily routine now became centred

around the cattle feeding and the potato riddle. Neil had the week off as he had RAF selection courses to attend. Mr Willis asked me if I would be able to drive the Fergy to keep the riddle clear of soil and chats. Bert had obviously told him I could drive. Of course, I jumped at the chance.

Tuesday morning, after helping with the feeding, I started up the tractor, hitched on the trailer and drove round to the Dutch barn feeling really cock-a-hoop. Now pulling a trailer going forwards is very little problem. It's backing the thing that requires a knack, as I found as soon as I tried to get it to where Neil had parked.

Much as I tried it went everywhere I didn't want it and my struggles were not helped by Bert bringing the whole riddle gang out to watch. Eventually I got it somewhere near where it was wanted and alighted, red faced, to cheers from the 'audience'.

Having loaded up with Bert's and Katie's help, I drove to unload and having done so spent some time practising on my own. Suddenly, like riding a bike, it clicked and from then on it became second nature and I could put the back of a trailer to within an inch of where it was required. Driving back to put away the tractor I felt as happy as it was possible to be: the weather had improved and it was very clear air after the rain.

Looking out across the lane I could see

two lots of bonfire smoke from where the rest of the staff were hedgecutting. Already I started to feel part of the farm, to be a small cog in what made it run.

The cattle were now able to look over their wall, since the muck in their yard was over 6ft deep with the two trailer loads of straw bales they were given each week. The fodder beet clamp was nearly empty and as I helped Tom one afternoon he told me that the next day the cattle would be going to market. I looked around at them quietly munching their hay. I had got to recognise them individually by now and knew which ones were quiet and which needed watching. I felt quite sad knowing that this would be their last afternoon in the yard but then I thought, that's what farming is all about, food production, and one cannot afford to be sentimental.

'I allus miss they old buggers when 'tis their time,' Tom said to me and I felt better about my feelings. He must have seen yardfuls of cattle come and go but still felt sadness at their departure.

Sure enough when I arrived the next morning two large cattle trucks were in the yard, their drivers talking to Tom. After some discussion one of the drivers went to his lorry, started up, drove up the yard and then reversed. Tom had the cattle yard gate open and called 'woah' when the back of the lorry was level with the gate. A couple of spare gates were found to make a 'lead in' to the lorry. A small crew were assembled.

Neil, Walter, Percy and a youngish chap called Roger that I had not met before squeezed past the lorry with me and quietly moved round the cattle. It was their normal feeding time so they were used to people about and moved easily. Tom counted out half and we moved through them to separate them and then moved the half nearest the gate towards the lorry. Some straw had been spread on the ramp to disguise it. The front animals stopped at the ramp and had a good sniff. We kept the back ones pushing on and soon they all clattered up and into the lorry. The driver and Tom had the retaining gates across and the back up in a trice and the job was done. The first lorry pulled away and the exact performance was repeated to load the second. With that the lorries pulled out of the yard and headed off down the lane.

The empty cattle yard looked huge with no cattle and the cribs with their dark, trampled areas round them looked lonely and forlorn. It was so silent. There had always been some sound either a moo or a cough, the rustle of straw as one or two fell out and chased each other. Now it was dead and still. Millions of motes of dust glinted in the rays of the early morning sun shining into the feed-trough area. This was the time of day the cattle would have been lined up eating their breakfast. Now they were being jostled about in a lorry bound for God knows where.

I turned away glad there was no one about to see my moist eyes. Sentimental fool!

January passed and by mid February the days slowly lengthened. I had found out from Neil that Roger drove the second Fergy. There were two parked where we left our bikes. He also told me that Roger was leaving for a better paid job driving a fork lift on the docks.

My delight can be imagined when Mr Willis called me from the riddle and told me Roger was leaving at the end of the month and would I like to take over his Fergy and do all the work he used to do.

'It will mean long hours at times,' he said. 'But I've been impressed with what you have done so far.'

I felt ten feet tall as I returned to the riddle.

'You look like the cat that got the cream,' Katie said.

I told her and Bert my news, adding that I hoped I would be up to doing the work.

'Yew'll soon git t'ang of it,' Bert told me, his eyes crinkling at the corners. 'Young Roger all 'e wanted ta do was tear aroun' tha' road an' when 'e were on tha' field ha tart 'e was on a bloody race track. He's busted a lot o' tackle I can tell 'e. I can't think as 'ow the Boss will be too sad to see back of un.'

Katie agreed, adding, 'I always thought he was a bit creepy. I wouldn't fancy being alone with him.' Then with one of her little asides so that Bert couldn't hear added, 'not like you.'

Again I was lost for words and flustered, hating my confusion. All I could manage was a smile and received one in return that tormented me further. I went to get on with my work feeling totally out of my depth and wondering what on earth was going on. Yes, I was that naive.

We were having one of those warmer spells that sometimes turn up in late February and inside the barn with the riddle it was quite mild. The women had discarded their long coats and were working in cardigans or pull-overs. Ruth called up to Bert to say she was getting too much straw coming down from the top of the store. The potatoes, as well as the bale walls, were covered over on top with loose straw.

Bert called me over. 'Go up on top o' 'eap an' rake bak tha' straw will 'e, Katie will give 'e a 'and; I 'spect you'll have ta push some outside as weem narly ta end.'

I went off with Katie, carrying a pitch fork each, and we started to scramble up the side of the heap using the side bales to hang on to.

'Don't be all bleedin' day 'cus ussel know what yew 'av bin up to,' Anna called.

'Shut your old yap, Anna, you're only jealous,' Katie called back, a big smile on her face.

I reached the top of the heap and held down my hand to pull Katie up the last bit.

Another shout from Anna: 'He's 'oldin 'er 'and again. Yew do watch out Missie it'll be up yer skirt next.' My face must have been a picture because there was general laughter from below.

We moved forward. There was three-quarters of a bay left to riddle so there was nowhere to push the loose straw ahead. For some reason I could not explain I felt nervous working alone with Katie, as if there was a tension between us. I was very conscious of her attraction and it bothered me.

'We'll have to take some top bales off the wall and push a lot of this loose out into the yard,' Katie said.

We set about the task, pulling out some bales and putting them back out of the way. It was warm work with little space to move in and the sun shining on the curved tin roof close above. Katie took off her jersey. She was wearing a man's-type shirt underneath and the top two buttons were unfastened.

We soon had enough room to start forking the straw outside. I pushed it across to Katie and she poked it out through the gap and down on to the ground. Every time I pushed a forkful over she would turn to take it and I would get a view of her cleavage. We had moved about half when Katie called a halt. We were both perspiring. She sat down on one of the bales.

'Phew,' she puffed. 'I'm getting baked under this tin roof.' She took a handkerchief from a pocket and wiped her face, then pulled the shirt out from the top of her skirt and fanned it up and down. She opened another button or two and wiped across the base of her neck and down her cleavage. She was wearing a lacy white bra. I was trans-fixed and I suppose a bit embarrassed, never having seen anything like that before.

'Mind your eyes don't fall out,' she giggled. 'You never see a pair of tits before?'

'Oh sorry,' I blurted, blushing furiously, realising that I had been staring. 'Er, no I hav'nt, only in pictures,' I went on, wishing I had kept quiet.

'Well that won't do will it,' she giggled, the tip of her tongue passing over her lips and her eyes holding mine.

She leaned forward a little and lifted the bottom of her shirt upwards. On the way up her fingers went into the bottom of her bra, which she pulled out and up.

'There now you can get a good look.' She was pouting at me, her face still flushed from the work.

Her breasts were naked, their whiteness emphasised by the rosy pink of her nipples that stuck out firmly.

I am almost unable to put into words my feeling at that time. I was totally speechless. My face must have reflected my amazement because she burst out laughing. She leaned forward again and slipped the bra back over her breasts and buttoned her shirt, stood up and tucked the shirt back in the top of her skirt.

'There, now you can't say you hav'nt seen a pair of tits,' she was still laughing, her eyes twinkling.

I had, by now, recovered some of my composure and was starting to smile but I could tell my face was bright red.

'Certainly a super pair to start with,' was all I could think to say and we both fell about laughing.

She came over to me and put an arm across my shoulders and moved her mouth close to my ear.

'I'll show you the rest another day,' she whispered huskily then gave me a peck on the cheek and returned to pushing out the straw.

It took another twenty minutes to finish clearing and to replace the bales in the wall.

When we reappeared and slid back down the heap to the floor there were more ribald comments from Anna.

'Yew both look bleedin' 'ot, yew bin at it up thar or summat?'

I was feeling quite elated after my experience and quickly came back at her.

'Well, I was keen but Katie chickened out.' This with a quick glance at Katie who burst out laughing.

'That's right, Anna,' she said. 'He's a big lad. I wasn't sure I could manage.'

Anna cackled and spluttered, 'Christ, that'll be the fucking day!'

There was general hilarity with Bert joining in and it was some time before order was restored and the riddling could continue.

I gave Ruth a spell on shovelling and every so often as I swung a load into the machine I would catch Katie's eye. They were certainly responsible for the difficulty I was having bending forward to shovel and for a certain shortness of breath.

Now I'm older I know it is called 'sexual tension', but back then I hadn't got a clue what it was but I was finding it very enjoyable and a super pair of breasts and some sparkling eyes featured highly in my fantasies when I went to bed that night.

Chapter 6

As February slowly eased into March, the warm spell had been followed by some rain and unsettled weather. Now, a few days into March, we were having some bright days with drying winds. Green patches were starting to appear round the yard and birdsong became more noticeable. Spring flowers were starting to speckle the lane banks and the air had a different smell and feel.

Roger had left to take up his new position, which meant that I was now the driver of the second Fergy. It was a petrol/tvo type, that is to say it was started on petrol and, by means of a two-way tap, once warmed up could be switched to run on tvo, which was basically paraffin. One had to remember to turn it back a short while before stopping the engine so that the pipe was full of petrol for the next start. If this was not done, it would be necessary to drain out the pipe. There were a few 'tricks' to driving it. If for instance it had been left ticking over on tvo and cooled down, some careful juggling of the throttle was required to get the revs up again. This accompanied by clouds of smoke from the exhaust.

Around the middle of the second week of March, arriving at the yard on a beautiful sunny morning, I found Mr Willis waiting for me.

'I want you to start on some field work today,' he said. 'You'll need to take one of the big Majors from round the other yard. I'll get Neil to show you how to start it. There are three fields we ploughed late last winter. We've put ferti on them, now they want heavy harrowing ready for drilling with spring barley.'

Neil arrived at this point and Mr Willis told him what was required.

I had seen Neil, Percy and Walter loading some sacks out of one of the store sheds alongside the yard. Each sack had 'De Passe Fertiliser' printed on it. They had put a full load on and gone off up the lane, returning a short time later with the trailer empty. Neil had then hitched on a wide box-like implement with big iron wheels, that Bert told me was a fertiliser spreader, and had gone scrunching off with it.

'Roger used ta do most of tha' ferti spreadin',' Bert told me. 'But bags is 'undredweight an' a quarter an I 'spect Boss thart yew might not manage they.'

I went with Neil round to the implement shed that made up the end of the yard between the big barn and the Dutch barn.

On the way I popped into the Dutch barn to tell them I wouldn't be with them today.

'Oh, we'll miss you,' Katie smiled. 'It's been a help having you around, especially clearing that straw from up top there.' Her eyes held mine and the blushing started.

I caught up with Neil. He was standing beside a big blue tractor, its rear wheels nearly as tall as me. It had 'Fordson Major' in red painted on the front and 'Fordson' written vertically down each side of the radiator. Neil told me it was a E27 model. We went through the starting drill. It was petrol/tvo the same as my Fergy but was started by a crank handle. There was no self-starter. Neil explained that it had an impulse magneto, that meant that half a turn on the crank handle should be enough to start it.

The knack was to make sure it was on petrol, turn off the fuel tap and drain out the fuel in the pipe, give it one or two swings and nine times out of ten it would start. It was then necessary to nip very quickly round the side and turn the fuel on to keep it going. If you tried to start it with the fuel on it would flood, which would require all the plugs removing and drying out.

Following Neil's instructions a couple of swings on the handle brought it to life. I climbed up beside him as he showed me the controls. They were fairly basic: a 3-speed gearbox controlled by a long lever on the left; throttle on the right which was a notched rod that pulled out for more revs; clutch by the left foot and, on the right, a foot-brake pedal that, by swinging over a locking bar, could be divided so that each rear wheel could be braked independently.

'Bring her up to the fuel shed and we'll top her up,' Neil called over the noise of the engine.

I engaged reverse and backed out of the shed (the steering was quite light for a big machine) and trundled up to the fuel shed. We filled up both tanks and Neil guided me round to the other side of the Dutch barn where assorted implements were rowed up, among them a dilapidated 4-wheel trailer that had on it four big harrows and a long angle bar with a wheel on each end that Neil told me was called a 'bat'.

I hitched on and followed Neil round to the main yard, where he collected his Fergy. I followed him to the first field to be worked down. We unloaded the bat which had a series of rings along one side. The harrows had hooks that located in the rings. Once all harrows were fixed on, I pulled the trailer outside the field and parked it to the side of the landway, drove back in and backed up to the bat.

On the front were two long rods that stretched to about two feet from either end finishing in a ring that was attached to the tractor drawbar. Neil dropped in the pin and all was ready.

'You'll find second the best gear,' he told me. 'Go round the headland three times and give yourself plenty of room to turn. Watch you don't turn too short or the rear wheel will pick up one of those rods and you'll have the whole lot on top of you. Work across the furrows. It'll do a better job.'

I engaged second gear, pulled out the throttle which sent a good puff of white smoke into the air and set off round the field. I found that it took a lot of concentration to keep the wheel on the bat near to the edge but soon got the hang of it. At the first corner I found out why the brakes needed to be independently operated because, when I went to turn, the tractor tried to go straight on. Stopping quickly I swung over the lock-ing plate and, by almost stopping the inside wheel, managed to make the turn. Neil watched from the gateway for a while then jumped on his Fergy and left me to it.

Once the first circuit of the field had been made it became a lot easier and I was able to look around a bit. It was a fine, breezy day and I found it marvellous to be out working the fields. The tractor exhaust had a very distinctive smell that today calls up a million memories of those days. The harrows clinked and jingled over the Kentish flints and the smell of freshly moved earth wafted over me.

Seagulls soon found me and swooped around picking up worms and titbits that the harrows fetched out.

I had not been going long when I saw Mr Willis's Land-Rover pull into the gateway. He walked over to me, dogs scampering everywhere, and looked at the harrowed land. I pulled up alongside him and got off the tractor.

'Them harrows are doing a good job. We shall be able to drill here without doing anything else,' he said as I came up to him. 'You seem to be managing that tractor all right.'

'Yes, no problem but it's got a bit of a mind of its own,' I replied.

He laughed. 'They are all the same those old Majors. You have to watch 'em all the time.'

He walked off, dogs in tow, and I returned to working down the field. Time for morning tea arrived. I had my haversack with me so stopped the tractor and had my very first experience of sitting by a machine, in the fresh air, having a cup of tea and a bite to eat. How many times have I done it since I wonder!

Morning tea over, I went through the routine Neil had showed me and the tractor started first pull, much to my relief. I stopped for lunch and by mid-afternoon had finished the first field. Neil had pointed out where the other fields were so I was able to move by unhitching the harrows and loading them on the trailer. This was a struggle. I could only lift one end and had to stand each one up and sort of walk it to the trailer and lean it on the side, then with all my strength, push it up and on. The same with the bat. I pulled it on its wheels as close as possible then lifted one end on and managed to slide it on enough to get to the next field.

I worked on after knock-off time to get as much done as possible, then unhitched and headed back to the farmyard. It was cold now the sun had set and mist was settling in the low spots. I was quite glad of the heat coming back from the engine and the warm transmission under my feet.

Biking home that evening it was hard to believe the changes that had taken place in my life in less than three months. A week or so before Christmas I was a schoolboy finishing term and now I was on the way to becoming a fully fledged tractor driver, accepted as one of the team on the farm, and learning new things about the countryside and life in general every day. To say I was happy would have been a gross understatement. I was like a cat with two tails.

The fine, breezy spell continued and I was able to finish harrowing the three fields, breaking the furrows down to a good tilth and mixing in the fertiliser. Neil was now following me round with the corn drill, sowing the barley seed. He had Percy riding on the drill platform looking after the little harrows that were fixed behind it and watching for any blocked spouts.

My next task did involve the Fergy. It was necessary to harrow in the barley seed once the drilling was finished. The little harrows following behind the drill did some of it but not all. It also needed harrowing across the rows to really cover it. The farm had a set of harrows made by the Ferguson company specially for fitting to their tractors, which were attached to the 3-point linkage. This meant they could be raised or lowered on the hydraulics for transport or for turning in the field. They were made in three equally sized sections with the two side ones able to fold upwards and fix for transport on the road and then be dropped down to working position again in the field. The actual tines or spikes of the harrows could be adjusted by a lever on top, straight down for heavy work or raked back for lighter applications. I was shown how to fit the implement to the tractor and how much to rake back the tines, then it was back to the first field to go over it again.

The field now looked totally different from when I first started working it down earlier. It had a smooth crumb of tilth which my second run with the Fergy harrows made even better. As I folded them up in the gateway, fluffy clouds chasing across a vivid blue sky in the bright March sunshine, I was struck by the contrast to my first few weeks when I was cutting cabbages in arctic conditions, at times ready to pack in, but spurred on by all my colleagues. For their encouragement and help I shall be eternally grateful as they got me started on a life that I have loved and enjoyed so much.

Looking at that field I had just finished I wondered what other line of work could give that much job satisfaction. The weather held just long enough to finish the drilling then, as is often the case in March, it turned bitterly cold. I finished harrowing in the seed in the last half of the last field in a dusting of snow and in a howling North Easterly gale. I think I was colder than on cabbage cutting days because there was no activity; it was a case of sitting there and taking it.

When I finished and got back to the yard I was so cold I could hardly stand but, as I soon found, it was a case of taking the rough days with the smooth. The bad days are soon forgotten but the good ones will stay with you always.

With field work at a standstill for a while Mr Willis decided we should make a start on clearing the muck from the cattle yard. My Fergy had some side tubes permanently in place that were part of the loader that fitted on to them. The jib and fork were propped on some 40-gallon drums in the yard, so it was just a case of driving into it and fitting the retaining pins. A special frame went on the linkage with a bar that fitted under some steel hooks protruding from a large block of concrete, which acted as a balance weight for when the fork was loaded. I got everything fitted and the hydraulic pipes coupled up ready to start. As I was filling up with fuel Mr Willis came over.

'We'll make a start tomorrow,' he said. 'Tony will be back today. Bert can leave the girls to finish up the spuds so we can get a full gang in the field unloading.'

When I saw Bert later I asked who Tony was.

'He be tha' Boss's son,' he told me. 'He bin away at college, an' then 'ad a bit of a 'oliday. Yew'l git on OK wid 'e.'

The rest of the day was spent with the riddle. During the afternoon Bert left me to help Katie with the weighing while he went to find the dung drags. These were long handled forks with the tines at right angles to the handle. One could stand alongside a trailer load of muck, swing the fork down into it and pull off a good lump with each swing.

I was quite happy working alongside Katie but she did nothing to ease my feelings and brushed against me where possible, and each time there would be that glance from her eyes...

It certainly made for interesting work and the time passed quickly. Bert returned after a while and beckoned me over.

'I've fixed wid Boss to git orf early today,' he said. 'Can yew shut down tha' riddle an' turn out tha' lights.'

'Course I can, leave it to me,' I replied, glad at the extra responsibility and not giving a thought to any ulterior motive.

'I'll git orf then. Katie will look arter 'e.' He waved to the girls and went to leave, as he passed Katie a look passed between them that I could not interpret.

'Where's 'e fucking orf ta this time o' day?' Anna called.

'Mind your own bleedin' business ya old tart,' a reply came that caused a gale of laughter.

Time came to finish for the day, Ruth stopped feeding the machine and soon the last of the day's spuds came up the elevator. Once all were clear the women quickly made their way out with calls of 'good night' and 'see you tomorrar'.

I went round to the engine that was tonking quietly away and steaming from its open water tank and flipped the lever to shut it down.

Quiet descended on the barn apart from

the ticking of the engine as it cooled and the occasional potato rolling down the face of the heap. The bulbs, hanging on their strings, seemed brighter in the fading light of day and cast dark shadows into the further corners. Katie had stayed behind to clear up as she always did when Bert was there.

'I think there's just enough to make up this bag,' she called looking in the box at the end of the elevator. 'Can you give me lift?'

I went over and we unhooked the bag and swung it on to the scales. I checked the weight and started to add some potatoes from the spare bag beside it. I heard a step behind me and felt Katie's arms come round me, the swell of her breasts against my back. She put her chin on my shoulder and looked over at the scales.

'Will you have enough?' she said, her voice husky, as she turned her head and started nuzzling my ear.

Nature was taking its course with my lower regions and I found myself unable to reply. She continued to hug me from behind but moved her hands lower, one going on down until she could be in no doubt as to my state of arousal. Events after that become a bit blurred. I remember her taking my hand and leading me to the stack of full bags and sitting beside me. She turned my head and kissed me at the same time placing one of my hands over her bosom. I was by now bewildered and surprised but at the same time excited beyond belief, my heart pounding. I felt her fumbling with my clothes and then her hand worked me to a shattering release.

I felt unable to move, Katie sat up and I managed to get myself together and my clothes fastened.

I was wondering what to do or say next but Katie made it easy. She put a finger under my chin and tilted my face upwards, kissed me again, and with a big chuckle walked out of the barn.

'Don't forget the lights,' she called back as she went out.

I was in a complete daze, all my feelings jangled, wondering what on earth was going on. Was this how grown-up people go on, I thought, or is it a joke on me? I had no idea, but decided that I had enjoyed it immensely and would see what happened tomorrow and sort of play it by ear.

I turned out the lights and went to fetch my bike.

I was not yet 17 but had the feeling life was good. When I arrived home my Mum looked at me and said. 'You know I think the outdoor life is doing you good, you look really well...'

Chapter 7

The next morning all was set to start clearing the muck from the cattle yard. Mr Willis was about with a very tall young chap in his early twenties. There could be no doubt they were father and son with the same country look about each of them.

'Tony, this is Graham the young apprentice I was telling you about,' Mr Willis said making the introduction.

'How are you making out?' Tony asked. 'It's all a bit strange at first isn't it?'

'I'm enjoying it ... apart from the cabbage cutting, that is,' I replied, a smile on my face.

Tony and Mr Willis both laughed.

'Well there won't be anything much worse to worry about,' Mr Willis said. 'Now are you going to be all right with that loader? It's a good old slog in there. If it gets too much I'll get Neil to give you a spell.'

'I'll manage,' I told him, thinking there's no way anyone else is going to drive my Fergy.

During our conversation Katie had arrived and put her bike in the shed before heading for the Dutch barn. As she passed she blew me a kiss and gave a quick wave. It was enough to start stirrings in my lower regions so I turned away quickly, after giving her a quick smile.

The field gang comprised Bert, Percy and Walter who'd be pulling the muck off the trailers into heaps five yards apart. As each heap was completed Bert would step out the next, keeping the row of heaps dead straight across the field. Tony and Neil were driving the tractors and trailers, Neil with his Fergy and Tony with the Fordson I had been harrowing with. It was awkward to begin with as there was only the gateway to work into.

Neil backed into a convenient position and we made a start. The fork bucket had no automatic trip, but had to be released by giving a fairly hefty tug to a rod that was fixed to the catch. The easiest way to close it again was to lower it on to the load or the ground and reverse. I managed to get the first load on fairly quickly as the muck was soft and churned up in the gateway. The field gang departed, all standing on the back of Neil's Fergy, and Tony moved into position. I soon found that it was not a good idea to trip the fork too high when it had a load of wetter, sloppy stuff. The first time I did so I received a good splattering back in my face and soon learnt to lower the fork right down and trip it close to the trailer, so that the tines dropped only a short distance, then raise the jib and let the fork load slide off.

Work continued with trailers going back and forth. I loaded each as fast as possible and it was not long before I had the gateway clear and was able to work inside with a trailer parked, for loading, across the gate.

It was hard going on the right arm, constantly tugging the catch to release the fork and also the left leg as there was continuous clutch work, going backwards and forwards. The Fergy's steering, even with the balance weight, required a good effort to turn so I was going to be pretty tired by the end of the day.

Morning break time arrived. The field gang had their bags with them and, as it was not too bad a day, elected to stay in the field. Tony arrived back and headed for the farmhouse. I collected my bag and made my way round to the meal shed, where the girls already had a fire going. This was something I wouldn't have dreamed of doing a few months back.

Walking into the shed Anna greeted me with 'Youm be makin' an fuckin' stink stirrin' up that bleedin' shit.'

'Good morning, all,' I smiled. 'Just giving you all an appetite for your break.'

There were shouts of dissent and waves for me to go away.

My eyes met Katie's for an instant and I felt my colour rise (among other things).

This was the first time I had been to a break-time with just the women and the banter soon started.

'I reckon as 'ow we'ed better watch out,' a woman called Flo piped up, 'we mightn't be safe er with this young buck.'

'With you about he's probably the one that's not safe,' Katie grinned at her.

'What chew mean by that, I'd never lead 'im astray,' Flo answered.

Anna cast her eyes to heaven. 'Fuckin ell, you got ta be jokin',' she started her distinct laugh and all joined in.

The girls were sitting in a semi-circle round the inside part of the shed. Katie had made herself at home in Bert's armchair. There was only one box to sit on and that was exactly opposite, so I sat down and undid my bag. The conversation turned to village gossip and seemed to be focused on who was having it off with who and where.

'We shouldn't be talkin' like this in front of a young lad, what will 'e fink?' Flo said, her hand to her mouth.

'From what I've 'erd youngens these days know it all aready,' another woman called Mary joined in.

Katie laughed 'Maybe not all of 'em, Mary, some of 'em still need a hand.'

There was a burst of laughter and I coloured wondering if Katie had told them of our encounter yesterday afternoon.

The general chatter continued and it was after a few minutes, as I leaned down to pick up my flask, that I noticed that Katie was leaning back in the armchair, engrossed in an old newspaper of Bert's. Her skirt was across the top of her knees and they were apart enough to give me an unobstructed view of her white panties. I looked away quickly and poured out a cup of tea but was not able to resist another quick look as I replaced the flask. A instant later she put the paper aside and pulled down her skirt, looking across at me she made an 'O' with her mouth and flashed her eyes.

I am pretty sure that was the moment that light dawned on me. I expect that loads of my readers, much more experienced and switched on than poor naive me, have twigged what was happening.

The fact was, of course, that I was being set up by the girls, probably with help from Bert, and had been almost from day one. It wouldn't have taken them long to realise that I was painfully shy and not at all used to females so it was easy for them to stage-manage my embarrassment and confusion.

It all suddenly dropped into place, I remembered the look that Bert had given Katie yesterday when he left early and now the strategically placed box. Looking back at the incident on top of the potatoes, I guessed was not a spontaneous event but had been discussed beforehand.

Suddenly I felt quite elated. OK, girls I thought, I'll keep playing along and see where we get. It could be a lot of fun!

The banter and laughter continued through the break until it was time to put out the fire and return to our separate jobs. Katie lagged behind the others as they went off to the barn.

'We'll need to move the riddle forward at the end of the day. Bert's busy, could you help me?' she said. 'None of the girls will want to stop.' She was standing very close and I could smell whatever she used on her hair, above the all-pervading aroma from the cattle yard.

'Course I will,' I told her. 'Can't refuse a damsel in distress especially one looking like you do.'

She flashed a smile. 'I'll see you later then. It will be a hand for a hand won't it?' Another smile and she followed the others, leaving me with a tightness in my chest ... and other places.

I gradually dug my way into the yard, the muck getting deeper with every load until, sitting on the tractor, I couldn't see over it. I had been thinking while I worked, about being set up by the girls, and another thought had suddenly hit me. I needed the lunch break to check it out.

The field gang returned to the yard for lunch leaving a loaded trailer in the field and I told Bert I would help Katie move the riddle.

'Good lad,' he said, 'twil save I havin' to leave 'em shart 'anded an come an 'elp 'er. 'Ow yew gettin' on down 'ere? Nearly cleared that yard, 'av 'e?' His eyes crinkled and gave him away.

'Well I would have if only you blokes would pull your fingers out,' I played him along.

He laughed. 'We darsn't want to git on too fast else us'll 'av fuck all left to do.'

'Not much fear of that. I'm not a quarter of the way in yet,' I told him.

'Ah, I reckons weem be a going to 'av too much for where weem to now. Boss'll 'av to decide where else to put un,' Bert stated before going for his lunch.

'You comin'?' he called.

'Won't be a mo,' I called after him.

With everyone now at lunch I quickly made my round the back of the buildings and came down the outside of the Dutch barn. Finding the spot I was looking for was easy. There was new straw on the ground where the wall had been tampered with and I could see where a bale had been cut and some pieces pulled out making a gap big enough to see through. The grass had been trodden down in the area indicating that several people had been here. I knew then that my guess had been right. Bert hadn't gone home early; he had come round here, with the girls, and they had all had a grandstand view of me and Katie.

I would not have noticed the gap in the bales as it was not on eye level and it was gloomy outside the circle of the electric light. Thinking back, where we had sat was almost right under one of the lights, so they all must have had a perfect view. Well, I thought, I suppose in a way something like this was bound to happen and I was certain there was no malice in it; it was just a bit of fun at my expense.

Clearing and loading continued through the afternoon, a trail of dropped dung leading down the yard and up the lane to the field entrance. I had got used to the smell and was hardly aware of it now. It was only if one walked away from the area and then returned, it was a bit overpowering.

Around 4.20 I sent Neil on his way with a load and, as there would not be time to load Tony, I parked up and headed for the potato barn. My thoughts were on what the girls might be setting up for me today.

''Ere's your young assistant, Katie, come to help you out,' Ruth called as I walked in.

'It's t'other bleedin' way round ain't it?' cackled Anna with a wink in my direction.

She laughed even more at my obvious embarrassment.

'Leave the poor lad alone,' Katie admonished. 'He's a good chap to come over. Somebody's got to help me push the riddle in.'

The women gathered in the end of the barn and with calls of 'bye' started to leave. Anna was last to go and as she left, called over her shoulder, 'Mind it's only tha' riddle what gets pushed in.'

'Piss off home you old bag,' Katie called after her. 'That Anna,' she said. 'She's always got to say something rude.'

She went off behind the pile of full bags and I shut down the riddle and pulled the boxes of dirt and chats clear so it could be moved. There were small iron wheels on each of the four legs that could be dropped and fixed with a pin. Katie returned and I got my back under each corner and lifted while she dropped the wheel and inserted the pin. There were two lengths of scaffold pipe which were kept handy and they were used, one on each side, to jack the machine forward. It was not hard to move and we soon had it repositioned. It was then a matter of taking the weight on each corner and putting up the wheels.

I was starting to think that perhaps there was nothing going to happen.

'I'm just going to make up the day book,' Katie said. 'Would you put the boxes back and Bert goes round with a grease gun every evening.' She went over and sat on a bale and picked up the book while I replaced the boxes. Without being obvious, I tried looking into the gloom to make out if the spy hole gap in the bales was open but it was impossible to see. Boxes in place I called to Katie to enquire the whereabouts of the grease gun. She was sitting sideways on the bale, one foot on the ground and the other on the bale and resting the book on her knee.

'It's in that tool box,' she called indicating a blue tin box at the end of the bale she was sitting on.

I walked over and lifted the lid. Inside with the gun were assorted chain links, tools, spark plugs for the motor plus assorted odds and ends. I picked up the gun and shut the lid and turned towards her. She had not changed her position and from where I stood I had a clear and unobstructed view up her skirt. She was not wearing the white panties I had seen earlier – she was not wearing anything – so I had my very first experience of the difference between the sexes. She was adding up in the record book and appeared not to be aware of my gaze or the fact that a short gasp had escaped my lips. After what seemed a lifetime I tore myself away and went over and greased up the riddle. On return Katie was back on her feet and looked ready to leave. I went to replace the grease gun. 'Thanks again,' she called, 'see you tomorrow and, Graham, I told you

I'd show you the rest.' I heard her giggle as she left.

I was sure in my mind that the whole episode would have been observed from outside and was able to smile to myself at the thought.

I turned out the lights and biked off home, going out of the yard just as the field gang drove in. I stopped briefly at the field and admired the dead straight rows of heaps that went across it, thinking of how there was even pride in the work of putting out dung. There seemed a lot of field to do yet and I also gave a thought to the fact that it had all got to be spread by hand, using just forks. Other images and thoughts came to me as I continued my ride home and I must admit that my fantasies went in directions that, until that afternoon, I had been unaware existed or rather, looked like!

Arriving home and walking indoors I found my Mum in the kitchen. At once she threw up her hands up in horror.

'What's that awful smell?' she exclaimed, holding her nose and trying to back away from me. 'You will have to leave those clothes in the shed. You can't possibly bring them in the house smelling like that. What on earth have you been up to?'

She fetched me a change of clothes and I had to stand in the cold shed among the garden tools and the mower and change. What was even worse I had to put them on again out there in the morning. The morning being the only time I could smell anything amiss.

The next day when I joined the girls for lunch I received a barrage of comments about the smell and my smell in particular.

Anna summed it up with, 'Effin 'ell, you don't 'arf pen an bleedin' ink.'

After the ribald comments on my personal odour, talk turned, as I guessed it would, to the evening before.

Katie had made eyes at me when I came in and I had, for probably the first time, no problem with blushing but returned her gaze easily with a smile.

'Got tha' riddle moved up all right then?' Ruth started. 'You 'ad no trouble seein' where it 'ad got ta go,' she said, trying not to laugh.

I've got to play along with this I thought and played dumb (not difficult for you I hear you saying).

'No, it was easy,' I replied. 'There seemed to be a ready made space for it to fit in.'

The girls fell about laughing and I forced myself to look round as if I was wondering what they were laughing at.

'What's so funny?' I asked.

No one answered but I noticed Katie look up at me suddenly, a questioning look in her eyes.

'You've twigged, haven't you?' she said,

causing the other girls to fall silent. 'I told you he would work it out soon enough.' She was looking round at the others.

'Yes, you've been rumbled.' I was making sure I had a big smile on my face, 'And I think you did a good job. No hard feelings whatsoever. You have probably done me a favour. I'm afraid I was a bit of a ninny where females are concerned.'

'Didn't take us long ta work that out. You must admit you were fair game,' Ruth said.

'That's for sure,' I told her. 'Anyway it's been as much fun for me as I bet it has for you lot. Wait until I see Bert. I can see his hand in a lot of what's been going on.'

'It weren't all 'e,' Anna spoke quietly for a change. 'We all as 'ad a 'and in it but we never meant no 'arm.'

'Don't worry, any of you, it was a good joke. I'm amazed I didn't guess before.'

'Well you sin more o' young Katie than you orter,' Anna piped up speaking usual volume now. 'Blokes ud walk bleedin' miles for a gander at a bit of neked fanny.' She cackled away her shoulders shaking.

'Shut up, Anna, you foul mouthed old troll,' Katie flared her eyes flashing, 'just let it rest, will you.' She smiled at me as if to apologise and, if I thought I had conquered my blushing, Anna had just proved me wrong.

Chapter 8

I had noticed when I passed the unloading crew the previous day that Bert had not been among them. He had obviously slipped away from the unloading gang on the pretext of moving the riddle. I caught up with him and we had a laugh together about the 'set up' he and the girls had worked on me.

''Ope yew ain't upset about it,' he said. 'We thart it might elp 'e in a way, not to be so shy like.'

'It did that all right,' I told him. 'After what I've had happen to me, it would be a job to embarrass me now.'

'Tell 'e tha' truth, I were a bit jealous at times,' Bert was starting to chuckle, 'specially when yew was standing thar wid your mouth 'anging open, looking at young Katie's fanny.' He was folding up now, the tears running down his face and I could do no more than laugh with him. He slapped me on the shoulder and walked off in that distinctive bow-legged action he had, his hand going into his pocket for his roll-up material.

That's odd, I thought, how could he be jealous? I saw him in a clinch kissing Katie not long ago.

Work on clearing the yard continued for the next week and a half and I was not sorry when it finished. Because of constantly using the clutch I could hardly walk on my left leg, and my right arm was painful from pulling the catch.

There was no stopping for wet days: just put a coat on and perhaps a sack across the knees and work on through. It could be a pretty miserable job in bad weather, not only for me, but the unloading gang as well.

Eventually it was all done, the yard looking strange and bigger still, empty of muck. The wall looked high and the top of my head came only half way up, yet the bullocks had been looking over it in their last days.

Bert had been right about the amount and for the last couple of days the muck had been carted to a heap in another field, to be used later in the year. We also put a few loads round the back of the buildings because Mr Willis said that local villagers often wanted a load for their gardens.

The girls had finished riddling potatoes. Any fall-out from their teasing soon passed and I found I could relax much more in their company. They seemed able to accept me now and we had a happy time together both working and during breaks round the fire.

I had wandered round to the Dutch barn

one break time and found it a bit like the cattle yard, looking huge with no potatoes. The riddle that had been in daily use was now stopped and quiet. Birds flew among the roof beams, many with lengths of straw in their beaks. Mice ran out in front of me from the base of the straw walls and scuttled quickly back again at my movement. A lone bale rested near the middle of the floor. My mind flipped back, was that perhaps the bale that Katie was sitting on the evening I helped move the riddle?

The images in my mind were vivid and clear and raised not only my heartbeat.

Our last action was to clean up the lane, which looked more like a landway, with dropped muck and mud from the tractor tyres.

The yard clearing had taken the year into the first week of April and the next task facing us was the spreading. It came down to myself, Tony, Neil, Walter and Percy to get the job done. Bert had returned to his girls who, he said, were going to be based at Hills Lea for a while planting beans.

We used Neil's Fergy for transport to the field, all of us standing on the drawbar or sitting on the wings.

Once there, we took a row of heaps each. With ordinary dung forks, it was a case of throwing the muck out in all directions half way to the next heap, making sure that all the ground was covered and big lumps were broken up. It was back-breaking work. The muck was heavy and needed a good flick of the wrist to throw it out and break it up. By the end of the day I was just about dead on my feet, and the bike ride home seemed never-ending. I changed in the shed, had my tea, a much needed bath, collapsed into bed and didn't stir until morning.

The next day seemed to go easier. One got into a certain rhythm with the work and it was possible to think of other things while working. It was a beautiful Spring morning with a warm breeze and it felt good to be outdoors. Hares chased about us, stopping every so often to stand up and box each other while plovers circled around giving their distinctive 'pee wit' call. Lark song filled the air and pheasants 'cock upped' from the field edges. We moved slowly across the field and it was as if nature accepted us as part of the natural scene and saw no harm in us.

It took four and a half days to finish the spreading and it was with some relief that we were able to put away the muck forks that now had tines that were shiny and polished. I recalled the words of that great country author Adrian Bell when he noted how 'metal things flashed and shone with use among the mire'.

The last two days we had had company in the field. Harry senior had pulled in with the Ford County crawler and his 4-furrow plough, so in a day or two all the muck would be under the soil and people living downwind could open their windows again. Not only that, I could stop spending so much time in the shed!!

The countryside was really waking up to Spring now. Primroses, daffodils and violets adorned the banks and the willows were showing a haze of green leaves. Buds were everywhere and a new sense of urgency appeared to be taking over from the cold-induced stupor of winter.

It was a pleasant ride down the lane of a morning and revel in the sights, sounds and smells of Spring. So different from my first rides back in January, it seemed a lifetime ago with so much happening and so many changes to my life. I felt full of a new confidence that had not been there before – the girls' campaign of setups had obviously worked wonders. Looking over the bank I was pleased to see that Tom's sheep had cleared the last of the cabbage field; they wouldn't get much off there. The thought that a new field would soon be planted ready for next winter sent a chill down my back.

Tony was in the yard when I arrived and after good mornings were exchanged said: 'Dad wants you to come with me and Neil.

We are going to drill some early peas for market. Most of our peas go to the new freezing works, but we are going to try some earlies. Harry is going to work down the ground so we'll get the seed and sort out the drill.'

The drill turned out to be right at the back of the implement shed and required several hitches and unhitches of Neil's Fergy to extricate it. It consisted of a blue tapered box with the word 'Suffolk' on a brass plate on the back. Four flexible spouts lead down to metal 'V'-shaped outlets that Neil told me were called 'coulters'. Two large wooden, iron-tyred wheels supported the box and at the front, where one would normally expect a drawbar, there were two smaller wheels, on a low axle, that could be steered by means of a long bar that projected out beyond the side. This could be swung over so the rig could be steered from either side. It was pulled by a length of chain which meant that the straightness of the work was controlled by the operator holding the bar and not, as is usually the case, by the tractor driver.

The seed was placed in the box and four discs, with little cups fixed to each side all the way round, picked it up and dropped it into the pipes and so to the coulters. The coulters made a groove in the soil into which the seed fell. They could be raised and lowered by means of two handles on the back that simply wound up a length of chain that raised them for transport or turning on the headland.

The discs that delivered the seed were fixed to a shaft that projected out of the side of the box and had a toothed gear wheel on the end. This was then driven by another gear rotated by the land wheel. The amount of seed sown could be adjusted by changing the size of the gear wheel.

We brushed the machine clear of pigeon droppings and the detritus of winter, greased and oiled it where required and loaded two bags of seed on the top. Harry, meanwhile, had clattered out of the yard with his County crawler towing a large set of disc harrows with a spiked set loaded on top. I guessed the County would be able to pull both, one behind the other, and so produce a seed bed in one pass. He would have to go the long way round as the crawler was not allowed on the road.

With everything ready we set off at a gentle pace so as not to lose the bags of seed with Tony having to walk and steer the drill. He had stuffed some pieces of paper in his pocket and laid an old walking stick in the box and I wondered what their use would be.

Arriving at the field, where Harry was working away, Tony called for Neil to stop in the gateway and set off walking to the far side.

'What's he up to?' I asked Neil.

'We've only got to drill part of this field,' he told me, 'from around here to the side that Harry is working toward. We need a straight edge to start from. Tony will put down some paper markers to give us our first run.'

Tony had, by now, reached the far side and had picked a mark on our side, probably the tree to the right of the entrance, and was walking towards it. Every so often he would stop and put down a paper marker and anchor it with a stone. When he arrived back we looked along the line and it was as straight as a gun barrel.

'See you didn't have too much down the pub last night,' Neil kidded him.

'Chance would be a fine thing,' Tony grinned back.

Neil pulled into the field and turned towards the markers. He then reversed against the frame of the front carriage and with a bit of manhandling we got the drill back against the edge and lined up.

After filling up with seed Tony said: 'Right Graham, what you need to do is to walk behind the drill and keep an eye on the four coulters and make sure that the seed doesn't get blocked or anything gets jammed in them. Take this stick and, if any weed or trash builds up on the front and starts flicking the seed out, you can poke it clear. If you see any problem at all, shout "woa". Each end lift up the coulters and take it out of gear.'

I moved the lever to put the box in gear, dropped the coulters and, with Tony taking his position with the steering bar, off we went. It was easy to see the seed falling from the ends of the pipes into the groove made by the coulter. Following each one was a little angled plate that neatly covered each row.

The lovely rich smell of the fresh earth that had been with me when I was harrowing earlier was a bonus to the sheer pleasure of being outdoors and actually planting seed. It was like sending a signal to all and sundry that you were going to be around on this patch of land for a good while to come. The walking was fairly easy as it was over a good tilth and one could always hold the back of the drill for a bit of a 'tow'.

The field had a slope, so one way was uphill but that meant it was easier coming down.

Tony steered so that each time we got to a paper marker the wheel of the carriage went over it. Neil drove to the edge and then turned hard, using the Fergy's turning brake, until he started to pull the drill off line at which point he stopped. I lifted the coulters and took the box out of gear. Looking back the wheel marks were dead straight. It was possible with the Fergy's great turning lock and with Tony turning the maximum on the front to rotate the drill in its own length. Then it was just a case of pushing back to the edge, coulters down, in gear and away with Tony steering exactly down the wheel mark from the previous run. I could see then why it was so important to get the first run straight, as all the rest depended on it. Each row of peas would now be exactly 2ft apart as the spacing from the outside coulter to the land wheel was 1ft. We had our morning break sitting on the bank at the side of the field but unhitched the Fergy and rode back to the farmyard for lunch.

When we returned, Walter followed us up the lane on his bike armed with a hoe and a small empty bag.

We had restarted when I noticed him come into the field, drop his bike beside the gateway and get some seed out of one of our bags into his small one. He then got busy with the hoe. Turning on the headland I asked Tony what he was up to.

He explained. 'When we drill away from the edge we can push the drill back and start right from the outside but when we come up to the other side we leave almost 10ft of ground unsown. Walter can see the marks where you lift up the coulters so he is pulling out four drills to the edge and sowing the seed by hand so everything is nice and even. He will catch us up that side then cross over and do this.'

Harry had finished by lunchtime and clattered off with the discs and we were done by four in the afternoon and left Walter to his lonely task. I could see that he had timed it well and would be finished by normal knock-off time.

We got back and cleared out the last of the seed from the drill. It was coated with a mercurial seed dressing that was supposed to stop pests eating it, but it tended to build up in the little cups and cake up the spouts, so we pulled it up to the hose and gave it a wash-out. Neil backed it just under cover as Tony said it would be needed again shortly.

'We'll get the light roller and harrows ready,' Tony said, 'be a job for you in the morning. The roller just spans four rows so you drive up between each set of drill wheel marks, miss a couple of runs to give yourself room to turn on the headland, and keep working round.'

The roller had at one time been horse-drawn and still had the seat on top, but had been roughly converted to be pulled by a tractor by sawing off the ends of the shafts, fixing a bar between and bolting on a plate with a hole in it. A set of very light harrows could be fixed on a chain to run just in front of the roller so two jobs were done at once: the peas would be properly covered and the ground firmed over them. I got my Fergy, hitched on the roller, and pulled it from where it had rested all winter, disturbing a couple of rats in the process, which lead to a temporary break in proceedings while we pursued them around the yard eventually dispatching them both.

I greased up the hub bearings and Tony showed me how to rig the harrows.

'If you want to take it up to the field now and get the harrows rigged you can get off to a flying start in the morning,' Tony grinned, rolling being one of the slowest jobs.

I scrunched and clanked my way slowly to the field and pulled in, lining up for the first run, unloaded and set up the harrows as Tony had showed me. Having checked all was secure I unhitched and walked round to get on the tractor, disturbing a cock pheasant that had come through the hedge. The bird panicked and took off back over the landway with a whirring of wings and loud 'cock ups' at which point there was a thudding of hooves and a female voice calling 'Steady now, steady girl'. A white horse appeared in the gateway bucking and prancing, obviously spooked by the noisy departure of the pheasant. Its rider was a stunningly pretty girl, perhaps a little older than me in usual riding gear, fawn check jacket and white jodhpurs inside black boots. She was hatless and had her hair tied back in a pony tail and I was quick to note that it was ash blonde, much whiter than the horse.

After a tussle she managed to control the frightened animal and it stood snorting and throwing its head up and down.

'Are you all right?' I asked. 'That looked a bit scary.' A while back I would have been blushing speaking to a strange girl but not now, not after, well, you know!

'She's fine now,' the girl answered smiling. 'I've seen you around the farm. Are you working here all the time?'

Her voice was devoid of Kentish brogue, instead there was an accent I thought might be foreign. She was obviously well educated and self-confident.

'Yes, I'll be around for a few years I hope. Do you live around here?' I asked smiling back.

'I've got a flat at the stables I share with another girl. It's up the lane and round the loop bit that joins the lane again.' She turned in the saddle and pointed back the way she had come. Her twisting in the saddle pulled the top part of the jacket open and I noted the obviously generous curves under her white shirt.

'My name's Tracy, by the way,' she said.

'Hello Tracy Bytheway. I'm Graham,' I replied smiling broadly. 'You certainly brighten anyone's day. I hope to see you around.'

She gave me a wide smile showing white even teeth. With a wave from a black-gloved hand, she moved out into the lane and, lifting in the stirrups, trotted off. I watched her go, wondering just how tight jodhpurs could get before they ripped. Shaking my head, I returned to the tractor.

On my bike ride home I took the loop lane. It took about five minutes longer that way, but I found the stables Tracy had told me about. She was just leading the horse to its box and we exchanged smiles and waves.

Well, you've got to start somewhere!

This route became my regular way to and from the farm and my days were made brighter by the thought of catching sight of this super-looking girl.

Next day dawned dull and overcast with a forecast of rain later. I hoped it would hold off long enough to finish the rolling. I parked my bike (no sign of Tracy at the stables) and was straightaway up the lane on the Fergy to get the job started. I hitched on the roller and, with a quick check round, I set off. It was quite alarming to see the harrows jingling along just 6in. in front of the roller but all seemed well.

The day grew gradually darker and a cold wind got up, blowing in my face one way and right behind on the return run. The dust from the tackle blew all over me and, if the old saying about a peck of Spring dust being worth a King's ransom were true, I could have made a fortune that day. I didn't stop for morning tea as the rain looked ready to start any minute, but I was in luck and it held off until the second to last run up the field. I just managed to finish with little bits starting to stick to the roller. I quickly pulled to the gateway and started to pack up the harrows when the heavens opened. I could only trundle along slowly pulling the roller and had to grin and bear it. As I pulled into the yard I saw Tony and Neil sheltering in the implement shed. I could see wide grins spreading over their faces at my sodden and bedraggled appearance. I parked up the roller, unhitched and drove in alongside them.

'Just made it,' I said to the grinning pair.

'Is there any soil left up there,' Tony said still smiling, 'or have you brought it all back on you?'

Looking down I could see mud in every fold and crease of my attire and I was dripping a pool of brown sludge on to the concrete floor. The dust that I had been liberally coated with had now turned into liquid mud and I was covered in it, as was the tractor that had more brown areas than grey.

The Land-Rover drove in at that moment and Mr Willis alighted and came over to us.

'Did you manage to get finished?' he

asked, his face also breaking into a smile at my mud-smeared appearance.

'Yes, it's done,' I told him. 'It's all right for you blokes standing around in the dry.'

'Well don't you stand around too long in one place,' Mr Willis retorted, 'or there will be a barrowful of mud to pick up.' This produced howls of mirth and I couldn't help but join in.

Mr Willis had a look round the sky and said: 'You did well to get that job finished. This rain will do more good than we will today, so get yourself off home and get dried out. Don't go walking indoors or your Mum will have a fit. I'll see you tomorrow.'

I collected my still-full grub bag from the tractor. Even that had a smeared muddy look, and headed home through the steady rain. I wondered how many more times I would get a soaking sitting on a tractor in my farming life. I didn't take the diversion past the stables not wishing Tracy to see my mud-smeared state.

Vanity, ah, vanity!

Chapter 9

The spell of wet weather continued for a day or two. Time was spent clearing up, picking up the loose straw that Katie and I had pushed off the potatoes. We cleared up the remains of the fodder beet clamp from alongside the cattle-yard wall. The boxes of chats from the last day's riddling were carted to the chalk pit and dumped.

During this spell Mr Willis asked me to clear out and tidy up a small store shed behind the granary.

I parked a trailer close to the door and started throwing out all sorts of accumulated rubbish, a lot of which looked as if it had come from the house. There was a broken chair, some carpet off-cuts – that sort of thing – plus bits from the farm, odd bits of seed left in bags and old sacks that the rats had chewed. I worked through to the back of the store. Hanging on the wall were traces and bridles and some collars plus assorted chains and bits. I had heard the Land-Rover pass on its way to the house not long before, so I walked over and knocked on the door, keeping a wary eye out for Smudge but, as Mr Willis was at home, he didn't even bark. The boss himself answered my knock. 'I think you ought to take a look at some of the things in that store,' I said. 'I'm not sure what's rubbish.'

He came over with me and went inside.

'It's all this horse stuff here,' I indicated the back of the store.

He stopped dead still, looking, the light from the grimy cobweb-filled window falling across his face.

'I'd forgotten all this was still in here,' he almost whispered as if he was talking to himself. He took a couple of paces towards the collars and ran his hand down over the nearest one, leaving a clean shiny mark through the dust.

'This was old Duke's. My father used to go to plough with him and Tammy.' He laid his hand on the next. 'This was Tammy's.' He looked up at the equipment on the wall no doubt with the memories of when horses provided the power to run the farm. Thoughts of his childhood brought up among their constant presence before tractors and economics gradually pushed them off the land.

He remained still for several minutes, the dust dancing in the light, the odd rustles and movements from rodents in the corners the only sound. He seemed to be steeling himself to speak, and when he did so his voice was croaky and tight with emotion. I could see the moistness in his eyes.

'They should be thrown out but I can't tell you to do it,' he paused as if to stop his voice breaking. 'Just leave them where they are so they won't be in the way.'

With that he hurried outside and walked down through the small orchard at the back of the buildings where he stood looking out over the valley. He was still there when, ten minutes later, I left with the trailer heading for the chalk pit.

I was quite shaken by his reaction to seeing the old horse tack but, thinking about it, I could well imagine the bond there must have been between man and horse – both sharing the nice sunny days and cold wet ones, plodding home at the end of a hard day's work both tired and looking forward to a break. I was sorry, in a way, to have been twenty years too late in starting a farming career and to have missed those days. On thinking further it is nice to be able to just press a starter or swing a crank handle in the morning and to park up at night and leave without having to groom, feed and water.

The few wet days turned to showers. Then bright, fine, breezy weather arrived. The women reappeared in the yard and I asked Katie what they had been up to.

'We've been dropping beans,' she said and, seeing my mystified look, explained: 'The Boss always grows field beans for market.

Since he's had Hills Lea they have gone over there. Ted's got an old cultivator frame with wheels on so as he can set the depth. It's got four tines with coulters on the end and he draws out the rows for us, then we come along and drop in the seed by hand. It's a back-breaking job but that's what we are here for.'

'Can't it be done with the pea drill?' I asked.

'Boss says it smashes up the seed,' she replied. 'Anyway us girls are used to sorting out seed by hand.'

She made big eyes at me and wandered off to find the rest. As for me, still a bit slow, I didn't cotton on to her mixed meaning for a second or two but when I did the memory of our encounter on the potato sacks caused pleasurable stirrings again in my nether regions.

Mr Willis now said it was time to harrow the winter-sown corn. Off we went in the Land-Rover and he showed me the fields to be done and told me their names for future reference.

'Why harrow a growing crop?' I asked him. 'Surely the harrows will pull it all out and ruin it?'

'Well, you don't want to hit it too hard,' he explained. 'Set the tines on the Fergy harrows two notches back and keep the weight on the hydraulics. Oh, and go steady, not like a mad thing like Roger used to. What it does is make the crop tiller: that means to shoot more than one stalk from a single plant and it also pulls out a lot of early weed seedlings. After it's settled down you can go over the fields you have harrowed with the ring rolls.'

Arriving back it was time for morning tea and there seemed quite a crowd with Bert and the girls back. The usual banter soon started with Anna's cackle sounding above the rest. Bert called to me over the fire.

'Ow's 'e bin gettin' on ower 'ere then, Graham? Was that 'e I seen walkin' ahind tha' pea drill? Yew must be findin' yewr way aroun tha' place a bit now.'

'Yes, that was me behind the drill,' I told him. 'I'm slowly learning my way around and (quick glance to catch Katie's eye) find-ing out how things have to be put in.' I leant down quickly to get my flask and to cover my mirth. The girls and Bert were falling about and Katie had developed a sudden fit of coughing.

Morning tea over, I went to collect the Fergy and hitch on the harrows. Katie was hanging her grub bag on her bike beside the tractor.

'Did you enjoy the pea drilling?' she asked.

Strange question, I thought, but replied: 'Yes, lot of walking mind. I was beat at the end of the day.' She was standing right in front of me her eyes on my face.

'If you ever fancy sowing a bit of seed without all that walking, just let me know,' her voice was husky and the trick of passing her tongue across her lips was working its magic.

'Katie,' I managed to say, 'is this a continuation of the set-up? Am I being spied on from somewhere?' I did a quick look round, but the yard was empty.

'No, that's all finished,' she said hesitantly, then went on: 'If you want to find out what it's all about, no strings attached, just for ... fun.'

'My God,' I said, 'how could I refuse an offer like that!'

'Leave it with me,' she said smiling. 'I've got an idea that should work. I'll let you know.'

With that she was gone, leaving me trembling, shaken, bemused and downright ... excited. Again.

Arriving at the first field to be harrowed, I set everything up as Mr Willis had told me and set off. I half expected bare earth behind me but all was well. It was more like raking a lawn and very little of the crop got pulled out. The harrows left light and dark stripes across the field and I concentrated on keeping them nice and straight to make it all look smart and tidy. I found that every different operation I did in the fields created its own unique smell, either the earthy smell when the soil is moved or in this case, the sweet distinctive aroma caused by the green leaves of corn being crushed under the tractor wheels.

I had to keep a constant look out for plover chicks of which there were many. They were doomed if the harrows went over them and they tended to run straight in front rather than out to the side. Every so often I had to stop and catch a chick and move it over on to ground that had been harrowed. The parent birds would swoop low over my head, not realising I was saving their offspring's life. These were happy hours, indeed, and I don't think I would have changed places with anyone. It was warm for early April. The fluffy clouds were about, drifting across the blue sky, while all around spread the multitude of greens of a burgeoning Spring.

The air was clear and almost seemed to sparkle. Other tractors could be seen on neighbouring farms, some of them doing the same job. The Fergy purred along, not under any serious load, and was not intrusive, so that the wildlife at the field edges seemed quite happy for me to be there. Beyond the fields, away in the distance, the tall chimneys of the factories along the Thames sent plumes of smoke straight up into the blue where they mingled into a white haze. For me they could have been on another planet, for here was peace and tranquillity and I had a feeling of being part of the unbroken continuity of farming life. Others had done this work before me and when my time was over it would still carry on. The countryside seemed like a separate entity, with us mortals its willing slaves, growing the crops, tending the livestock, improving the soil and keeping everything neat and tidy.

Sitting on the bank eating my lunch I could see part of one of the fields I had harrowed back in early March that had been drilled with barley. It now had a green tint and I promised myself I would drop by and have a look on my way home. Having finished eating and with my last cup of tea to hand I lay back on the bank and listened to the birdsong and watched the clouds floating gently across the sky.

I was disturbed from my daydreaming by a clinking and the rattling of stones and lifting my head found that Tracy and her white steed were standing beside me.

'You got nothing else to do?' she said, her eyes twinkling. I noticed they were a deep green and had an almost hypnotic quality.

'It's lunchtime, a man's got to eat,' I said with a smile, finding my cup of tea. 'I hope you aren't making big hoof prints all over my nice neat harrowing.'

'You can hardly see where she's been,' she

said moving the horse a pace sideways and looking behind her.

'What's her name?' I asked.

'Moonshine,' she replied. The horse swung its head up and down as if agreeing and champed on its bit as if anxious to be off.

'You've got amazing coloured hair; it matches the horse,' I told her, hardly believing that I was calmly chatting to a girl without blushing or being self-conscious.

'It's always been like that, right since I was a little girl,' she told me. 'Drop in the stables sometime and I'll show you our flat.'

'I'll do that,' I said getting to my feet and stroking Moonshine's nose. 'Might be working on for a day or two but first chance I get I'll call in and see you.'

'Good,' she smiled. 'I'll make us some coffee. See you.'

She gently pulled Moonshine's head round, turned on the spot and trotted off towards the gateway.

I watched her go, again noticing how well she filled the jodhpurs.

I finished the first field by mid-afternoon and moved on to the next, worked on until 6.00, folded up the harrows and called it a day. Leaving the yard, I made my way to the fields I had worked down in March. Sure enough there were frail green rows visible right across, highlighted by the low sun. I felt quite elated that something had actually come up and delighted that I had been a part of its arrival. Because of me and my workmates this bare ploughed field was now becoming a green productive area with the prospect of a valuable harvest to come. I lingered for some time until the gathering gloom sent me homeward. To this day I have never lost that sense of pleasure at seeing a newly emerging crop of any sort, be it mine or my neighbours'.

Next day saw the harrowing finished and I was back in the yard with the tractor parked up soon after 4.00. There was not a soul about. The Land-Rover was in the lean-to and Mr Willis's car was missing from by the back door. There was not enough time to start another job so I wandered over to the big barn that was the centre of the farm-yard. It was a typical tythe barn with a big tall double door on one side and a smaller lower door on the other. The idea of this was that a full waggon load could be driven in through the tall doors, unloaded, and drive, straight out. Inside it was like a church with its high roof and curved trusses, narrow slits in the thick walls projecting shafts of light onto the dusty concrete floor. There was a small stack of hay bales down the cattle-yard end left over from the winter feeding. The other end had a couple of weighing scales and several 56lb weights. There were also a couple of piles of corn sacks and I could see stencilled on the top ones 'On Hire from the West of England Sack Co'. I remembered on my first day coming into this barn via the tall door from the cattle yard so I walked right down there to take a look. I was about to return when I heard voices and laughter and realised that someone had come into the barn. It was quite dark where I was so anybody walking in from the daylight would not see me at once. I took a couple of quick paces to the hay bales and climbed up a couple to where I could see over.

I was surprised to see Bert and Katie holding hands and walking towards one of the piles of sacks and was even more surprised when, on reaching them they went into a long kiss. Katie finally broke away and dropped back on to the sacks, pulled up her skirt and Bert, after a bit of fumbling, went down on top of her and they had sex there and then. I heard Katie give a little cry, then it was all over and they were on their feet adjusting clothing and heading for the door. I stayed where I was for a least a quarter of an hour and then came down from the bales and, after a quick look round, scampered across to the tractor shed.

These events had brought the time close to knock-off and, as there was no sign of Tony or Mr Willis, I made my way home. I didn't know what to make of what I had witnessed in the barn. Was it just sex or was Katie exchanging her favours for easier jobs with Bert or were they having a full-blown affair? I decided it would be best not to mention anything of what I had seen to anybody using the 'least said soonest mended' policy.

Being more or less on time knocking off I decided to take the loop road past the stables. There was no sign of anybody around so I coasted down the drive way and into the stable yard. I lent my bike against some straw bales in the small barn and walked around. Moonshine suddenly appeared, looking over her stable door and seemed to recognise me. I spoke to her and stroked her nose. There was a brick-and-stone building making up one side of the yard with a flight of wooden stairs at one end leading to a landing with rails round it and a blue-painted door. The windows of the second storey had chintzy curtains, so I guessed that was Tracy's flat. Taking the bull by the horns and doing something I would never have dreamed of doing a few months back, I mounted the stairs and knocked on the door.

There was a short delay then Tracy's voice from inside called, 'Who is it?'

'It's Graham, haven't you got anything to do?' I called back.

I heard her laugh, then the door opened and her head appeared, the white blonde hair wrapped in a towel.

'I'd just got out of the bath,' she said. 'Come in, you'll have to excuse me.'

I slipped off my boots and went inside to find her wrapped neck to toe in a large white bathwrap.

'I'll just go and get dry and put something on,' she said.

'Don't bother on my account,' I heard myself say without really thinking.

She side-glanced me and went into the little kitchen area. 'I'll put the kettle on,' she said a bit breathlessly.

There was a small blue table with two wooden upright chairs, also painted blue, to the right of the door, so I pulled one out and sat down. She filled the kettle and put it on. She opened a cupboard below where I could see mugs and china but, not being able to bend and get anything without loosening the towel, she shut the door again, flustered.

'Just be a tick,' she said heading for a door to one side that I guessed was the bedroom and bathroom. The kettle had just started to sing when she reappeared in a blue print dress with white edging, her feet bare and the towel still wrapped round her hair. She took off the kettle and opened the cupboard door again and, in that clever way that women have, turned slightly and bent one leg so as not to show too much, and came up with a couple of mugs.

'Sugar?' she asked.

'Yes, honey,' I replied quickly. She cast her eyes heavenwards.

'No, idiot, do you take sugar in your coffee?'

'Two please, not much milk.' I felt quite relaxed in her company, a fact I found hard to believe, even though we hardly knew each other.

'Is Moonshine the only horse here?' I asked. 'You can't be overworked.'

'There are five others that belong to the stables' owner but we often have eight or nine sort of in transit,' she replied.

She brought over the coffee and put the mugs on the table. I caught a whiff of the bath oil or soap that she used.

'I didn't think you would call in,' she said. 'I thought you might think it a bit forward of me asking you.' She was flustered again and lowered her head, blushing.

'I might only be a farm boy,' I smiled at her, 'but I'm not so silly as to turn down an invite from a beautiful blonde.' It was my turn to blush a little, me blush, unheard of!

She laughed out loud. 'Thanks for the compliment, just remember the invite was for coffee.'

She got up again and moved towards the bedroom door. 'I'll pop and fix my hair.

Make yourself at home.' She disappeared through the door and I sipped my coffee and looked around. The room I was in was obviously a kitchen/diner. There was one other door, apart from the one Tracy had just gone through, that I assumed was to a sitting room as it was in the wall dividing the length of the building. The walls were painted a sunshine yellow and the doors were blue to match the table and chairs. There were some pictures on the wall mainly of horses and there were wall lights with cream tassled shades. It was small but functional. The stove that Tracy had boiled the kettle on was gas so obviously from bottle supply.

I had all but finished the coffee when she returned and I'm sure I gasped as I got to my feet. The blonde locks were loose over her shoulders held back from her face with a blue and white band that matched the dress.

'My God, you look like a million dollars!' I told her. 'If that invite was just for coffee I had better be going. I'm only a mere mortal you know.'

She laughed again. 'How old are you? You seem to have the knack of saying the right things.'

'Guess.' I was in trouble and needed time to think.

'Well,' she looked at me quizzically. 'I would

say between seventeen and eighteen.'

'You guess as good as you look.' I thought that would save me having to lie to her.

'What about you then?' I asked quickly, moving the spotlight off me.

'Guess,' she shot back at me, her lips twitching at the corners. It was a good excuse to slowly look her up and down and I took full advantage.

'I would say, without looking at your teeth, around twenty eight.' I had a job keeping a straight face as it was obvious she was much younger.

'You pig!' she cried out but unable to keep a straight face. 'I make you coffee and all you do is insult me.'

She pouted and folded her arms as if in a huff.

'Sorry.' I tried to look repentant. 'I would say you are maybe just a bit older than me.'

'I'm twenty in a couple of months,' she told me, 'but you don't deserve to know.'

She picked up her coffee and took a long drink.

'Where's your flatmate?' I asked.

'Oh Sue, she's away with the other horses. We usually take it in turns to go.'

'So do you stay here alone when she's away? It seems a bit risky.'

'I'm OK, I can look after myself. My Mum and Dad live only about five miles away and there's a phone.'

She was speaking quickly as if not quite sure of herself and her cheeks were flushed.

I looked at my watch and said, 'Well I'd better be off. Talking of phones, am I allowed the number?'

'Only if you give me yours,' she replied coyly.

'Deal.' She found paper and pencil and we exchanged numbers.

'I think your flat's super,' I told her, moving towards the door.

She moved across and opened the door and I noticed she seemed even more tense.

'You must call in again, perhaps for an evening. I could cook a little meal. I'm very good with a tin-opener. A weekend evening, perhaps? Can I ring you?' She almost raced out the words and looked at me through her eyelashes, her head lowered.

'That would be nice. I'll look forward to your call.' I smiled at her, wondering why she was so wound up.

I moved through the doorway and slipped on my boots.

'Thanks again,' I said standing up and without warning she put one arm round the back of my neck and kissed me full on the lips. Not a peck, a full-blown kiss.

'See you,' she said and, quickly moved back inside, blew another kiss, and shut the door.

It was a few moments before I could gather

my senses and go down the stairs, wondering what the hell was happening in my life.

I had left school four months ago, got a job that had led to a fairly key position, had the offer of sex from a very attractive older woman I work with and now seemed to have made a bit of a hit with a stunning ash-blonde stable-girl.

I walked back to my bike. Moonshine was still looking over her stable door expect-antly. I thought perhaps she had another meal to come and was looking for Tracy. But then Tracy wouldn't have got all dressed up if there was another feed to do ... or did she dress up just for me...?

Any car drivers coming towards me as I cycled home must have wondered about that young chap riding along with a great big grin on his face. If only they knew!

Chapter 10

Work on the farm seemed to move up a gear now that Spring was well and truly with us. I finished the corn harrowing. Harry, meanwhile, was deep cultivating the fields where we had spread the dung ready for planting potatoes. I had the job of carting the seed to the field and dropping the bags in 'stations' along each side so that the planter could be refilled either end. It had a wooden box holding the seed that was tapered to three outlets that let the seed out into trays in front of the women operators. Under each tray there was a circular plate that rotated and had small flat cups attached round the edge with bottoms that would swing open when the cup was over the tube that led to the ridger.

Each operator had to take the seed from the tray and put one in each cup as the plate rotated. It was a noisy, tedious and dusty job. The cups opened and shut with a clang and, with three of them going plus the dust from the seed and the tractor wheels, it was not something that one would want to do for long at a stretch.

The girls used to swap over several times a

day and would come off the planter covered in soil and dust and have difficulty in standing up for a while, I shudder to think what all the dust did to their lungs.

One of the E27N Fordson Major tractors from Hills Ley had been fetched over to pull the machine as it had a special reduction gearbox that enabled it to go very slowly.

I remembered from helping my Dad in the garden that we always left the potato ridges in place and earthed them up even more as the crop grew. This didn't happen on the farm. The ridges were harrowed flat on completion of sowing and the field ring rolled in the direction of the ridges. I found out why later in the year.

In the corn fields I had harrowed I now had the job of ring rolling. The rolls were in a gang of three, one 8ft wide and two 4ft. They were pulled one behind the other to the field and then the two smaller ones could be attached to the outside of the wide one to give 16ft of working width. There was quite a knack in getting them ready. The two short ones were too heavy to be pulled about by hand so they had to be unhitched and then the wide one pulled round in a circle so the attachment point came right to fix one of the smaller ones. The same procedure was used in the other direction to pick up the second. It was a slow second-gear job with the Fergy, but as the rolls covered a wide area it didn't take long to do a field. They made lovely light and dark stripes, like the harrows, so the job looked great when it was finished.

The spring barley was given the same treatment as it was now growing on strongly.

Several days had passed since I had called in on Tracy and, although I had caught the odd glimpse of Moonshine in the distance, we had not spoken. I had been working until dark most evenings so had not had the chance to visit the stables.

Another job that came my way at this time was assisting Tony with drilling the plant bed. The farm grew a variety of green vegetables such as brussel sprouts, cauliflowers, Christmas cabbage, January King cabbage and others, all of which were grown from seed. All the different varieties were planted in a bed in separate rows and, when big enough, were pulled and bunched and then hand planted in the field where they were to grow until fit for market. The tiny seeds were planted by a 4-row drill driven by a chain from one single front wheel. The depth of planting was controlled by the operator (Tony), who had two handles exactly like a wheelbarrow with which he could push down or lift up according to the hardness, or otherwise, of the ground. It was called a 'barrow drill' and could be pulled by hand but the plant bed was on quite a slope so we used a tiny Ransome MG2 crawler tractor. I had the driver's job. The little crawler had a small, single-cylinder, air-cooled engine and was steered by two levers that simply braked the track on one side or the other. There were no independent clutches. It had two gears, one to go forward and one reverse, and the throttle was a simple lever of the type that could be found on an average lawnmower. The seed barrow was pulled by a piece of chain, thus giving Tony control over direction and straightness.

The seed bed was at Hills Ley. Tony had use of the Land-Rover for the day so we loaded tiny cotton bags of seed, marker discs and a can of petrol and set off.

Ted was in the open shed working on the engine of a small elevator. Greetings were exchanged all round.

''Ow yer makin' out then, Graham?' he asked me.

'Fine, gradually finding my way around,' I replied. 'Haven't got this way much as yet, except for some harrowing and rolling.'

'Thart that was 'e,' Ted said. 'Don't see too many folks ower 'ere, 'tis like one o' lay frontear outposts.' His lined face crinkled into a grin showing brown tobacco-stained teeth. 'Yew'll 'ave come ta drill tha' plant bed I'll be bound.'

'You're right,' Tony said. 'Think the little Ransome will start?'

'Carse it'll start yew,' Ted looked disdainful, 'little ole tacker loike that, thare be fuck all to go a'kilter. Did yew remember ta bring some petrol?'

'In the back.' Tony indicated the Land-Rover.

'Fuckin 'ell, fings be lookin' up yew remembering summat!'

Ted wandered off and came back with the can.

We went round the side of the big barn to a smaller weatherboard shed that had double doors fastened with a padlock. Ted retrieved the key from its hiding place on top of one of the side beams and unlocked the doors. The Ransome was to one side partly buried under an assortment of bits and pieces and the seed barrow even more deeply buried behind it. We set about shifting everything and finally got the tractor clear.

'If you were a bit tidier over here it wouldn't take half a bleedin' day to get our tackle sorted out,' Tony said with a wink in my direction.

'Oi this bain't all my rubbish,' Ted cried, trying to look serious. 'Thar be t'others about 'ere as well as I.'

We filled the tank and Ted brought over a grease gun and oilcan and busied himself firing grease into various nipples and squirting oil here and there. The engine was started by winding a piece of cord round an outside pulley and tugging firmly. Tony found the cord and wound it on, checked the tractor was out of gear and gave a pull. Nothing happened so the process was repeated several times with no success. Ted removed the plug and the motor was spun over to check the spark.

'She's sparkin' OK,' he reported, replacing the plug. 'This'll get the fucker goin'.' He soaked a rag with petrol and held it over the air intake, Tony wound up the rope again and pulled and with a roar the motor sprang to life and ran smoothly.

'Loik I sed thar be fuck all to go wrong wid these,' Ted shouted over the beat of the engine.

'I'll show you how it works,' Tony said to me. 'It's got a centrifugal clutch so you can only get it in gear when it's ticking over. Once it's in gear speeding up the motor will make it go along. The more revs you give it the faster it goes.' He moved the throttle lever backwards and let the revs die to an idle. On the front bulkhead was a little lever with a spring-loaded, lift-up, knob that engaged a pin in holes in a slightly curved plate, one to the left and one to the right. He pulled up the knob, and moving the lever to the right and engaging the pin in that hole, opened the throttle and the machine started to trundle forwards. A gentle pull on the side lever caused it to turn (both levers together would override the clutch and make it stop).

'Yer das'nt need ta be a genius to drive tha' bleedin' thing,' Ted observed wisely.

Tony stopped and dismounted and waved me over. 'Give it a try while we sort out the drill.'

I stepped aboard. The top of the tracks only came up to just above my knee, and I followed his movements.

I found it easy to control once you got used to a gentle touch on the steering levers as they tended to grab, leading to violent changes of direction.

The seeder was out and brushed off so I trundled back and turned in front of it ready to hitch on. Tony got the bags of seed along with a canvas sheet and a soft brush and, laying them all on top, hitched up the chain and off we went. The seed bed was just across the lane and had been worked down to a very fine tilth and rolled. I guessed Neil had been doing that. We pulled into the nearest corner and unloaded the seed bags and canvas. Tony opened one of the bags and poured about half into the box. There was a shaft that ran through the box with grooves, like keyways, cut into it and these picked up the tiny seeds and dropped them down the tubes to the coulters. A rod across the back of the box slid out and fixed and another rod went from that down to the ground. This made a mark that guided the wheel of the drill up on the next run and kept evenly spaced rows. The seeder was put in gear and we were off at a slow walking pace. We would drill perhaps eight rows of one plant, then upend the seeder over the canvas and carefully brush it out, tipping that seed back in the bag it came from and filling up with a different seed, then off again.

It was, of course, essential to mark what had gone where, so not only were marker discs put down but Tony also noted in a pocket book exactly what was where. Plants all tend to look the same when they are small. It took nearly to lunchtime before the bed was finished and we went back across the lane to park up the tractor and seeder.

Ted appeared as we drove in, coming out of the shed.

'Yew bin all this time just drillin' that little plant bed,' he tutted. 'Could a done tha' 'ole bleedin' field by this time.'

Tony laughed. 'Never mind, Ted, we've done so you can doze off again now.'

'Fine chance o' lat,' said Ted pulling the shed doors shut and snapping the lock.

Tony and I got back in the Land-Rover with what was left of the seed and the can and, with a wave to Ted, set off for our lunch.

After lunch I took the Fergy back to the

plant bed. Neil had left the light flat roller there, and went over the bed again to firm up the soil round the little seeds. It took longer going to and fro from the yard than it did to do the job, especially as I had to bring the roller back. But I didn't worry as it was a nice sunny afternoon.

On the way back I met Tracy coming the other way so I stopped to say hello.

'Not seen you for a while. I hope I didn't upset things last time,' she said, looking worried and blushing a little.

'Of course not,' I replied quickly. 'It was just a bit of a surprise that's all, a very nice surprise, I might add.'

'I'll be at the stables all weekend if you're not working,' she said, her colour rising still further.

'Well, Saturday's out, but I could come over Sunday after lunch if that's OK,' I told her.

'Fine, I'll see you then,' she smiled and, pulling Moonshine's head up from where the horse was trying to have a quick graze but getting tied up with the bit, tapped her heels and moved on past me.

I drove on back to the yard, the roller chinking and rattling behind, parked it up and put the Fergy away. Coming out of the shed I met Mr Willis driving in and he stopped and beckoned me over.

'Remember that bit of muck from the yard

that we put round the back?' he said. I nodded.

'Tomorrow's Saturday,' he went on. 'Would you throw on a good load and take it round to Katie's house?'

He explained how to find the place, which was about a mile and a half away towards the next village.

'They've got a good-sized garden and she has a load nearly every year,' he told me.

'By the way,' I said. 'I'm not old enough to have a tractor driving licence. Am I OK driving on the road that far?'

He laughed. 'You'll be all right. Most of the cops round here get several free pheasants and spuds when they want them. I don't think they will bother you too much.' He drove off still chuckling.

Cycling home my thoughts were again on girls – yes, I know – but they were a bit new to me and I was still trying to understand them. Now fifty years on I'm still trying to understand them!

Katie's on Saturday and Sunday afternoon with Tracy. I expected the trip to Katie's to be innocent enough, just a routine thing by the sound of it. I knew she was married so her husband was sure to be there.

Tracy I wasn't too sure about. She obviously did things on impulse so who knows what might happen...

Saturday was wet, very wet, and cold. I rode to work in my full waterproof kit, overtrousers and oilskin coat. My 'good mornings' to others arriving were met with 'what's fucking good about it!'

I filled the Fergy, hitched on the wooden trailer, collected a muck fork from the tool shed and drove round to the heap. What a dismal sight, puddles everywhere round it and the rain slanting down on the strong wind!

I parked the trailer in a handy position for loading, covered up the seat on the tractor to at least keep that dry and set about forking on a load. The trouble with working in wet gear is that as soon as you start to get warm the perspiration can't get out and your ordinary clothes get damp and clammy.

It took about three-quarters of an hour to throw on a good load, by which time the rain was easing a little. I had hopes that the old saying of 'rain before seven, fine before eleven' might be coming true, especially as there were signs of brightness downwind. I stuck the fork in the load and, driving through the yard and out onto the lane, slipped the Fergy into top and made my way towards Katie's. A steady stream of water came off the front wheels which rattled against my wet gear, and every so often the wind would catch not only that but the stream off the rear wheels and throw the whole lot over me. It was not a pleasant ride.

By the time I had located Katie's house the rain had stopped and the sun was trying to emerge from the overcast sky. The house was a semi-detached property on the end of a row of six at the edge of the village. There was a drive entrance with no car in the way so I reversed the trailer into the driveway and went in search of someone to see where to unload. I followed the path at the end of the drive through a wooden gate and round to the back door which opened before I could knock. I almost didn't recognise Katie. Her hair was loose, no sign of the usual bandanna, and hung in dark curls and ringlets to her shoulders. She had made up her face and was wearing a figure-hugging red blouse tucked into a black skirt. Her feet were bare. Totally different from her usual work attire.

'Oh, sorry to trouble you,' I said. 'I must be in the wrong place, I was looking for Katie.'

'Nutcase,' she laughed.

'Well, I must say you look real pretty,' I said, putting on an American accent.

'You look like something the cat dragged out of the pond.' She was still laughing.

I put on an aggrieved look. 'That's a nice way to greet a guy who's gone through storm and tempest to bring you a nice load of shit.' I couldn't keep a straight face and was laughing with her.

Recovering, I asked, 'Where would madam like the aforementioned load deposited?'

'If you back in a bit more and dump it by the path to the veg garden, I'll get Alan to move it when he gets home. Do you want a cuppa now or when you've unloaded?' she asked.

'Sounds like a bribe to me,' I told her. 'When I've unloaded will be fine. Milk, one sugar.'

I left her still smiling in the doorway and, returning to the tractor, located the spot she had mentioned, backed up and started forking off the load.

It took less time unloading and, having scraped off the trailer and taken off my wet gear, I once again went round to the door. I saw her through the window as I got there and she called for me to come in. Easing off my boots on the outside doormat I stepped into what was obviously the kitchen.

'Well that looks a bit better,' she said over her shoulder as she poured tea into a couple of mugs that were on a small tray. 'Come through.' She lifted the tray and I followed her into a bright sitting room with leafy pot plants dotted around and a black cat asleep in front of a small log fire.

'Have a seat.' She indicated an armchair by the fire.

'Thanks,' I said, 'but I'd better not, my

things are a bit damp and not too clean. I'll perch here.' There was a wooden upright chair against one wall. She brought over the tray and indicated one of the mugs.

'That's the one with the sugar,' she said.

'Thanks, I'm about ready for it,' I said, looking up at her.

'So am I,' she replied, her voice low and husky and the eyes sparkled.

I took the mug carefully, hoping that my hand wasn't shaking too much, and took a good mouthful.

'It's a nice place you've got here, Katie. What does your husband do?' I was desperately trying to make small talk. She frowned as if not wanting to have this discussion.

'He's a long-distance lorry driver. He's away an awful lot, and I won't see him until the middle of next week.' She put the tray down, walked to the window and looked out.

'Must be a bit lonely. You got any children or your family local?' I asked.

The little frown again before she replied. 'Yes, we've got a little boy, Tim. My folks live in Devon. Tim's gone to a birthday party, one of his pals from...' her voice tailed off.

'It's a job to talk at work.' She looked nervous and not too sure of herself. 'But I just wanted to say sorry about, you know, what me and Bert and the others did to you. It seemed harmless and I played along and you were so nice about it. I shouldn't have let them talk me into, well, showing so much. Oh, hell, I'm making a complete mess of this.' She was looking at me almost pleadingly.

My body was, at that instant, in two halves. Below the belt it was saying 'Go for it Graham, what an opportunity, she's dying for sex. She's an older woman, think what she could teach you, you would be crazy to miss out, you might never have this chance again.'

Above the belt my calmer, more sensible and reasoned half was saying, 'She's a married woman. Think of the possible complications. You've seen her with Bert so you know she puts it about. She's got a child, for Pete's sake, you would be raving mad to go with her. Think what your folks would say if they found out.'

So, having mentally weighed up, in an instant, what my separate halves were telling me I came to the decision that there was really no contest. I got up from the chair and put my tea mug on the tray and walked over to where she was still standing by the window. I took the mug from her hand and put it down.

'Katie.' I kept my voice low and tried to maintain eye contact. 'I'm sorry, I'm not going to be very good at this but ... if you want to lead the way.'

She must have been holding her breath because she let out a short gasp, then reached out and took my hand.

I thought it possible that she would be able to hear the pounding of my heart. She guided me out into a hallway and up the stairs to a bedroom. The curtains were drawn back and a lacy net let the light in. There was a double bed and a dressing table with a mirror and lots of girly things, perfume, brushes – little boxes that sort of thing – and a chest of drawers to one side.

The next half hour or so is a wonderful memory of the making of a man from a simple boy, of soft flesh against mine, of nuzzling between those breasts that had amazed me before, of Katie's whispered instructions and, while she made little mewing noises, a final coming together that took me to what seemed like the gates of heaven itself.

We lay entwined, the sweat cooling on us, until thoughts of search parties being sent out looking for a lone tractor driver last seen heading West with a load of dung brought us apart and back into our clothes.

Back down in the hallway we stood holding hands and looking at each other. The black cat came out from the sitting room and brushed round our ankles. Katie released my hands and we went back into the kitchen. She opened the door and let the cat out.

I took her hands again. 'I don't know what to say, it was so...' I started but she put a finger on my lips and stopped me.

'Don't say anything.' She came into my arms and whispered in my ear, 'It was just between you and me and nothing needs saying. No stupid I love yous, all that stuff. You had better get going.' She hugged me and stepped back.

I leaned over and kissed her. 'Thanks, Katie,' I whispered. I opened the door and pulled on my boots. The cat was sitting on a low wall that edged the path, watching me, I gave it a stroke at which it stood up and its tail went straight up in the air.

She giggled, her eyes sparkling. 'Push off, don't tempt me.' Her voice full of promise. We waved and I walked away round the side of the house and back to the tractor. The rain was back and the lane was wet and there were puddles everywhere so I pulled on my wet gear to keep off the spray from the tyres, started up and drove out of the drive. Katie was watching from the downstairs window so I blew her a kiss.

It's a wonder I fitted on that little Fergy. I felt about ten feet tall and I knew that life would never be quite the same for me again. I was, perhaps, a bit too young to grasp the 'sex for sex's sake' thing that Katie had muted and I was probably having deeper feelings for her. All sorts of crazy mixed-up thoughts were going through my head like the fact that we hadn't taken any precautions and she might have got pregnant or her neighbours might have wondered why I was so long indoors.

I got back to the yard at 1.00 and, fortunately, there was no one about so I parked up quickly and left. It wasn't until I came to the loop lane to the stables that I remembered my date with Tracy the next afternoon.

I was, of course, late home and my Mum was waiting dinner. We had our main meal at 1.00 on weekends.

'You're late,' she scolded. 'Did something come up at the farm?'

'Well, not exactly at the farm,' I told her. 'But connected with it.'

I hid my smile.

Chapter 11

I had a bit of a lie-in on Sunday while I went over the previous day's events in my mind. It was going to be difficult at work not showing any extra affection for Katie, but our secret had to be kept. I'll just have to do my best I thought. It was bright and sunny after the rain. I helped with a few odd jobs round the garden and then wandered down the local woodland with my .410 shotgun. There were rabbits everywhere and I had some good sport before going home for dinner.

During dinner I told my folks that I was going out that afternoon. Their interest was immediate.

'Meeting a friend?' Mum enquired.

'Yes, I met her at work. She works at the stables down Oldbarn Lane,' I told her.

'Oh, a young lady,' my Dad joined in. 'It's about time you started to take an interest in the fairer sex. They don't seem to have featured much in your life so far, do they?'

'No, that's right,' I agreed, nodding my head. 'Got to start sometime.' Thoughts of a pair of soft breasts and some smooth thighs flashed through my mind and I felt my breathing quicken. Once again my smile was well hidden.

Lunch over I went for a wash and change of clothes, said goodbye and set off to bike to the stables. It seemed quite strange to be cycling along my usual route to work but to be in decent clothes.

I left the bike in the same place and walked across the yard to the stairs. There was no sign of Moonshine, but rustling and munching from her stable indicated she was in residence. Tracy came out on to the landing at the top of the stairs.

'Hi,' she called. 'Come on up.'

I climbed the stairs. 'Sorry, I haven't changed or anything but I've got to give Moonshine her tea later and just give her a muck out for the night,' she said. 'Hope you don't mind.'

'Of course not,' I replied, smiling at her.

The hair was tied in its usual pony tail but she had made up her eyes and put on some lipstick so she had gone to a bit of trouble to make herself look good.

'Come on in.' She held out a hand towards the door. 'And tell me what you've been up to.'

I went inside thinking that it would probably, no definitely, not be a good idea to tell her everything I had been up to. She left the door open as it was a warm spring day and it made the little room seem less cramped.

'Would you like something?' she asked. I

looked at her and grinned broadly.

'I meant, would you like a drink?' she huffed. 'Coffee, tea or there's a beer if you prefer?'

'Tea would be fine. Thanks,' I told her. I sat at the table where I could admire the view from the window beside the door.

'I didn't realise you could see over part of the farm from here. Those are the fields at the back of Hills Lea. I harrowed and rolled them a few days back, you can still see the stripes.' I pointed them out.

'Do you sit up here spying on me?' I asked smiling.

'Well, I have seen you once or twice, or I thought it was you. It's too far to see properly, I'll have to get some binoculars.' She was busy with the tea.

'That could be embarrassing. I have to stop some time during a day you know,' I said.

She looked mystified for a moment then light dawned and she laughed.

'Don't worry on my account. I've seen it all before,' she was still smiling.

'Oh, a lady of experience,' I exclaimed. She coloured a little as she set the full cups on the table.

'I wouldn't say that but, you know, a girl riding alone round the woods and landways, there are some queer folk about. It's not very nice but it happens to all my friends.' She looked pensive as if not sure how much to say.

'We've drifted on to a funny old subject for openers,' I said trying to lighten things up.

'Haven't we,' she agreed. We went on to chat about her horses, other things, back to horses until I was getting desperate. She was obviously mad about the things and it was difficult to get her off the subject. We were sort of sparring round each other like young couples do, unsure how to make the first move.

Totally different from being with Katie where there was one object, sex with no ties.

The afternoon passed pleasantly enough, I went down with her and helped with giving Moonshine her tea and we wandered around the property for a while. On the way back to the flat I casually put an arm round her shoulders and pulled her close. She responded with an arm round my waist. I stopped at the bottom of the stairs and moved round to face her, my arm still behind her head and before she had a chance to move I bent my neck and kissed her.

The response was incredible, she crushed herself against me and I felt the tip of her tongue move into my mouth probing and exploring. Her arms were round me hugging me tightly. Of course, him below, that had led me astray at Katie's had a field day, leaping to attention like a demented guardsman.

I moved a hand so as to cup a breast and

she gently pulled away.

'Graham,' she seemed breathless as if steeling herself, 'it's too soon. I want what you want but we need more time. Can you wait a while?' She was looking at me under her lashes and there was a hint of tears.

'Of course,' I said quickly. (I could almost hear him below saying 'Oh, for Pete's sake!')

'I'm sorry, I shouldn't have got so carried away,' I said trying to look repentant.

'It was both of us. Let's go and have some more tea. I've made a little salad stuff.' She took my hand and we went back inside. It did seem as if a bit of tension had been released and we chatted lightly about horses, and she made more tea and produced plates of ham and salad and drew the curtains as the light faded.

We moved into the little sitting room where there was a two-seater sofa in a big flowery pattern, some little tables and a radiogram with a drop-down door and a stackable turntable. She put on some music and we cuddled up on the sofa.

'This is cosy, isn't it?' she snuggled up to me 'It can be quite lonely here in the evenings.'

The evening passed very quickly, we had the odd kiss and cuddle and I found she was fond of reading and music and, once I had got her off the subject of horses, she proved knowledgeable about a variety of topics. The amazing thing was the instant rapport we had, as if fate had meant us to meet. We soon were totally relaxed in each other's company, like we were old mates from years back.

Eventually I had to say it was time to go. She came out on the landing and flipped on a floodlight that lit up the yard. We kissed and made promises to contact each other. I thanked her for the meal and went on my way, giving her a wave as I left.

Riding home through the dark, I reflected on the weekend. The experience with Katie would live with me for ever, of that I was certain. It had given me more, much more than just sexual knowledge; it had given me confidence and self-assurance that had already been awakened by the girls and their 'set up'. I felt able to look the world in the eye for the first time and not to regard girls as an alien species. Tracy was altogether different. My feelings for her were set to go much, much deeper. I had heard of the expression 'love at first sight' and wondered if this was the case. It was impossible to get her out of my mind and thoughts of her gave me a warm glow. Our next meeting could not come soon enough.

Monday was a perfect Spring day. The April sun was still low in the sky as I coasted down the lane to work and the air sparkled as if washed clean by Saturday's downpour. There seemed to be a general feeling of goodwill among my co-workers as we gathered in the yard waiting for Mr Willis and the day's orders.

''Ow were yous weekend then, Graham?' Bert asked. 'Don't suppose you cud git up ta much on Saturday, t'were a right bugger of a day.'

'No,' I replied catching Katie's eye as she stood nearby. 'It didn't seem to matter where I got to, it was still wet.' I risked another glance and I could see she had her head lowered and was laughing.

The Boss arrived with Tony and for him, Neil and me it was more pea drilling, to be followed by a small acreage of beetroot and then a tiny field of about a half acre that they told me always went in to marrows.

So plenty of walking for Tony and me this week. I would have been interested to know how many miles we covered each day. All I do know is that I slept like a log and ate like a horse. They were long days starting at 7.30 and working until there was just enough daylight to get back to the yard, as there were no lights on the tractor. Riding home at night I was on autopilot, my legs just about able to turn the pedals. Every day's walking, however, seemed to get a little easier as the muscles developed. The week turned showery and by Friday it was too wet to continue drilling, so a temporary halt was called.

The Boss found me early in the day. He had left the dogs indoors and was in his shoes, not the usual gum boots.

'There's a job in the dry I'd like you to do. If you come with me I'll show you what's wanted,' he said.

We went up towards the house to the flight of stone steps leading up to the granary above the mill that Tom used to grind and roll cattle feed. The Boss led the way up the steps and we went inside. There were four big wooden bins lined with tin, leaving a passage way down the middle that opened into a storage area at the end. The bins had a sloping floor that led to a pipe down to the mill below, each controlled by a sliding shutter. Three of them were empty but the last had a small amount of barley in the bottom. The whole place was coated in white floury dust and was festooned with cobwebs, also coated with dust. The glass roof window was too grimy to let in much light. The Boss had switched on a single electric bulb hanging from the rafters and this was casting dark shadows in corners of the store room. Scamperings and rustlings indicated that we were not alone up there.

'We need to get this place cleared out like you did that one at the back,' the Boss said. 'It's close to the house and it's only harbouring rats and mice.' There was a sudden patter of feet and Smudge flew in through the open door. He must have seen us come up here out of the office window, cried to go out and torn across.

'Smudge you bugger,' the Boss shouted, 'you're not supposed to be over here.'

The terrier shot past both of us, ignoring the shout, and in an instant dived behind a pile of old sacks in the corner, came out with a rat in its jaws, dispatched it with a scrunch and shake of its head, tossed it aside and dived in again.

This time, however, it was not so lucky and the next instant all hell broke loose. A rat had fastened on to its lip and Smudge was yelping and throwing his head around trying to dislodge it, at the same time tearing around the store like a demented dervish. The Boss grabbed an old broom and was trying to hit the rat and in doing so welted Smudge round the ear which only added to the dog's discomfort and to the decibels of its yelping. After several circuits of the floor which, by now, was impossible to see across for dust, I managed to grab the dog's collar and the Boss got his broom on the rat and dispatched it. There were trails of blood around the floor and Smudge was licking rapidly at his torn lip.

'Let's have a look at you,' said the Boss, picking up the dog and examining its muzzle. 'You'll be OK. Teach you a lesson, I shouldn't wonder.'

We became aware of a female voice calling from outside and went out onto the square landing block. Mrs Willis was below, looking up at us anxiously.

'What on earth's going on?' she called but before a reply could be made she started to laugh. Tony, Neil and Walter had also heard the commotion and arrived and they also dissolved into gales of laughter.

'What the hell are you daft buggers laughing at?' the Boss admonished them and then we caught sight of each other and in no time were joining in the mirth.

We were both coated from head to foot in white dust. It was everywhere, our white faces and hands stood out and our eyes were like dark holes in the snow. Caps, coats, trousers and footwear were white like a miller at the end of the day. Smudge, apart from having a red muzzle, looked like a Yorkshire terrier and when the Boss put him down he shook himself, causing a white cloud to go drifting away on the wind. This increased the laughter and the tears cut clean lines down our faces making us look like circus clowns. At last we recovered enough to make our way to the yard tap and wash off. Several minutes were spent beating caps and clothes before some resemblance of order was restored.

'You had best wear a mask when you clear out up there,' the Boss said. 'I should put a trailer at the steps and chuck everything in.

There's nothing any good up there – I've checked with Tom, it can all go.'

I walked off to get the trailer and the Boss went back to the house. As I crossed the yard I could hear him and Mrs Willis laughing again. I guessed the story would be retold several times to friends and relations.

I completed the clean-out with a hand-kerchief tied over my mouth and nose and finished up nearly as dusty as before. It turned out later that Smudge's bite was more serious than the Boss thought and a couple of visits to the vet were required. He got well in the end but always had a turned-up lip on one side that exposed a couple of teeth, so if you happened to approach him from that side he looked as if he was snarling.

The pea drilling had meant that it was now nearly a week since my never-to-be-forgotten experience with Katie. I had not even had a chance to speak to her. Neither had I seen Tracy apart from a wave across the field, so my love life was in tatters! I was pleased, therefore, on Friday lunchtime, to meet Katie in the shed collecting her bike.

'Hi, gorgeous,' I greeted her. 'I thought you stayed to lunch.'

'I've got to go early. Timmy's got a routine injection at the doc's. I've missed you. What have you been up to?' She was looking good and him below was running through his usual routine.

'Pea drill mostly,' I told her. 'Did you get the muck moved?'

'I've been wanting to see you about that. Alan's pretty much worn out when he gets home. I told him I thought I could get someone to do it but it would cost him a quid.' She looked at me her tongue passing over her lips.

'Would you be able to come and do it for me?'

'I'd love to,' I heard myself saying, my sensible practical half screaming in horror.

'When do you want me?' I asked.

'All the time,' she replied, the eyes saying everything.

'I meant to move the muck,' I laughed. Not many days ago I would have blushed but not now, no way.

'Oh, I'll let you know. Is that OK? Look, I must go 'cus of Timmy.' She wheeled out the bike and put a foot on the pedal.

'Give me a shout when you are ready,' I called as she pushed the bike and passed a leg through to the other pedal in that very awkward start that women seemed to have, not being able to swing a leg over the cross-bar like men. She waved over her shoulder.

The sun had returned with a light breeze, which was just what we needed to continue with our drilling. I decided not to join the rest for lunch but took a box and, setting it against the barn wall in the sun, sat there enjoying the warmth and the feel of Spring. Birds were rushing about with beaks full of grubs. Pigeons and doves cooed around. The smell of hay and the cattle yard, the buzz of insects, the whole joy of country life seemed to be there with me as an integral part. That lunch break is still remembered and feeds my love of the countryside and the people who work the land and tend the livestock.

Tom came across the yard as I was about to move.

'Tis a grand arternoon,' he said coming over to stand by me. 'They tells me tha' bin doin' one o' lay himpercynations.'

'Sorry, Tom,' I said mystified. 'I'm not with you.'

'They tole me thee were lookin like one o' lay abominable snowmen, thee and tha' Boss.' He was chuckling now his face a mass of wrinkles.

'Cor bloody hell!' I exclaimed. 'That soon got round. Me and the Boss were going to sing "It was dust one of those things" but we couldn't remember the words.' We both had a good laugh and he went on his way.

The sun and breeze continued and we worked right through the weekend to catch up. Monday saw the peas finished and we cleaned out the drill and moved on to the beetroot. It was quite a small piece, about two acres, so it didn't take us long to get finished.

We cleaned out the drill again and Tony said: 'I'll see Bert and tell him we will be on the marrows first thing tomorrow.'

'Why does Bert need to know?' I asked.

Tony smiled, 'You'll see tomorrow, it's easier than trying to explain.'

'You might as well knock off,' he went on. 'It's only half hour to time, forecast is OK so should be able to get on tomorrow.'

I took the loop lane on the way home and dropped into the stables. There was a big horse box parked beside the one that was usually there and entering the yard I could see horses' heads looking out from a number of the stables.

Tracy was there with a pail of water in one hand and a hay net in the other. Her face broke into a smile on seeing me.

'Hi, stranger,' she called.

'Hi, yourself,' I called back. 'You're still looking as sexy as ever, got a bit more to do now by the looks of it.'

The smile turned to a laugh.

'Yes, they are all back. The owner and her husband have just left but Sue is here and will be for a while.'

'I just wondered if you might have time to go to the pictures – maybe on Saturday afternoon – I think there's a bus?' I asked her.

'I'll have to check with Sue,' she replied. 'Can I ring you?'

'Sure can. I'd better be off and let you get on.'

We waved and I left her to it. I had no idea what was on at the cinema but if she was able to get away I thought it would make a change.

Next day we moved on round to the field where the marrows were going to planted. Bert and the girls were already there, having been told the night before, their bikes lined up along the hedge. We had brought the seed with us and having got the drill lined up I went to pour some in the drill.

'Hang on,' Tony called. 'The girls are going to do the sowing, all we are going to do is mark out the rows. It's the easiest way to do it. They will plant the seeds in our coulter marks but only in every other one so the rows are four feet apart.'

We took off the little plates that covered up the drilled seeds on two of the coulters and away we went. I didn't have much to do – just keep an eye on the coulters making the drills to be planted and ensure no stones or weed trash got caught on them and that they were making a nice neat job. Turning on the end I could see that two of the girls had set in behind us dropping in the seed and each time we turned more joined in until they were all involved. I had no chance of a word with Katie but she did manage to make eyes at me as we passed with the drill. With the field marked we left them to it. I returned later in the day with the light roller with the harrows in front, and covered up the seed and firmed up the soil.

Chapter 12

Spraying the young corn in Spring was a fairly new operation and only selective weed-killer was used at Manor Farm. Neil had the job as his Fergy had some permanent fixings that fitted the sprayer. This was a linkage mounted model, with booms that were lifted up by hand and fixed in a vertical position behind the tank for transport. The nozzles delivered a high-density spray, so filling up was a regular occurrence and was achieved by bucketing water from a big open-topped tank that sat on an old 4-wheel trailer, into the top of the sprayer. It took the best part of a day to fill the big tank but, as the forecast was good with light winds, it was decided to fill the tank overnight. I had knocked off and gone home after harrowing and rolling the marrows, so Tony and Neil had towed the trailer round to the tap and started filling the tank ready for spraying the next day.

When I arrived in the morning, a small stream of water was running out the yard gate and down the side of the lane. Tony arrived at the same time and quickly turned off the tap. The tank was brim full and overflowing across the yard. He explained what was going on.

'Neil filled up yesterday evening so is ready to go,' he told me. 'He's going to start in Barrowfield. Would you hitch the rubber tyred small Fordson on this tank trailer and take it up to him? I should park it about a third of the way along the headland, then he can move it when he gets to it. It will mean walking back but it's not that far. You are going to spill quite a bit because it's too full, but don't worry there will be plenty left if you go nice and steady.'

Neil had arrived and was backing out his Fergy with the sprayer and set off up the lane. I went over and checked over the Fordson for oil and fuel. Tony had left with the Boss in the Land-Rover. I started up and reversed over to the trailer. This had been horse-drawn at one time and had been crudely converted for towing with a tractor by bending a piece of 2-inch pipe into a loop and then fixing it to the front.

Instead of a clevis hitch the Fordson had just a flat plate with quite a large hole in it for towing. This left me with a dilemma: how to fix a trailer with just a loop to a plate with, in turn, just a hole. In the end I decided that a big shackle would do the job and found one hanging on the wall of the implement shed. It had no screw pin. Another search located an old bolt that was long enough but wouldn't screw in. I looped the bow of the shackle through the loop on the trailer, put its legs over the hole in the tractor drawbar and dropped in the pin. I was getting in a bit of a rush because I thought Neil would be running out of water. Easing the tractor forward, all was well, and I moved down the yard, water slopping everywhere, and out on to the lane where the going was smoother.

The route to the field was a short way up the lane and then a left turn onto another lane that led up a short hill, over the brow, and down the other side. All was going well. I was getting splashed a little now and again but not too much. Reaching the brow and starting down the other side, however, the trailer started to go faster than the tractor and overran it. This should have been no problem but the shackle turned under the tractor drawbar and the bolt dropped out. The trailer drawbar dropped on the road and ran on under the rear axle of the Fordson, lifting the rear wheels off the ground.

I was now in big trouble as I had only rear wheel brakes and the wheels they worked on were not on the road. The hill was twisty and steeper further on, but ahead of me on my right was a field entrance with low banks leading off the lane. I steered for the bank on the far side and let the tractor run into it. The front reared up a bit and then everything came to a very abrupt halt except the water in the tank.

The ensuing wave would have gladdened the heart of Guy Gibson and his Dambusters. It hit me in the back, washed me head over heels off the tractor and out into the lane where I came to rest sitting in the middle and watched my cap, surfing on the top of a whitewater wave, disappearing down the hill.

Sod's law decreed that at that moment Tony and the Boss would turn up. I was staggering to my feet, water pouring off and out of me as they stopped by the trailer in the Land-Rover. They both got out but could not remain standing for long and they both collapsed in gales of laughter. Personally I was having a job to see the funny side of it as I sat on the bank and poured a gallon of water out of each gum boot, but their laughter became infectious and soon I was joining in. We were in that condition when Neil turned up, having run out of water. The outcome was that the Boss drove me home for a change of clothes while Neil and Tony sorted out the Fordson (which was totally unmarked) and the trailer. The Boss drove right to the bottom of the hill where my cap had finally dropped anchor and that set him off again laughing and it was some time before I made it home. At least home was deserted and I could go and change without answering a lot of questions.

After I had got changed, the Boss drove me back to the farm where Tony was just walking in the gate and in answer to our questions told us that he and Neil had pulled the trailer back and recovered the Fordson. They had to pull that back as well because the starting handle was in the hedge. After drying out the plugs it had fired up all right and Tony had pulled the trailer and tank on down to where Neil was spraying. He said it was about half full which meant that around 500 gallons had washed over me. He had to stop at this point as he and the Boss leaned against each other totally paralytic with mirth again. I must admit that, now I was in dry clothes, I was more able to see the funny side of it.

When he recovered enough the Boss said: 'As you are such an expert with water, Graham, would you wash my car for me? I've got to go to London tomorrow to see the salesman.' He was still having difficulty in keeping a straight face. 'And when you're finished could you walk out to Barrowfield and pick up the water tank and we'll fill it up for tomorrow? It will be empty so you should be safe enough.' This started us all off again and we stood like idiots, tears running down our cheeks.

Next morning I delivered the water tank safely to Neil, with only a few splashes, after being shown the correct way to hitch up the trailer. I was in good spirits as Tracy had phoned to say she could get off on Saturday afternoon if I still fancied going to the pictures. We arranged that I would cycle to the stables and drop the bike. Then we could walk to the end of the loop lane where the bus stopped.

The year ticked on into May and all the fields seem to be growing something. Soon it was time to start on lots and lots of row-crop work.

Tony helped me fit the steerage hoe to my Fergy. This was designed to hoe four rows of crop. We were going to do the early peas that were now showing, and the hoe could be adjusted to run very close to the plants. Also, although fitted to the tractor linkage, it could be independently steered by an operator sitting on a seat that projected from the back of the hoe. It was a fairly slow job that required concentration by both operators. There was no time for looking around. If a stone lodged across the hoes, it could rip out the row until noticed and cleared.

The farm had two of them and from then on we were almost non-stop, going through various crops. Of course, the hoes could only do between the rows, so the girls were also very busy with hand hoes doing the actual rows. There was a very prevalent weed in Kent called 'Fat Hen' that looked rather like a tall dock and this had to be hoed or pulled before it seeded.

Steerage hoeing called for a good feel for the slope of the land. It wasn't simply a case of driving up the middle of the row because, on sideways-sloping ground, the tractor would tend to crab and the hoe operator would be pulling hard one way. It required a quick glance back every few yards to see what was happening and to make adjustment if things were off line. I found I was just as tired at the end of the day as I had been walking behind the drill, only this time it was mental rather than physical. After a day or two I found that I could tell what was happening behind without looking and could drive to make it easy for the hoe operator.

I had fixed with Tony to have Saturday afternoon off. He didn't mind because we had hoed the early peas and the maincrop were not quite ready. I had an early lunch and set off to the stables. It was a fine warm May day and the countryside was in bloom. In the stable yard there was no sign of Tracy but a dark-haired girl in shirtsleeves and a bib and brace-type overall was doing the usual with water and hay. I dropped the bike in its usual place and went over to her.

'Hello,' she greeted me smiling. 'You must be Graham. I'm Sue. I share the flat with

Tracy. She's told me all about you.'

'Hello Sue,' I smiled back, doing a rapid appraisal, like you do, and noting the green eyes, generous mouth and the fact that the shirt buttons were under a considerable load.

'Tracy's a lucky girl if she shares a flat with you.'

'Oh yes, Tracy said you had a knack of saying the right thing.' Her smile was broader, showing white even teeth. 'She's in the flat if you want to go over.'

She had put down the pail of water and hay net as I had approached and now stooped to retrieve them giving me a good glimpse of why the shirt buttons were under such a load. I opened the stable door for her and stood aside for her to enter.

'Thanks,' she said and as she passed added, 'yes, Tracy *is* a lucky girl.'

I walked across to the flat, ran up the stairs and rapped on the door.

'Coming,' Tracy called from inside and after a second or two the door opened.

She looked fantastic, the long locks were twisted into a thick plait that hung over one shoulder and she was wearing a tan jersey that showed off her figure. The jersey was tucked into a cream pleated skirt and she had tan-coloured sandals on her feet. The plain colour of the jersey was relieved by a sparkly brooch in the shape of (you guessed) a horse's head. When I remarked on it she told me it was Sue's.

'I can't take you to town looking like that,' I said. 'How am I going to fight off the hoards of guys that will be chasing you?'

'Crazy man,' she laughed. 'I'll just get a mac in case it rains and then we had better go.'

She went back inside and came out again with a light waterproof.

'Right let's go. I'll just get you to meet Sue,' she said.

'We met on my way in, she's nice,' I told her. We walked out on to the lane and headed for the bus stop.

'She's a good pal,' Tracy said. 'This skirt is hers. We share everything.'

'Do you now?' I looked at her, a grin on my face. It took a second or two before she slapped me on the arm.

'You keep your hands off,' she said in a raised voice. 'I'm not sharing you with any-one.'

The afternoon went well. There were four cinemas in our local town and we settled on a western, mainly because of (you guessed it again) the horses.

After the film we had a half hour to spare before the bus so grabbed a quick cup of coffee in a local cafe. I took pleasure in notic-ing the envious glances of other young guys.

The bus dropped us off at the end of the loop lane and we strolled back to the stables in the gathering dark stopping for a kiss and cuddle along the way. The yard floodlight was on and Sue was around finishing the evening chores.

'Had a good time?' she called. 'The kettle's not long boiled if you fancy a cuppa.'

We waved and went up to the flat, where Tracy added some water and put the kettle on. As she did so I came up behind her and put my arms round her waist, nuzzling the thick plait to one side and kissing the nape of her neck. She responded by grinding her backside against me and then grabbing my hands and moving them up over her breasts. Him below was having a bloody field day and was obviously transmitting his manoeuvres to Tracy.

'I'm supposed to be making tea not whoopy,' she said, taking my hands away and turning round.

The door opened and Sue walked in. I turned away quickly to face her and Tracy went to the teapot.

'Oops, sorry,' Sue said, her eyes moving down me. 'I should have knocked.' Her cheeks coloured.

'Don't be daft,' Tracy said. 'We were only having a cuddle.'

Tracy made the tea and produced some plates of pork pies and sausage rolls and a

180

chocolate cake.

'I'll just wash and change,' Sue said. 'Only be a mo.'

A few minutes later she was back, transformed, the dark locks combed and glossy and held back with clips decorated with butterflies. She was wearing a short-sleeved green dress that heightened the colour of her eyes. She was barefoot. I was in heaven dining with two super-looking girls and the conversation was light and varied until, suddenly, there was a problem.

'How do you get on with those women that work on the farm?' Tracy asked. 'They look a pretty rough lot.'

'Oh, they are OK,' I told her. 'They've got hearts of gold. I was pretty shy when I started there but they soon sorted me out.' Both girls were laughing.

'You, shy?' Tracy said still laughing. 'I can't believe that.'

'If you were, which I don't believe either,' Sue asked, 'how did they change you?' I could see we were getting into awkward territory and tried to make light of it.

'Oh, they just worked out little set-ups between them and Bert – he's the foreman – you know, just daft things to make me embarrassed,' I told them.

'That must have been a problem. I can't see you being embarrassed about anything,' Sue said.

'See what a good job they did,' I said, holding my hands wide. The girls wouldn't let it rest and I inwardly cursed myself for mentioning it.

'What sort of things did they do?' Tracy asked, looking doubtful. I was trapped and had to think quickly.

'Well, let's just say they showed me in no uncertain manner that there is a difference between men and women,' I said, praying that would finish the conversation. Both girls took time to digest what I had said until Sue's hand flew to her mouth.

'You don't mean... Oh my God,' she cried, 'how awful! What did you do ... think, I mean?' She was floundering for words, her hand still up to her mouth.

'That's the whole point,' I told her. 'I was embarrassed but I wouldn't be now, so you can see it worked.'

Tracy had caught up now and, of course, had to ask the question.

'How did they do it ... was it just one or...?' she was also struggling for words. Damn girls I thought, they are going to pester me now!

'Let's just drop the subject shall we?' I said, hoping to put them off but to no avail.

'Oh, you've got to tell us,' Sue cried. 'You can't leave it there.' Tracy was nodding in agreement.

'OK, OK, I'll give in,' I said and went on

to explain about the spy hole and staying on to move the riddle. I was careful not to mention names. I told them about how I had fetched the grease gun and been confronted with a woman astride a bale with one foot up and no knickers. They were wide-eyed and I was getting a lot of 'Oh no' and 'that's awful' comments.

'There's a young, pretty one among them, has a scarf round her hair. I bet it was her,' Tracy gasped, her eyes wide.

'That's the end, I'm not saying another word. Any more questions and I'm away,' I told them and they looked at each other and agreed to leave it.

With our tea finished we moved into the sitting room and sat listening to music on the radiogram until around 9.00 when Sue said she would not play gooseberry any longer and was going off to read a new book she had bought.

I snuggled up with Tracy on the sofa and after some kissing and fumbling, things moved on to what I believe is called heavy petting. There was no embarrassment between us. It all seemed so normal but was a bit restrained because Tracy was worried about Sue overhearing her whimpers and kept burying her head in a cushion. We were both keenly aware that it would only be a short time before we became lovers in the true sense of the word. I thought she was just the most fantastic person I had ever met.

I left the stables around 10.45 and enjoyed the ride home in the cool night air.

My folks were still up and I was lucky as they had just made tea. They knew I was taking Tracy to the pictures.

'Was it a good film?' Mum asked.

'Yes,' I replied, 'a western. Tracy likes the horses.'

'She must ride well, working at a stables,' Dad observed.

'Well I'm no expert but I'm sure she does,' I answered.

Chapter 13

May was spent almost non-stop on the steerage hoe. The maincrop peas for freezing were up and it was a bit like painting the Forth Bridge – no sooner had we got through everything once, it was time to start again. We worked on every fine evening until dusk so my meetings with Tracy were limited to a quick call on the way home. Katie caught up with me one morning soon after the start of the month.

'Any chance of moving the muck for me this weekend?' she asked.

'I'm sorry, love,' I replied. 'I'm working right through and Tony's relying on me. I'd love to but there's no chance.'

'I guessed you would have a job to get away,' she said with a pout. 'I was going to provide tea and ... but it will have to wait. I think one of my neighbours might shift it for me. I promised Alan I would get it done so I can't leave it.'

'I'm real sorry to let you down,' I told her, knowing what I was missing.

'Never mind, can't be helped,' she answered. I got the feeling she knew our sexual relationship was going to be a one-off.

185

I did have a short break from the steerage hoe around the middle of the month. Tony was going on a course at his college so I was given the job of what was called 'potato break'.

The idea was to loosen the soil between the rows of potatoes that were now just showing, I had one of the big Fordsons and a cultivator with three groups of three tines with wide points fitted. Each group of three ran between the rows and were dropped on the linkage as far as the tractor would pull. It was a slow, first-gear job with the tines in the ground at least two feet. The rows of freshly showing potato shoots actually lifted up as I passed and settled back down again. The soil around and under them loosened for them to grow into and to make it easy to baulk up the rows later. They would be moved like that only once, the points then being changed for narrow ones and just the soil between the rows kept loose.

The women could be seen now in different fields almost daily, spread out in a long line moving slowly across, prodding with their hoes. I often thought that of all the personnel on the farm, the women worked the hardest and, I expect, for the least money.

We had a good run of weather to start the month and were on top of the pea hoeing and then it turned wet, so we were stopped.

There were several jobs around the yard to do. The bale walls in the Dutch barn that held the potatoes were renewed every year. I was told they fell apart because the rodents chewed the strings. I worked with Neil loading and carting the old bales to the cattle yard where they would form the base for this Autumn's intake of new stock. The whole barn was then swept out and the riddle cleaned up and parked out of the way. New walls would be built as soon as harvest was finished and bales were available for the job.

The first wet day was the also the first time I had knocked off on time for a couple of weeks. I had spoken to Tracy on the phone a few times and had the odd quick chat on the headland as she stopped by on Moonshine, but that had been the limit of our contact. So I was quite excited to be able to drop in and see her on my way home. Approaching the entrance to the stables I saw a man, on his own, drive out in a big Jaguar car and speed off. I rode down the drive and into the yard and saw Tracy and Sue close together by the first stable, so coasted straight to them. Neither of them heard my approach and they looked up startled as I pulled up alongside. Tracy was crying, the tears running down her cheeks. She was wearing a light-brown shirt, the collar and top of the front of which were wet. Recovering from the surprise at seeing me, she fled for the stairs to the flat, rushed up them and inside. I looked at Sue who also was close to tears and feared that perhaps they had lost a horse. God, not Moonshine I thought!

'What's going on?' I asked Sue.

'Tracy will kill me if I tell you but I'll have to take the risk,' she replied, her voice croaky with emotion.

She took out a hanky and blew her nose and gave her eyes a quick wipe, composing herself.

'Its a bit of a long story.' She was steadier now, her voice controlled. 'The stables belong to a Mr and Mrs Williams. He's got the money and he bought them for her. He's the boss of a haulage company. It was fine to begin with but then he started coming round here on his own and being a pest. Silly things like putting his arm round you while he's talking.' She stopped as if wondering if she should go on and looked towards the flat.

'So then what?' I prompted her.

'Well, it's been getting worse. He started groping Tracy, until last week he put the hard word on her. He wanted her to...' She paused trying to find the words. 'He asked her to, you know, use her hand on him.' She was biting her lip and gazing at the concrete.

'He knows that she just loves the horses

here and it will take something really bad to make her leave. He knows that. That's why he approached her and not me, he knows I'd tell him where to go, and quit.'

'So what happened?' I asked my mind spinning.

'Tracy tried to laugh it off. She told him not to be silly, that he was married, all that stuff and he went off in a huff. Today when he arrived we tried to ignore him but he followed Tracy into a stable and came up behind her. He grabbed her hand and pulled it back against him and he had his ... thing ... out.' Sue stopped, and her eyes were moist again. She took some deep breaths and I could see she was trembling with emotion.

'He pushed up against her and told her she either did what he said or she was history. What a bastard that man is! You can see what a state she's in. She won't leave these horses.'

'He didn't rape her did he?' I cried, alarmed at what I was hearing.

'No.' Sue was shaking her head. 'Can't you guess from her shirt what he made her do?'

'There's no way a guy can get away with that.' I was livid and shaken with what I had heard. 'Can't you tell his wife?'

'If we did she would like as not tell us both to get out, so the end result would be the same.' Sue looked totally miserable. 'He's got all the angles covered. If we complain to the police, he'll just deny it and again we would be out. I don't care, I'm only doing this to earn some money to get by with but Tracy...' Her voice tailed off and I could see tears starting to well down her cheeks. 'I can't go off and leave her to that animal.' She was sobbing and shaking. I left the bike where it was and, putting an arm round her, led her towards the flat, helping her up the stairs and inside. Tracy had left the door ajar. I got her to sit down at the table and, as I did, Tracy came out from the bedroom. She had changed her stained shirt and was looking more composed. Hurrying to Sue she put her arms round her and tried to comfort her so I left them together and went out on to the landing outside. I leaned on the handrail and thought the problem through.

I gave it half an hour and then looked back inside. They were both now steadier and Sue had regained her composure and had also changed her top and washed her face.

'Right,' I said. 'There is a way out of this.' I explained exactly what they must do and I could see the light begin to come back in their eyes.

'I'll be away,' I said, 'but I'll call you this evening or tomorrow, and don't worry, it will be OK.'

Tracy came out on the landing and took my hand.

'Thanks, Graham,' she said her voice

almost a whisper. 'I wasn't sure you would want to be ... to have anything to do with me after...' I stopped her saying anything else by kissing her and she folded herself around me like a limpet. It was a minute or two before I could surface for air and depart.

I rushed off home and dashed indoors to the phone. My Dad was still at his office and I quickly explained what had happened and suggested my idea.

'I think I might be able to go one better,' Dad said. 'I'll call you back in five minutes.'

He duly phoned and as a result I was able to call Tracy and tell her and Sue to expect a visitor or two tomorrow.

I was troubled all the next day, hoping that the wheels I had set in motion were still turning. It was not a wet day but the soil was too sticky for field work. We moved what was left of the hay in the big barn as close as possible to the big cattle yard door so that it would be the first to be used when new stock arrived. There were no hay fields at the farm. Our hay was brought in by the neighbour that owned the sheep and he stacked it in the barn for us. How the financial part worked I never found out but it must have been a tad complicated. There was a bit of building repair work to do in the cattle yard itself. Some of the feed troughs were a bit worse for wear in all the jostling that went on and some weatherboard needed replacing and tarring. I also took the chance to change the oil and filter on my Fergy.

Five o'clock seemed to take forever coming but at last I was able to get to the stables. Tracy rushed over as soon as I got in the yard and after a long kiss started gabbling at twenty to the dozen and pulling me towards the flat. On the way Sue caught up with us and I actually got another kiss but without the tongue treatment Tracy had given me. On the table in the flat was a document folder and inside were typed details of exactly what had happened to Tracy and Sue at the hand of Mr Williams – every word with regard to his threatening the girls with eviction and dismissal and full details of his behaviour with Tracy. Everything was signed in the presence of a solicitor, who was also a Commissioner for Oaths, and witnessed by a police superintendent.

The policeman had told the girls that they (the police) would take no action unless an official complaint was received. There was no doubt in anyone's mind that, once Williams received a copy of the document, he would know that any further messing about would lead to him being taken to court and as a prominent businessman he would not risk that.

'How on earth did you manage to get those people here today, so soon?' Tracy asked.

'The solicitor does all my Dad's work and

the copper is a personal friend of the family. I suppose you'll find out anyway, but my Dad is also a businessman. He employs over a hundred people,' I told them.

'I thought you were an unusual farm apprentice,' Tracy cooed.

'Well that's what I am, usual or unusual.' I smiled at them. 'Now I'm going home for my tea but with your permission I'd like to come back for the evening.'

'Don't come all high horse with me,' Tracy was laughing. 'You don't have to ask ever, we'll always be happy to see you. Just call on in.'

I duly returned to find the girls in jubilant mood.

'I'd love to be a fly on the wall and watch that disgusting creep open his post. Is he going to get a shock!' Sue said fiercely.

'Let's hope that's put paid to Willie Williams,' Tracy laughed.

It was a fun evening with a lot of friendly larking about until around 9.30 when Sue said she was going to read some more of her book.

'G'night Graham,' she turned to me. 'Thanks for what you've done. I should hate to lose my pal.' That said, she leaned over and kissed me until Tracy shouted, 'Oi you, get your mitts off my bloke, you little trollop,' and the two of them started a cushion fight with me in the middle. We all finished up on the floor in a mad tangle during which I discovered why Sue's shirt had been under such strain the first time we met.

Eventually order was restored and Sue left for her book and Tracy and me cosied up on the sofa. Because of Tracy's jubilant mood and the happiness between us, our kissing and petting led to us finally taking that last step and we made love. This time Tracy didn't seem to mind if Sue could hear or not and squealed away with gay abandon. To say it was exquisite would be a gross under-statement. We were both aware that some-thing quite incredible had taken place. We were madly, impossibly and totally in love. It was quite late when I got home but my folks were still up.

'I hear it all went off well,' Dad said. 'What a pig that chap is! Let's hope that's the end of it. I bet Tracy is pleased. You must bring her over some time. Your Mum and I would love to meet her.'

I had told Dad her name and a bit more about her when I phoned him the day before.

'Yes, she was happy this evening, both of them were. Perhaps she could come over one Saturday or Sunday. You could pick her up in the car,' I suggested.

'Good idea,' Dad replied. 'Well, we are off to bed. You look tired yourself.'

'Yes, I do feel a bit drained. Good night,' I

said. Did I hear a little voice saying, 'drained is right!'

I called in again the next evening to check there had been no reprisals and to give Tracy her birthday present. I had twisted Sue's arm to tell me the date. They told me all was quiet and they hadn't heard a peep out of Willie Williams, which was great. I then produced Tracy's pressie.

'How did you find out the right date?' she cried.

'Well, a little bird told me,' I replied. Sue was gazing at the sky and whistling to herself.

'Yeah, a little bird not too far away at the moment.' Tracy was jabbing her finger in Sue's direction. She opened the little parcel and gave a whoop of delight. I had noticed that the black riding gloves she used daily were worn through where she held the reins, so had got her some new ones with a little silver horse motif on the back. She threw her arms round me and I received a big kiss. The gloves were well worth it.

Monday morning I managed to have a word with Katie. 'Did you get the muck moved?' I asked her.

'Yep,' she answered. 'Got the muck moved but the earth stood still.' The look she gave me sent tingles everywhere.

'Sorry again, but, Katie, I think in a way it

was for the best.' I was upset and she could see.

'Don't worry about it,' she was smiling. 'The jungle drums have been beating, I know you've got a girlfriend. I always thought it was the *guy* that galloped up on a white horse and swept up the maiden. Trust you to be different.'

'Well, you know me,' I smiled back.

'Intimately,' she said huskily, moving off with the other girls.

Katie and I never got together again sexually but we remained the best possible pals at work. The memory of that half hour together I am sure would last forever. I felt eternally grateful for all her patience and for all that she taught me in that all too brief but joyful encounter.

Towards the end of the month and running into June, it was time to put out the plants from the bed we had drilled at Hills Lea. The girls had been hoeing them from time to time to keep the bed weed-free, and the seeds had now grown into plants 6 to 9in long. I took a load of boxes over to the bed where Katie and Ruth were pulling the plants for the next day's planting.

The planter itself was a 4-row machine on the tractor linkage. It had a seat for each operator that was only about 18in off the ground and foot rests like a motor bike out in front. A coulter made a groove in the soil and right in front of the seat were two angled rollers about a foot in diameter that allowed room for the operator to put a plant between them. These then squeezed the plant into the groove and at the same time, it was given a shot of water from an onboard tank. There was a little bell on each position that could be set to give the correct moment to insert the plant to get the right spacing. The machine could be heard operating from some way off with these four bells dingling away as it crossed the field. For the women operators it was yet another back-breaking, dusty job. The boxes of plants were on a tray in front of each position so the procedure was to have a bunch of plants in one hand and to continually pass them, one at a time, to the other hand and so to the soil.

There was quite a logistical operation keeping the thing going as it had to be supplied with water. The big tank that I had had problems with earlier was used for that, the planter tank being filled with a bucket when required. Boxes of plants had to be fetched from Katie and Ruth and empty ones taken back. Tractors seemed to be going all over the farm as the steerage hoeing was still going on where it was possible to get through the peas. The beans now had to be tractor hoed between the rows. Beetroot had to be steerage hoed and the potatoes done with the deep break. There was plenty of variety in day-to-day work and I enjoyed it immensely. The only problem was that I was spending so much time at the farm that the only moments I got to see Tracy were on the headland, with her sat on a horse and me on a tractor, which is not too conducive to an active sex life. Him below was thinking he had been given early redundancy. It almost got to the point of praying for a wet spell to give everyone a break. June has a reputation for being a dodgy month weatherwise and this one lived up to it so our prayers were soon answered. The rain was welcome for the freshly put-out plants; it was just what was needed to get them set and growing.

I had been steerage hoeing with Tony when the weather broke. We carried on until it became too sticky and then gave up. It was just before lunch break when we got back to the yard, both of us wet and muddy.

The Boss was about and came over.

'You've been just about living here the last week or so,' he said. 'Push off home. This rain will do more good than any of us will out there.'

It poured heavens hard when I left the farm and I cycled head down up the lane sloshing through the puddles. Wet as I was I couldn't resist taking the loop lane past the stables and as luck would have it, Tracy was in the yard, kitted out in waterproofs and waving for me to come in.

'What a day!' she said holding her arms out and looking skywards. 'You're off early, are you OK?'

'Yes, fine. The Boss said to knock off as it was so wet and I've put in a lot of hours lately. You on your own?' I asked.

'That was good of Mr Willis. Sue's brother has had an operation. She caught the early bus and won't be back until the five o'clock. He's OK but Sue thought she ought to go and see him,' Tracy explained.

We were sheltering under the corner of the barn, the rain hammering on the iron roof and pouring out of the downpipes to rush across the concrete and disappear down the drain in the corner.

'Any problems from Willie Williams?' I asked.

'He's not been near the place,' she grinned.

'I think he knows we've got him by the balls.'

'Do you want to come in and eat your lunch here?' she asked.

'Well, I'm pretty wet, I ought to get home and dry out,' I said.

'Oh come on in,' she took my hand. 'You can dry out just as well here.'

We went out into the downpour and made our way to the flat. On the way Tracy picked up a dry sack from the feed store and when we opened the door to the flat she spread it on the floor for us to take off our wet gear on. She hadn't been out in it very long so was reasonably dry under the top layer but the knees and backside of my trousers and sleeves and collar of my shirt were wet. She made me take off the wet things until I was down to vest and pants. There was a lot of giggling and horse play. She put a match to the Aladdin paraffin heater that provided the main warmth for the flat and draped my damp clothes over a wooden clothes-horse and stood it by the heater.

'They can be drying while we have our lunch,' she said. 'I'll find you something to put on. There should be something in here.'

She went into the bedroom and I followed her.

After our love making she found me a big sloppy jersey with a girly pattern on the front, but refused to provide anything for my lower regions. So that's how we had lunch, her in her dressing gown and me in the jersey that caused her to giggle every time she looked my way.

She was in mid-giggle when Sue walked in.

'Oh,' was all Sue could manage, then it was, 'I'm so sorry,' then it was the hand to the mouth and then, damn the woman, she burst out laughing! Tracy joined in at once; that left me sitting there tugging the front of the stupid jersey down as far as possible and wishing I had put my pants back on, instead of adding them to the rest on the clothes horse. With the girls squealing with laughter I found I was unable to keep a straight face in such hilarious circumstances.

When some recovery was made, Sue explained that she had caught the early afternoon bus as morning visiting was restricted to one hour and she wouldn't be able to see her brother in the evening.

'Right,' I said to Tracy. 'You've had your laughs, now would you get my clothes.'

'They can't be dry yet,' she said.

'Don't bother on my account,' Sue said still chuckling.

'Well, I can't sit about like this all afternoon,' I told them, still dragging the front of the jersey downwards.

'Know what, Trace?' Sue said, looking at me, her head on one side. 'That sweater looks better on Graham than it does on you.' More laughter.

I got up carefully from the table and reversed towards the bedroom door, grabbing my trousers and underclothes off the dryer one-handed as I went. Unfortunately in trying to do it one-handed, I unbalanced the thing and one side of it fell towards the heater. I grabbed it quickly and set it upright again. Then realised I had used the hand that was holding the jersey. The squeals and giggling reached unbelievable levels as I fled through the bedroom door.

The girls had more or less recovered when I returned, rather sheepishly, to get the top half of my clothes.

'If you are going to wear those you had better go and change, they are very damp,' Tracy said.

'You are probably right,' I agreed.

'It's still pouring so I guess I won't come back today,' I added looking out of the window.

I climbed back into my wet coat and leggings and kissed Tracy goodbye.

'Bye,' I called to Sue.

'Bye, Graham, nice to ... *see* ... you,' she giggled.

Damn the woman again (no, not really, she's too much fun)!

Chapter 14

One result of the wet spell was that the heavy rain had pushed the earlier sown peas over so we were unable to drive through with the steerage hoe. These fields were passed over to the girls, who would have to walk them with a bag and a hoe pulling out the fat hen and thistles and putting them in bags. These were then emptied in heaps on the field edge for collection and burning after the crop was harvested.

The later peas we could still get through, so many hours were spent on this. The middle of June was nice and sunny and our neighbour was able to make some good hay, some of which he delivered and stacked in the big barn ready for the coming winter's cattle feed. Its scent filled the air around the yard and seemed to impart a general 'feel good' ambience to the whole area. Even Anna, whom I encountered briefly one morning, said: 'I loves tha' smell o' that 'ay, makes yew fink it's nearly bleedin' summer. That's if we ever fuckin' git one.'

There were a few changes for this year: the Boss had decided not to grow fodder beet for the cattle but instead to make more use of the feed value of barley straw. They'd still get their chat potatoes and, as Tom said, 'Twill be one less job ta do I zuppose, them used ta loik they beet choppins mind.'

The next change would be Neil. He had passed his tests for the RAF and would be leaving at the end of the month.

The next personal change would be my seventeenth birthday, I had been saving my wages to the point of Scrooge-like meanness with the intention of buying a motorbike. My folks had promised me money for my birthday so it was a case of seeing what I could afford when the day came.

I had talked to Tracy about the idea, being careful not to mention it was my seventeenth birthday, and she was delighted. It would mean we could get out for trips once I had passed my test and I would be able to ride it to work and not have to cycle home when I was dead beat at the end of a long day.

I was now busy tractor hoeing between the rows of plants that had been set out. The plants were in 2ft 3in rows as against the peas in 2ft so I had to change the width of the wheels on my Fergy.

Tony showed me how it was done and from then on I could do it on my own in about an hour, even though the rear wheels were water ballasted.

The hoe had five tines for each set working between the row of plants with right-angle blades on the first four and a duck-foot point on the last one. Each set of tines could be widened or closed by means of a screw adjustment on the top. This meant that when the plants were tiny it was possible to have the sets quite wide and cover nearly all the ground. They could then be closed up to be narrower as the plants grew.

It was a maximum-concentration job with the plants passing through a gap in the hoe that, when they were small, was no more than 4in wide. Constant attention was required not to dislodge them and the crabbing of the tractor allowed for. Fortunately steerage hoeing the peas had given me a good feel for this and I had no problems.

I had met young Harry, the lorry driver, one afternoon as I was knocking off. I had hardly seen him since my first week. We chatted for a while and he suggested again a trip to the markets overnight. I was in full agreement so it was left that he would have a word with the Boss and fix it up.

My birthday on 28 June duly arrived and I was truly delighted to receive a surprise from my folks in the shape of a BSA Bantam 125cc motorbike.

'Spend your money on a crash helmet and the gear you need for riding,' they told me.

'I'll get one as soon as possible,' I promised.

Next day, L plates affixed, I rode into the

yard to surprised smiles from all and sundry. Everyone gathered round to admire my new wheels and to pass comment.

'That thar'll save 'e some toim,' Bert observed. 'Yew'l be a'gettin' 'ere afore yew've left 'ome.'

I was still sitting on the bike and felt someone climb onto the pillion. It was Katie.

'Cor this is cosy,' she told everyone. 'First chance I've had to get close to young Graham.'

My face was difficult to control but I did just manage to laugh it off.

The change the bike made would be tremendous. I had independence, I could go where I liked. I could work late and still get back to Tracy's for a short while.

My brother had a motorbike before he joined the Merchant Navy so I had learned how to ride one when I was twelve. I put in for a test straight away when I got the bike, so hopefully would not have to wait too long before I could take a passenger.

However, there were other things to sort out first today. In the yard were two huge lorries standing waiting with 18 tons of fertiliser on each. It was all in 1¼cwt sacks that had to be carried on one's back and stacked in the store.

'Do you think you'll be able to manage?' the Boss asked. 'Give it a go, but pack up if it gets too much.'

Apart from myself there was Tony, Neil, Percy, Tom and Walter to manhandle the loads off. The driver put them on the lorry edge for us and it was a matter of walking to and fro bringing in a sack each time. The first one I took off the lorry didn't seem too bad but, as the day wore on and the number carried increased, they seemed to get heavier. We got the first one unloaded by morning tea, which meant we got a break before starting on the next.

"Ow yew makin' out?' Tom asked me, concerned. 'Don't 'e go an burst yewr boiler.'

'Thanks, Tom,' I replied. 'I'm OK so far.' My shoulders ached and I found that sitting down having our break I had a job to stop my legs trembling. I mentioned it to Tom.

'If yew be thinkin' these be 'eavy,' Tom said, 'wait til yew git on ta arvest an git some o' lay two an a quarter 'undredweight buggers. They'll mak yewr legs tremble,' he chuckled at the thought.

The next load seemed to take forever, but I stuck with it and had the honour of taking the last sack.

'Shud be a fiver under that un,' Tom observed. 'That must be tha' reason we bin a'movin' all they others.'

We all laughed and I found this was a stock remark among the workers on completion of an unloading job. The Boss arrived soon after we finished, as the drivers were folding up their canvas sheets, to be greeted with ribald comments from the guys.

'Cor, that do tak years o' practise ta turn up jist as job be finished!' Percy joked, to much laughter.

'A lifetime more like,' the Boss said laughing along with them. 'I would have been here sooner but I got held up on the phone.' There were shouts of derision at that and some cries of, 'likely story'.

'Be yew a fan of that 'Ans Christian Andysen, guv'nor? 'E were good at fairy tales too,' Tom called, causing more mirth.

'Well,' the Boss said, 'this isn't a fairy tale. There will be two more loads, same size, tomorrow.'

The men groaned and went off to their separate jobs. I went and started routine morning checks on my Fergy, oil, water that sort of thing and the Boss came over.

'Tony tells me you stayed the course. Well done. You'll have muscles where you didn't even know you had them,' he grinned.

'Well, at the moment I ache all over,' I told him. 'But it's wearing off slowly.'

It did too. After an hour or so on the tractor, apart from a bit of a stiff neck, I was fine, then Tracy turned up on the headland and it wasn't only the neck!

'I'll be working on a bit I expect but I'll call in and see you on the way home,' I told her. 'I've got something to show you.'

'Oo,' she replied making big eyes. 'Promises, promises! Happy birthday, by the way, I've got something for you when you call.'

'Oo,' I said smiling. 'Promises, promises!'

'Don't push your luck,' she smiled back as she turned Moonshine away.

I worked on until I had enough daylight left to get to Tracy's. I wanted her to see my new wheels without the floodlight. She heard me arrive in the stable yard and came out on to the landing outside the flat with Sue close behind. They were both soon down the stairs and admiring the bike. Then they wanted a ride and I explained I shouldn't take a passenger until I passed my test, but I finished up giving them a quick flip round the loop lane. Tracy first and then Sue. Tracy put her arms round my waist and away we went, round the yard, out on to the lane and off round the loop, Tracy giving little whoops of delight. I did a repeat run for Sue who was just as enthusiastic and wanted an extra circuit of the yard.

Tracy then produced a neatly wrapped parcel and gave it to me with a kiss.

'Hope you like it,' she said looking worried. I quickly ripped off the wrapping and opened the small box inside. It was a wallet made of really soft black leather and I just loved it.

'Thanks, darling,' I said, pulling her to me and hugging her. 'It's so nice of you to get it for me.'

'Wish I could afford more,' she said. 'You have done so much.'

I left them and rode home to get my tea, going a long way round just to enjoy the bike. I was delighted with the present and so pleased with the way my relationship with Tracy was developing. My God, I thought, I do really believe I'm in love!

That evening, as I relaxed at home, I felt that great sensation of muscular tiredness that one gets from a day's hard physical work and strangely enough the prospect of two more 18-ton loads to carry off in the morning didn't bother me.

The farm now looked terrific with crops expanding in every field, so different from my first days back in January when all was bleak and these same fields brown and empty. The only relief then being the frail green trembling plants of winter sown corn: how they survive the winter I shall never know. Now they were half a hedge high, the heads of barley or wheat standing up proud to the strengthening sun. In another field the shaking dance of a crop of oats would catch the eye. Straight rows of cabbages, cauliflower and numerous other 'greens' marched across the acres, now big and strong with heavy veined leaves, cupped to catch the rain. The lighter green of the peas showed up, some still in flower, while the earlies were carrying pods nearly ready for picking. The haulm of the rows of potatoes almost met across to form a solid mass, and it would soon be time to earth them up as a final act before harvest. Then there were the beans, beetroot and marrows all adding to the wonderful variety of colour and feeling of productivity that the farm gave as a whole. The immense satisfaction of looking at it all came from knowing that in numerous ways I had helped to bring this about and that people somewhere would be sitting down to a meal and enjoying what this farm had produced and would produce.

My Dad had spoken to me the previous evening.

'You've been with John Willis for nearly six months now,' he had started, 'and I must admit that I never thought you would stick it. I gave him a ring last week and called round to see him on the way home in the evening. He has been more than pleased with what you have done so far, and he too, thought you would never last out.' Dad paused to fill his pipe and then went on.

'He thought that week just after you started when you were cabbage cutting in that freezing weather would be the end. You seemed to get through it and since then have progressed well. He mentioned that you might have had a problem with the women

on the farm. He had heard that they had...'
Dad paused again to get the pipe drawing,
'...what was I saying? Oh yes, have you had
trouble with the women?' he asked.

'No trouble at all,' I told him. 'They are a
terrific bunch and as tough as nails. They
thought I was a bit shy to start with but they
soon cured me.'

I laughed it off and Dad did not pursue
the subject – thank goodness.

'How's the Bantam?' he asked.

'Goes like a dream,' I replied. 'Tracy was
impressed.'

'Nothing to stop you bringing her over
once you've passed your test,' he said. 'Your
mother and I would love to meet her, as I've
said before. I must say Giles and Howard
were very impressed.'

Giles and Howard were the solicitor and
police superintendent who had fixed up the
paperwork that seemed to be keeping Willie
Williams at bay.

'Yes,' I said, 'they would be. She's a bit of
a stunner. She's got white blonde hair.'

'So they said,' Dad told me. Yes, I thought,
I bet they were perving over her, probably
jealous of Willie.

A couple of weeks later in early July I went
for my motorbike test. This involved riding
up and down the street in front of the test office and doing an emergency stop when the

tester stepped out and held up his hand. A few minutes later and it was ditch the L plates and away. I called in to the stables to be greeted with squeals of delight from the girls. I'd told them of my appointment for the test. I asked Tracy if she'd be free on Sunday, to come and meet my folks and stay to lunch.

'Yes, she will,' Sue replied on Tracy's behalf. 'I'll cover for her here, no problem.'

'Looks like my Sunday is arranged for me,' Tracy smiled. 'Thanks both of you. I'll have to dig out my best gear and try and make myself presentable.'

I arranged to pick her up on Sunday morning on the bike but if it was raining I would come over with Dad in the car.

Everyone at the farm knew I had gone for the test, as I had to get time off to go, and the absence of the plates drew some cheers and backslapping from those about. The girls were just finishing lunch and Katie came over all smiles and clapping her hands.

'Well done!' she beamed, adding in a low voice, 'I could have told them you were a good rider.' She made big eyes and pouted.

Work-wise, I had been almost non-stop tractor hoeing between the plants. Almost all the peas were now too big to steerage hoe and field work was beginning to slow down on the run-up to harvest.

I had a change for a day and a half, earthing up the potatoes. The farm had a 3-row baulker, each one like a pointed snow plough that pushed the soil up into the familiar ridges of a potato crop. The haulm was almost meeting across the rows but after going through with the baulker, just a small amount of green peeped out of the top of the ridges. From the tractor it looked as if the plants were being buried never to emerge, but within a couple of days they had shaken off the soil and were standing green and healthy on top of the ridges.

Another job and there was another distinctive smell as the tractor wheels crushed a bit of haulm and released that unique aroma.

What a pleasure it was now to be able to sit on the tractors in shirt sleeves and feel the heat of the sun on your back. My arms and face were as brown as could be and I was putting on weight, but it was muscle and not fat. Things that had been a problem lifting or moving about a few months back now seemed easy, and the tractor driving had become second nature and did not occupy all my attention as it had early on.

I was able to look around and see what else was going on and enjoy the wildlife and birds. I was happier than I had ever been and delighted in my new career. My love for Tracy was growing stronger by the day. She was rarely out of my thoughts. Life was sensational!

Chapter 15

A new man started early July as a replacement for Neil. His name was Andy; he was in his early twenties and had worked on a local farm since leaving school. He had not been able to get on with his previous boss who was, by all accounts, a bit of an eccentric. He was an affable, easy-going guy, nearly 6ft tall, dark-haired and with a ready smile. Everyone soon took to him. I was sorry to see Neil leave as he had been a good mate and had helped me settle in. He had also been great at showing me how jobs were done and how bits of tackle fitted and worked. I wished him well in his new career and I was sure he would do well in what ever he chose to do.

With the arrival of Andy another big event occurred in the shape of a brand new tractor. It was a Fordson Major diesel and had, of all things, a self-starter, also full hydraulics and a power take-off for driving things like balers or mowers. Andy was appointed its regular driver and he was like a cat with two tails. The old Fordson on spade lug wheels was taken away but the one on rubber tyres was kept as a stand-by and for odd carting jobs. Not long after the arrival of the tractor a new plough turned up specially for the new machine. It was a Ransome 3-furrow, fully mounted. That meant it fitted directly to the tractor's 3-point linkage and could be lifted in and out of work simply by moving a small lever that operated the hydraulics. It was a great advance from all the other ploughs that were trailed and were lifted in and out of work by means of a ratchet on the plough wheel, operated by a rope to the tractor. I had seen pictures in the *Farmers Weekly* of a tractor like the one just arrived, fitted with a cab and wondered what it would be like to operate shut into one of those. I couldn't see that ever catching on.

Later on, some workmen installed a large tank on concrete block pillars to take diesel fuel. The Boss was convinced that all tractors in future would be diesel and he was proved perfectly correct, unlike me with the cab.

Harry, the lorry driver, finally fixed it for me to ride to London on the Friday night before the weekend Tracy was due to come to dinner at home. He arranged to meet me at 9.00 in the evening in the farmyard, as it would be a good place to leave my motorbike. He told me to come in work gear so I could give him a hand unloading.

I duly arrived at the arranged time and not long after, Harry pulled in with the lorry. It was a flat-fronted Ford with the engine back in the cab between the seats and the gear lever back behind that, so one had to reach backwards to change gear. I had a light coat with me in case of rain so with that over my shoulder I went round to the passenger door and climbed in. There was a double seat on the passenger side. I said 'Hi' to Harry.

'I suppose you mostly make this trip on your own?' I asked.

'Sometimes on a Friday when thar's no school next day one o' me daughters might come,' Harry said. 'I've got two, nineteen and sixteen and tha' lad he be twelve.'

'That's a nice family,' I told him. He went on to explain that he didn't only haul produce for Mr Willis but for lots of smaller local farms that could not afford their own lorry. When there was nothing for the markets he did general haulage.

'Got a regular pick up on tha' way,' he said. 'Small place, grows mushrooms in special sheds. We'll pick up thare an then 'it the A2.'

We had left the yard and were driving through the village where Katie lived. I noticed there was a small red car parked in the driveway. A few miles further on we pulled into a small yard and alongside a pair of garage-type doors. Harry stopped and jumped out.

I opened the door to get out but Harry called me to stay as there was not a lot to load and he had left a space for it. Evening was starting to fade and the smell of dew came in the open window.

Harry soon returned and we set off again, out on to the A2 and heading for London. The number of times I had been to London was negligible despite living only 35 miles from the centre. I had the very occasional trip with my folks to the theatre and we once drove up to see the Christmas tree in Trafalgar Square. It was noisy in the lorry cab with the engine between me and Harry so conversation was limited. Darkness slowly pushed away the last glimmer of evening to be replaced with the glow of street lights as we neared London. Our first drop was at Boro & Brentford Market and what an eye-opener it was! Lorries seemed to be everywhere and the place was a hive of activity at 10.30 at night.

We drove into the market where each sales retailer had his own specific area marked out in painted lines with his name board hanging above.

Harry knew exactly where to go, having done the job hundreds of times before. We joined a short queue of lorries unloading at the area we were aiming for and then, after half an hour or so, we were able to draw alongside. I hopped out and helped Harry with the unloading, having taken the ropes off while we were waiting. There was a card on the ground with 'J. Willis. Manor Farm' painted on it which Harry moved to one side and then set about stacking some of the bags of peas on the spot where it had been. I passed them off the lorry and the unloading soon progressed. Around half of the boxes of mushrooms we had picked up were stacked where another printed card was waiting. A quick count to make sure we had left the right amount, then Harry attached dockets to the cards with a clip that was on the top.

Moving forward out of the way to allow other lorries to unload, we re-roped what was left of the load and set off for Covent Garden market. There it was almost a replay of before, another mass of lorries and people. It was hard to believe that while I was asleep at night all this was going on and, as Harry pointed out, this was just the vegetables. Other markets were doing the same thing with meat, fish, flowers and all sorts of perishable items.

We had to wait a bit longer here to unload and by the time we were finished it was nearly 2.00 in the morning. Harry suggested a cup of tea and he found a spot to park not far from a tea stall in the market. The tea was hot and strong and I suggested a bacon sarnie which Harry welcomed.

It was quite a pleasure to listen to the Londoners gathered around us. They laughed a lot and seemed to me to be a really happy bunch. With the tea drunk and sarnies eaten, we returned to the lorry.

'Right, let's go 'ome,' Harry said, starting the motor. 'I expect you're tired. I've 'ad a sleep during the day.'

'I'm OK,' I told him. 'It's certainly been something new, I had no idea this all went on.'

Harry pulled out of the market and we started to thread our way back to the A2, the street lights illuminating the dozens of street girls that still hoped for a late trick. 'Cold old job that, even in Summer time,' Harry observed.

The engine noise put off further chat and I started to feel a bit drowsy. Soon we were in the suburbs and moved out on to the A2. The engine settled to a steady drone, a half-moon gleamed over the countryside as the street lights were left behind. Harry was a vague shape the other side of the engine cover. I rested my head against the side pillar and must have dozed to come awake when we were only about five or six miles from the farm. We pulled back into the farmyard as dawn was tinting the eastern sky. I hopped out and held the door open.

'Thanks for the trip, Harry,' I called, 'it's

been great. Perhaps we could do it again later in the year.'

'Any time ya like, nice ta 'av a 'and unloadin',' Harry called back.

'I'll look forward to it,' I told him, shutting the cab door and waving as he drove off.

I rode home in the gathering light and crept indoors. My folks knew where I had been and would not disturb me in the morning, as the boss had given me the time off. Hunger got me up around midday and I went downstairs for lunch and a cup of tea. Mum and Dad were interested to know how the trip had gone and I explained to them about the workings of the markets. They were fascinated by my description of the crowded state of the area and the huge number of people about.

Sunday dawned fine sunny and warm and my Mum was in her usual tizzy if anyone was coming to lunch. Did Tracy like this or that? I told her all I knew was that she definitely wasn't vegetarian and as far as I knew had very few dislikes.

'Well, I'm going to do roast beef with Yorkshire pudding,' Mum declared. 'I do hope she likes it, and I thought apple pie for dessert. Do you think that will be OK?'

'I'm sure that will be fine, Mum,' I told her. 'She's just an ordinary girl, not royalty or anything. I'll go and fetch her about eleven.'

I gave the bike a bit of a clean and polish and around 10.50 set off for the stables. I drove in and round to the bottom of the stairs to the flat and put the bike on its prop stand. Tracy answered to my knock and I was stunned.

'My God,' I gasped. 'You look absolutely mind-blowing.'

She was wearing a black-bolero type jacket with a red and white silk scarf knotted round her neck – I could see the edge of a red shirt or blouse under the jacket. A knee-length suede skirt made up with different coloured patches and light tan slip-ons. Her hair was tied back in a head scarf obviously with the motorbike ride in mind. She was carrying a small tan handbag. Sue appeared behind her.

'She scrubs up quite well doesn't she?' Sue observed. 'Mind you, she's been doing her face since first light.'

Tracy swung the handbag at her but Sue dodged back easily, laughing.

'Thanks for holding the fort, Sue,' I said. 'You've got the number if you have a problem. Just call and we'll cut 'em off at the pass.'

'I'll be OK,' Sue smiled. 'I've got both Winchesters loaded and I'm the fastest gal West of the Klondike with a six-gun. You two have fun now.'

I escorted Tracy down to the bike and with

waves to Sue we set off for the short, 2-mile, ride to my home. My Dad had bought a ¾-acre piece of land around six years previously and had a 4-bedroom house built there, more or less to his own design. We had lived there now for 3½ years. That had given time to establish lawns and an orchard, a decent-sized veggie garden and a fish pond. There was a drive that came off the road and round to the front. I turned in and stopped by the front door. Tracy dismounted and looked around as I propped the bike.

'You didn't tell me you lived in a place like this. My God, it's super!' she exclaimed.

'Glad you like it,' I replied, trying to sound casual but secretly on a little ego trip. 'Come on in and meet the folks. Sounds like something out of a Yankee B movie, doesn't it?'

She laughed a little nervously and removed the scarf from her hair letting it fall loose down over her shoulders. The door was on the latch so I was able to open it, and hold it open, while ushering her inside.

My folks came out into the hall to meet her and she shook hands all round. My Dad's face was a picture. I don't know what he had been expecting, but Tracy sure took his breath away and Mum adopted that rather defensive attitude that women have when confronted with a 'rival'. I thought Dad's eyes would pop out when she slipped off the bolero jacket to reveal a tight red stretchy blouse that emphasised her figure and showed just a respectable inch or so of cleavage.

The day went well, we had drinks on the terrace before lunch and Dad monopolised Tracy as I knew he would. Mum was very impressed when she turned up in the kitchen asking if she could help.

During lunch there was general chitchat and then my Mum happened to say: 'We didn't really want Graham to have a motor-bike but it will give him some independence. He could hardly wait for his seventeenth birthday so he was old enough to get one. I just hope you are careful on it.' The last bit directed at me.

Out of the corner of my eye I saw Tracy's fork stop halfway to her mouth then go on again and I didn't dare look in her direction. Oh God, I thought, Graham's in for a kicking when we get back to the stables.

Once the meal was over, Tracy insisted on helping Mum clear away and wash up and I could hear them chattering away in the kitchen.

Dad settled down with his pipe and, when it was drawing well, said: 'You were certainly right about her being a stunner,' he observed. 'I don't wonder Giles was impressed. Fancies himself as a bit of a ladies' man I think. That hair is amazing. Doesn't it get in the way when she's working? And what a colour!'

'She winds it up into a single big plait and fixes it up somehow,' I told him.

We had the usual coffee and things after the clearing-up and relaxed, chatting until around 4.30 when Tracy said she should be getting back so as not to leave all the evening feeding and chores to Sue.

Goodbyes were said and promises to come again were made, then it was on the bike and off back to the stables. Sue had just started her rounds.

'With you in a tick,' Tracy called, heading for the stairs in a rush leaving me to follow at a more leisurely pace. She had left the door of the flat open and rushed straight into the bedroom pushing the door to, but not closed. I pushed it open and walked in.

'Do you mind!' she said. She was in bra and panties and about to put on her work trousers. 'I'm not sure you are old enough to see me like this.'

'Balls!' I replied, a bit pissed off. 'I've seen you in a damn sight less.'

She pulled on a shirt and tucked it in the trousers. 'I've got to help Sue. Make yourself some tea or coffee. I'll be back in a while.' She moved past me to the door. 'We can talk then.'

I did as she suggested, made a cup of tea and relaxed looking at the view. Some time later I heard their voices and they came up the stairs and into the flat.

'I'm going to have a bath,' Sue declared, heading for the bedroom. I guessed Tracy had asked her to give us time for a chat.

She got right off with it.

'You told me you were seventeen going on eighteen, you lied to me,' she flared.

'No I didn't.' I kept calm. 'If you remember, when I asked you to guess my age, you said between seventeen and eighteen and I told you it was a good guess. It was – you were only a year out. That makes it a very good guess.'

'You were just being a smartarse,' she scolded. 'You could have told me your proper age.'

'Look, Tracy,' I reasoned, 'would it have made an ounce of difference if I had told you? Would you have shown me the door and told me to get lost? I don't think so.'

She thought about that for a while, her face softening. 'Damn it, you're right as usual! I don't think I would have worried if you were fifteen. Come here and kiss me, young man.' She was smiling now and I did as I was told.

I stayed for tea and we went for a walk in the fine evening air. It was an idyllic summer's twilight with bees buzzing around and the air full of bird song. We got back to the flat and Sue had her feet up on the sofa reading and records playing.

'I've just got cosy here,' she said. 'Can you

two find somewhere else to go?' That Sue, what a babe! We shut the door and moved to the bedroom where Tracy went to great lengths to convince me that all was forgiven, and how!

When I arrived back home my folks were full of Tracy's visit and delighted that I had found such a wonderful girl.

'She is so easy to talk to,' my Mum enthused, 'and so willing to help. Most girls these days don't seem to want to get off their backsides and do anything. Has she got any brothers or sisters?'

'She's never mentioned any,' I replied, 'but I've never really asked her.' My Dad was having the late evening cup of tea and was equally impressed.

'I don't know about a stable girl, she looks more like a film star or a model,' he said. 'I still can't get over how lovely her hair is and there is so much of it.' They carried on in a like vein until I took myself off to bed, delighted that the day had gone so well and that Tracy had impressed my folks so much.

Chapter 16

With the year moving into August even more changes were apparent around the farm. The cornfields were now starting to change to golden from their familiar green. The heads of the barley drooped over and hung down the stalks, and the wind, which before had silently rippled across them, now rustled among the stems and the heat of the sun had them cracking and snapping.

The oats were ripening the quickest with their dancing chandelier heads swinging in the breeze and seeming to make the whole field quiver, the straw up to one's armpit. The fine spell that had started midway through July, apart from the odd day or two, continued into August and hurried on the day when harvest could begin. First though were the freezer peas. The man from the freezer works was around the farm every other day with a gadget called a tender-ometer. He would pick a sample of peas from different areas of a field, shell them and put the peas in a stainless steel cup. He then pushed down on a lever which forced some curved metal fingers through them. The amount of force required was registered on a dial which indicated the tenderness of the crop. Once certain parameters were reached then harvesting could begin. The whole crop had to go to the freezing works, bine and all. The peas were then threshed out at the works, cleaned and flash frozen.

I was still managing to get through some of the cabbage plants with the tractor hoe but soon they would be too big. The girls were sometimes in the same field spread out in a line pulling the fat hen and dropping it down. It was only in the peas they carried it to the headland. On one of these occasions the Boss turned up to see how things were going. He walked behind the hoe for a little while and then stopped me.

'Better make this the last time through,' he told me. 'They are getting too big now.'

While he was speaking the line of girls passed, bent over and working away. The Boss looked at me and grinned.

'Listen to this,' he said.

He moved across behind the girls until he was in the rows that Anna had been working on and found a big fat hen plant that Anna had pulled out. He turned his back to the line and picked up the weed and quickly heeled it back in, upright.

'Hoy, Anna,' he called. She stopped, stood up and looked back. 'You're missing a whole lot here. Look at this.'

Anna looked at the weed sticking up by the Boss and twigged straight away what he had done – then she started. I must say I was impressed as would any squaddie or docker have been. She went on for what must have been a couple of minutes and never repeated herself, taking care of the weeds, the boss, the field, men in general and anything else that had crossed her path in the last month. I won't try to reproduce it all here out of respect for my readers. The Boss was holding his sides and rocking with laughter – some of the girls were laughing as well, Katie stood with her hand to her mouth in amazement. I must admit it was too funny a scene for me not to join in the laughter. It finished with Anna telling the boss exactly where he could go in no uncertain terms. She then turned away and carried on working.

He came back to me his face streaked with tears from laughing so much.

'How would you like to be married to her?' he asked.

'I would never have guessed she was married,' I replied.

'Been with Charlie now for, oh must be over forty-five years. She's got five kids and I've lost count of the grandchildren. I remember when she had ... I think it was the third. We were potato harvesting in the field next to this one. Anna was huge, having a job to bend over and pick up the spuds. The other girls kept telling her to give up and go home but she said she needed the money, so kept on. Anyway,' he went on, 'soon after lunch her waters went there in the field – we got her on the trailer and back to the yard. Missus phoned the midwife and she had the babe in the farmhouse around four o'clock. We managed to get her back to her place in the evening, baby was fine. You know what...?' The Boss tapped me on the arm to emphasise what he was going to say. 'She was back in the bloody field picking up spuds the next morning and worked a full day. Brought the baby with her all swaddled up and laid it in a box on the headland. T'other girls covered her land when she was seeing to it.'

I was totally amazed by his story and it made me realise even more what an incredibly tough bunch the farm women were.

Around the second week in August the tenderometer readings were right for the first field of peas. A day's notice was given for the arrival of lorries to transport the crop to the freezer works. I hitched on to the big elevator which was folded up in three sections for transport. Once in the field the side poles were put up and by a system of wires and pulleys the sections unfolded to form a straight elevator. Andy stripped all the tines from a mounted cultivator and replaced them with a wide blade that had a leg at each end to fit to the cultivator frame. The two Fergys were fitted with rear-mounted buckrakes. They had long, round-pointed tines with a frame at the back. The tines could be adjusted so when the buckrake was lowered on the hydraulics, the points ran along level with and against the ground and were angled up slightly, back to the frame.

It was arranged for Andy to make an early start with the new Fordson and the blade. The blade itself was slightly tipped downwards so that when lowered it drew into the ground. It was wide enough to cover four rows of peas. In action it was adjusted on the tractor hydraulics to run just below the roots of the crop. Walking alongside it was possible to see the four rows lift up over the blade and then drop back down where they had been, the difference being that they were now just virtually lying there and not rooted into the soil.

Reversing the buckrake across the rows lifted them right out and they slid up the rake, each row pushing the previous one further on until the whole rake was full. Tony showed me how it was done and told me he was going to drive the second Fergy.

We cleared an area round the gateway to give the first lorry room to pull in and get under the elevator, picking up rake loads and putting them to one side ready to pick up later. Right on time it arrived and I was surprised to see it was a big flat-bed artic. I had expected a lorry with high sides.

The driver had done it all before and drove round and under the elevator. All was set. The elevator was belt-driven by one of the older Fordson Majors. This was swung over and started up and reversed to tension the belt.

The rake loads that were set to one side were picked up and brought in to the base of the elevator where Walter and Percy were waiting, pitchforks at the ready. To start with it was quite a slow job on the Fergys; only one load at a time could be dropped for the two forking so there was a bit of waiting time. Once the immediate area had been cleared, however, things hotted up and the last third of the load meant using top gear to and fro from pick-up to elevator and back as quite a large area was cleared. With the rake full of peas the front wheels had minimum contact with the ground and steering was only possible with the independent brakes. It was not unusual to reverse through the crop and fill the rake, lift up and pull away, the front wheels perhaps nine inches off the ground. Change up through the box and hurtle in to the front of the elevator and only then, on dropping the load would the front wheels come down again. It was exciting stuff and not for the faint-hearted as over-exuberance could finish up with the tractor going over backwards.

The lorry driver positioned the crop as it came on board, placing it out to the edges and keeping them upright and straight, filling in the middle to hold the outside. There was quite a knack in loading but when carried out properly it looked neat and tidy. Having done it before he knew when he had his weight on and called a stop. Once loaded, he pulled a heavy net across the top to stop any over-hanging trees pulling bits off. Then started up and slowly made his way to the field gateway, the lorry swaying and springs creaking under the load. We had a quick tea break before moving the elevator out into the field and up to the edge of the uncleared peas. We were just setting up the Fordson and belt to drive the elevator when the next lorry arrived. The freezer pea harvest took around a week to complete. In that time we cleared 62 acres and loaded usually three lorries a day. There was always a bit of a delay when we had to move fields as it meant sometimes packing up the elevator and re-erecting. Close contact with the lorry firm was essential so as to avoid their vehicles waiting about.

Personally, I was quite sorry when it was over. The usual sedate tractor work had given way for a short time to almost manic driving and an appreciation of just what the little grey Fergys were capable of. One of the advantages of clearing the whole crop was that it left a clean cultivated field with just the wheel marks to work over before it was ready for Autumn drilling. In later years, of course, mobile viners like huge combines would travel round the farms working 24 hours a day, but for the moment, the freezing operation was in its infancy.

Corn harvest started as soon as the peas were finished. Some would be cut with the combine, the oats and some of the wheat with the binder. While we had been busy, Tom, Bert and Harry Snr had been scything round the outside of the oatfield, a couple of the girls following on tying up the sheaves. This made it possible to make a start with the binder without the tractor running through the crop.

I had the tractor job with Harry Snr riding on the binder and watching over the cutting. He had three levers in front of him, one to adjust the height of cut and to lift the cutter bar while turning at the ends. The second adjusted the height of the sails that swept the crop on to the knife, while the third corrected the position of the string round the sheaf. The binder itself was quite a modern one and, although pulled along by tractor, the actual workings were driven by a power take-off shaft using the tractor's power to operate it, and provide mobility.

It was handled quite comfortably by the Fergy and was a very pleasant job. In total contrast to the racetrack driving of the pea harvest, this was a slow, steady operation with the almost hypnotic swish of the sails, the steady chatter of the cutter bar and the clink-clunk of the knotter and ejection of a neatly tied sheaf.

The girls followed us round stacking the sheaves into stooks to finish drying before carting to the stack. Tea and lunch breaks were taken in the field, sitting around the binder and leaning back against the tractor wheel or any handy spot. They were great times, full of laughter, as the men teased the girls unmercifully but finished up getting as much back as they gave. Tracy turned up on Moonshine and said hello to everybody and I walked over and held her stirrup while we chatted. There was some fairly lewd comments after she went as I expected, with Harry suggesting that he would like her to get her legs round him instead of 'that oss'. Dream on I thought.

It wasn't a big field and late morning on the second day saw us getting to the end. The Boss and Tony turned up with a shotgun each and had tremendous sport knocking over the rabbits that had gathered in the last bit. Even a fox broke cover but was allowed to run free. I asked Tony why.

'This is hunting country,' he told me. 'I might have fired at that fox and only wounded it. It could then get into cover and die a lingering death. Much better to leave it to the hunt because if they catch it, it's clean killed in a few seconds and much more humane.'

The combine was now brought to life. It was a Massey Harris 726 and required two people to operate it, one to drive and the other to bag off the corn and tie up the sacks. I got the bagging-off job as the rest of the wheat that was to be cut with the binder wasn't quite fit.

A good quantity of sacks were hung over the seat at the back of the bagging platform. Why it had a seat I'm not sure, because all the time I worked on it I never had time to sit down! We were going to cut winter-sown barley. Tony showed me how the sacks fitted on. There were four outlets, one for weed seeds and tiny bits, the next for tail or chipped corn and then two for the good crop. The sacks were fitted onto two hooks at the back and slipped between two plates at the front. The operation of a little lever pushed out pegs to hold them in place.

We trundled up the lane, filling it from bank to bank, and turned up the landway to the first field. Running up the engine to operating revs and putting the threshing mechanism into gear seemed to create a cacophony of noise and dust. Moving into the crop, it was only a few seconds before corn began to pour out of the first outlet into the sack. Once that sack was full a simple swing shutter changed the flow to the next. Then it was all go to get the first sack tied and down the shoot to where it could be held for a while. The sacks weighed over 2cwt and moving one about on a swaying platform was no easy task. It was usually a case of just about getting a new sack fitted before the previous one was full. Dust swirled around all the time and the awns from the barley ears were itchy and seemed to get everywhere. However, like most jobs one found the easiest way of working and, after an hour or two, I found I could keep up easier. The shoot down which the full sacks were slid would hold two and one balanced at the top. Once that stage was reached, a hard tug on a rope opened the stop at the bottom and the three sacks slid off to be picked up by tractor and trailer later. I found that by 'walking' a full sack to the top of the shoot, I could slide down with it and keep it upright. Doing each sack this way meant I could get three sacks on the shoot and one balanced, meaning fewer stops for the carting gang. Tony used to moan because the combine got so hard to steer with three sacks on the shoot putting extra weight on the steering wheels.

The header on the 726 had an unusual operating system. It had heavy springs that held it in the up position and it was pulled down into the working mode by a chain, driven by an ordinary car-type starter motor. This was operated by a little switch in front of the driver. It was not very reliable and gave regular problems – mainly the solenoid burning out through overheating. It was unusual to run for more than a few hours without something breaking or coming apart, but for its time it was a good machine and produced a good clean sample without too much waste over the back. The farm did not have a dryer so it was not possible to run too long into the evening. When the dew started to gather, the knife would start banging and you would know it was time to stop. Once stopped it was all go to get the sacks picked up and carted in. It took three men lifting each one on to the trailer and a man on the trailer putting them in place. The method used to pick up $2\frac{1}{4}$cwt-sacks from the ground was for two men to face each other one on either side of the sack and the third at the tied-up end. The two either side would bend their legs and get a grip on the top and bottom of the sack, jam the top of their heads together to form a lock, and then lift. As they lifted, the third man would help by pulling up on the end. Once upright, the heads parted and it was not too much problem to walk to the trailer carrying the sack. Once there and stopped in the right position, the sack would be swung backwards a short way to give impetus to the swing onto the trailer. Once the base was on, the three men would quickly get behind it and push it upright. The man on the trailer then had to move it into position on his own. This was achieved by wrapping your arms round the top and digging in the knees. It was then possible to slide the sack in a series of 2 or 3ft heaves.

Once the trailer was full, the whole team would hop on and ride back to the barn for unloading. I can well remember the first time I had one of those sacks on my back. All the crew stood around to watch and to give advice, most of it useless! I reached up and got hold of the top and, pulling it over off the trailer, staggered to the drop point, the men shouting approval and clapping.

'I never new yewr legs could bend sideuds as well as to an' fro,' Tom laughed.

The strange thing was that by the end of unloading the first trailer, as I took my turn in the line, the sacks didn't seem so heavy. It was like all other farm jobs. There was a definite knack to how it was done. The sacks were stood down singly, the tie strings undone and the top of the sack rolled down level with the corn to assist with final drying.

The final load of the day would usually be

late evening. What pleasure it was riding on top of the sacks as the trailer creaked and swayed towards the gateway, the smell of the dew and the low sun highlighting the wheel-marks through the stubble. Then out onto the lane and the quicker ride, the breeze drying the sweat and that wonderful relaxed, tired feeling seeping through one's body. The last load was backed into the barn for un-loading in the morning and we all dispersed to our homes. I was mightily pleased to have the motorbike. I wouldn't have fancied push-biking home.

The corn harvest started well with a fine spell of weather giving us an unbroken run of ten days. During that time we managed to cut most of the winter barley with the combine. The sun had also quickly finished drying the oats in the stooks and, while we had been busy on the combine, the others, with help from the girls, had carted and stacked them. A neat oval stack with a tidy sloping top now stood in the corner of the field with a temporary cover over. It would be thatched as soon as there was time avail-able.

Harvest came to a halt for a short while due to the weather, giving everyone a welcome break, I had spoken to Tracy on the phone lots of times but hadn't seen her for ages. It seemed almost strange to leave the farm at

5.00 normal time. I had been working until nearly dark for what seemed like weeks. I rode to the stables and on arrival found that Tracy wasn't there but Sue was.

'Hi, how's things?' I greeted her.

'Do I know you?' she enquired.

'Hell, it's not been that long,' I replied laughing, 'or perhaps it has. I had forgotten just how gorgeous you are.'

'Just because your bird has gone up the shop on our jointly owned bike doesn't mean you can try out your chat up lines on me,' she fake-scolded.

'Well, at least you could make me a cuppa while I'm waiting,' I suggested.

'Well,' she mused. 'I expect I could go that far. Just give me five minutes to finish off. In fact, why don't you go up and put the kettle on and I'll be up.'

'I'm nothing but a skivvie to a couple of tarts,' I moaned to her. She bent down and grabbed a wet sponge from the bucket beside her and hurled it at me.

'Piss off and put the kettle on, and not so much of the tarts,' she laughed. 'We are respectable, well-behaved girls, I'll have you know!'

'Yes, damn it, I'd have much more fun...' I couldn't finish because this time it was a pitchfork she grabbed. I stopped my sprint at the bottom of the stairs and, strolling up to the flat, found the kettle and put it to boil. There were some dirty mugs in the sink so I washed them up and put them to drain. The kettle had just started to sing when Sue appeared. She took off her light waterproof (it was drizzling out but very muggy), to reveal a check short-sleeved shirt with the bottom part pulled up and knotted under her bust leaving a good nine inches of bare middle showing between it and a pair of elastic-waisted shorts.

'Whew,' I gasped, 'it's got ever so warm in here all of a sudden!' She saw the direction of my gaze and laughed.

'I can't believe that I turn you on when you've got Tracy,' she said. 'She's too hard to compete with. The blonde hair, the great figure and legs. It's a...' she shrugged as if lost for words. 'It's a "no competition" package.' She threw up her hands in a helpless sort of gesture and moved across to the kettle, her back to me as she made the tea.

'Don't ever put yourself down, Sue,' I told her. 'You are one hell of a good-looking girl. Any guy would be made up to be seen out with you.'

She was a few minutes finishing off the tea and stirring the mugs and when she turned and brought it over there were tears in her eyes and they had started to creep down her cheeks.

'Thank you for what you said,' her voice

was husky with emotion. 'It's tough sometimes working with someone like Tracy, although I love her to bits. I just feel like the ugly duckling ... you know?' She started to sniff and searched for a hanky, finding one on the side shelf.

I went over to her and put my arms round her.

'You should never feel like that, honestly.' I tried to comfort her. 'I meant what I said. You're a real smasher.'

'Thanks for that,' she said returning my hug.

Tracy walked in carrying a bag of groceries.

'What the bloody hell is going on?' she demanded, her face angry.

'Woah, steady on!' I held out my arms with the palms of my hands towards her. 'Sue's got herself a bit upset, that's all. I was just trying to help.'

It sounded lame but Tracy could see Sue's red eyes and calmed down a little.

'Tracy, you know I wouldn't cheat on you,' Sue said between sniffs. 'And you must know Graham wouldn't either.'

'So, what's it all about?' Tracy asked, calmer still.

I took the bag of shopping and drew up one of the chairs for her to sit on.

'How about some more tea?' I suggested to Sue and she took the hint and went off to pour it out.

Meanwhile I explained quietly to Tracy how Sue felt.

'She feels overshadowed by you,' I told her. 'In her own words, she feels she's the ugly duckling.'

'I had no idea she felt that way,' Tracy said, aghast. 'She certainly has no need to.'

'Look in the mirror, darling,' I told her. 'You are one sensational-looking girl. I don't know what the answer is with Sue. She's going to have to get over it or change her job.'

Sue returned with a cup of tea and seemed to be back in control, with even a bit of a smile on her lips.

'She's got a real sweet and ladylike turn of phrase hasn't she?' Sue smiled, referring to Tracy's outburst previously.

'Not half!' I smiled back. 'Looks of an angel, mouth of a docker, that's Tracy.'

I just managed to avoid a flat-handed swipe that headed my way and the laughter that followed finally put things back together. What the final solution was going to be I could not work out, but the germ of an idea was born in my mind.

Chapter 17

Like all dull spells, this one eventually cleared and the sun arrived again to dry things out. It was now into the last week of August. We were able to get started again cutting with the binder, as the last bit of drying could take place in the stooks. Once the first headland had been scythed round we made a start. Going was quicker in the wheat than in the oats as there was less straw and the wheat was easier to cut. With the girls once again stooking, the end of the day saw nice neat rows across the field and a good acreage covered.

Next day dawned fine again and it was now possible to combine the last of the winter barley.

We would cut with the binder until 4.00 in the afternoon, giving the girls time to catch up and knock off on time. They didn't work overtime because they had children and homes to look after. Then we would make up a gang to cart in the sacks of corn from the combine. Andy had gone bagging off with Tony, so Percy, Walter, Tom and me made up the team. The Boss decided that the corn coming off now was dry enough to tip in the bins in the granary. This meant that each sack had to be carried up the flight of stone steps and in the door. This door was just too low to get through with the sack on one's back so you had to stoop to get through and then straighten again. The sack was then rolled off the back onto the edge of the bin, untied and tipped in. There were lots of knacks to learn. If you miscalculated and the sack didn't lay nicely on the edge of the bin, perhaps dropping on the floor, it then took the whole gang to lift it up again and tip it, causing delay in carting in the rest. I dropped several, some in the bin and some outside before mastering the art.

A lot of the sacks, as they were straight off the field, were over 2½cwt and carrying one up a flight of steps, ducking through the door and then getting it to drop in exactly the right place time after time was no joke. The most noticeable thing I found was that after a few loads it seemed to get easier as knacks and skills were honed.

The year moved into September and the harvest rolled on. We cut one more full day with the binder, and with the winter barley finished the Boss thought there would be enough storage room to cut the rest of the wheat and the spring barley with the combine. There had been some hot dry days and so we started on carting and stacking the first field of wheat. Tom took over from

Andy bagging off on the combine so that we had both Fergys on the trailers. Bert built the stack, with Katie and Ruth supplying him with sheaves. Percy and Walter pitched up on to the trailers where two more girls built the load, an art in itself.

There were some straw bales in the Dutch barn unused from last year and they were fetched to form a base to build the stack. There was something peaceful and traditional about bringing in a load of sheaves to the stack. The tractor had to be eased quietly along so as not to tip off the load and then pulled alongside the stack and the sheaves, pitchforked off to the waiting girls who would pass them on to Bert. Returning for another load one would meet the second trailer coming in loaded. The rest of the girls were looked after by the Boss and were busy picking beans and keeping on top of the rest of the work. Once the stack was two-thirds complete, the elevator we had used for the peas was fetched up and rigged. This made it easier for the stacker as the sheaves were delivered to the middle and not constantly pitched on one edge. Bert took great pride in his stacks, and every so often he would come down and walk round it; eyeing it up from all directions. The outside sloped very slightly outwards so that when it was thatched the water would run clear. We still had to stop early because the combine was also going and there were sacks of wheat to be brought in. I thought the barley sacks were heavy enough but of course wheat is even heavier. At least they didn't have to be carried up the granary steps!

Sitting in the harvest fields having tea or lunch breaks with the whole crew gathered around are some of my happiest memories. Jokes were exchanged and there was always some new item of village gossip to discuss. These break times gave me a chance to chat and get to know Andy.

We had only met briefly in the yard and had not worked together before. I found out that he lived with his Mum and Dad and had a couple of younger sisters. He was keen on cars and had bought a little Morris that he spent all his spare time working on and hoped to soon have on the road.

'That will please the girlfriend,' I said.

'Haven't had much time for girls,' he replied. 'Don't get out very much and there's only the village birds.'

'Well, you get that car going and you'll be beating them off,' I laughed.

'Do you think so?' he said, looking surprised. 'I must get my finger out then and get the job done.'

A notable event at this time was the arrival of a new yard full of cattle. They looked very small. I had got used to the ones that were there when I started. The boss had seen to their arrival as we were all busy and they were then left alone for an hour or two to settle down before Tom started his feeding routine. All the staff became stock experts and leaned on the gate to cast their eye over the new arrivals and to voice an opinion as to their quality. It was nice to come into the farm and hear them rustling the straw and giving the odd moo. It sort of completed the rural feel and took me back to my first days. They now seemed an age ago but it was only ten months.

By the end of the second week in September we had two decent stacks of wheat built, all the winter barley cut and only around 25 acres of winter wheat left to harvest plus the spring barley that I had been involved with planting. Another dull damp spell moved in so the opportunity was taken to get the stacks thatched. There were the two wheat we had just built and the oats from back at the start of harvest. Bert again was the man for the job. In the last bay of the Dutch barn, the far end from where the potatoes had been, was a pile of wheat straw trusses. These were loaded on a trailer and I carted them first to the oat stack where Bert unloaded some and then on to the wheat stacks where I dropped the rest.

In the shed where the cabbage bags were

kept Bert had a freshly cut stack of hazel 'benders', small branches light enough to twist and bend into a staple shape. These were loaded on the trailer along with a bucket and a drum of water plus a large comb, some clippers and a sort of wooden mallet. The long wooden ladder was laid through the top sticking out over the tractor and poking a long way out the back. Arriving at the oat stack, we unloaded the trailer and set up the ladder against the sloping top.

'Cut tha' string orf some o' lay trusses,' Bert said. 'Lay 'em out side by side an chuck a bit o' water ower 'em.'

I followed his instructions and he then showed me how to pull the wet straws through my hands to straighten out any bends or kinks. Once done it was retied in much smaller bundles. Once Bert was happy that I had got the idea, he started carrying the bundles up on to the stack and securing them in place with the hazel branches and baler twine.

''Tain't loike thatchin' a 'ouse,' Bert told me. ''Tas only got ta last til Christmas, then us'll be a threshin' of 'e.'

I was surprised how quickly the job was done. By the end of the day the stack was waterproof and all that was left to do was trim round the edge with the clippers and tidy up. This we left for the morning as light was fading and we needed to get the tractor and trailer back to the yard.

''Ows yer 'ands?' Bert asked. 'Can make 'em sore keep a pullin' that straw through.'

'OK so far,' I told him. 'Ask me again when we have done the next two.'

There was, however, a change of plan for the next day. The boss was anxious to get the combine going, as time was getting on. As it had been a breezy day previously, he wanted me to go with Tony bagging off. Katie would take my place helping Bert. I went off to move the ladder and clear up after Bert had trimmed the bottom edge of his thatch on the oat stack. When we arrived at the wheat stacks Katie was waiting, her bike leaning on the hedge. We unloaded and I helped to rig the long ladder and then I left to join Tony. I don't suppose Bert will be too upset to have Katie with him, I thought. It might just take a little longer to thatch those two stacks!

Climbing onto the combine and looking round it was amazing to see the change a few weeks had made to the scene. Where there had been golden fields of standing corn, the wind swirling the tops like an ocean swell, now there were bare stubbles or rows of straw left by the combine. In the distance I could see Andy with the new Fordson making a start on the baling, a cloud of dust following him along, and the thump of the ram could be heard on the breeze. The new corn stacks stood out as if someone had built some houses on the farm. I could see the ladder leaning against the wheat stack but no sign of Bert. For a brief instant, jealousy reared its head! Tony had greased up the machine and was all ready to go but, to allow a bit more drying time, we had a cup of tea first. The ears of wheat popped and crackled as the sun made brief appearances in gaps in the cloud. Tea finished, we started up and the noise and dust became our workplace for the day. We cut until 5.00 in the afternoon and then had to stop to make up the sack carting team as Bert was thatching. By this time we were both black like tinkers and blowing one's nose gave some idea of the dust in our lungs.

This wheat we carted to the big barn and stood the sacks singly with tops open to help with the drying. A passageway was left between the sacks of barley which I was told were now dry enough to be weighed up and stacked two sacks high to give more room. This would be either a wet-day job or in the early morning when it was still too damp with dew to combine.

The weather improved and the last little piece of winter wheat vanished inside the combine. We then moved across to the spring barley and it was such a pleasure being able to bag off the corn from fields that I had worked down during my first-ever tractor job. It seemed such a short while ago. Two and a half more days saw the end of harvest, and the last small triangle of barley seemed to mark the culmination of a year's endeavour and of success in seeing the corn harvest home. The mixed farming that was carried out at Manor Farm, however, meant that this was just one harvest of many. Next on the agenda would be the potatoes.

Trundling back to the yard on the combine seemed to mark a milestone in the farming year and to park it up in its usual bay in the Dutch barn, the end of Summer with Autumn close at hand.

That evening as we brought in the last trailer load of sacks the Boss took me to one side.

'I think you ought to have some time off,' he said. 'I've been most impressed with what you have achieved and I would like to offer you a full-time job as tractor driver and I'll pay you man's rate starting at once. That's if you want the job.'

'Thank you, Mr Willis.' I was almost too choked up to speak. 'Of course I want the job and I'll do the best I can. I've enjoyed it so much and they are all a great bunch of people to work with. Thanks again.'

I had what was for me an early knock-off and left the yard at around 7.00, the Boss's words still ringing in my ears. I rode straight to the stables and flew up the steps to the girls' flat. The door was open as it was a fine evening and Tracy and Sue were both in the little sitting room when I knocked. Tracy appeared first and with a little whoop ran into my arms for a big kiss.

'To what do we owe the honour of this visit?' she said, pulling back. 'You're as black as a sweep.' She was looking down at the front of her blouse to see if it had got dirty against me.

'Have you got the sack or something?' she asked. 'I mean ... it's not even dark yet.'

'Sarcasm,' I told her, 'is the lowest form of wit.'

'Blimey, you can tell he went to a posh school,' Sue called from the doorway to the sitting room.

'In fact, far from getting the sack, I'm no longer the farm apprentice. The Boss has offered me a full-time tractor driver's job on man's rate.' I rattled out the words in excitement.

'Well, congratulations!' Tracy said, giving me another kiss, this time from more of a distance.

'That's great news,' Sue joined in, coming over and giving me a kiss as well.

I went on to tell them that the Boss had said I should have some time off and, as luck would have it, Tracy was intending to do the next weekend alone so that Sue could spend time with her mother who was unwell. I arranged to come over both days to help out with the horses and to spend time together. Next day I asked the Boss if I could have the weekend off and he readily agreed. Time up to the weekend was spent carting in bales. The first task with the new bales was to build the walls for the new potato crop. Each bale was tied to the one next to it to add strength and the actual wall was two bales thick in order to make it frost-proof. We built the walls right up to the eaves. The top layer could then be cut and spread over the potatoes. The rest of the bales we stacked in the big barn up against the hay and, as there were no fodder beet this year, the remainder were made into an outdoor stack alongside the cattle-yard wall.

Friday evening Tracy phoned me at home to say how much she was looking forward to the weekend.

'Graham,' she said, her voice quiet, 'couldn't you possibly stay the night?'

'Good God woman!' I fake scolded. 'Have you no morals at all? Of course I'll stay. I was too chicken to ask, so I thought I'd leave it to you.'

'Rotten pig!' she cried. 'You just wait, I'll get you for that!'

She told me what time she would be seeing to the horses in the morning and I said I would be there. I told my folks I was staying with Tracy for the weekend, which caused some raised eyebrows and a word of caution from my Mum telling me to 'be careful' like Mums do!

I packed toothbrush, washing and shaving kit and a change of clothes in my haversack and was at the stables before Tracy had started.

She was saying goodbye to Sue who was being collected by her Dad so I wandered over to see her off.

'Have a great weekend,' Sue said. 'Don't wear yourselves out now.' She rolled her eyes and looked sexy.

'Hope your Mum's OK,' I said, giving her a little kiss. She hopped in the car and we stood waving her off.

As the car turned onto the lane Tracy moved into my arms and we kissed like there was no tomorrow. Breaking free she moved towards the stables.

'I must see to the horses first,' she gasped.

'You mean before breakfast,' I answered.

'It's not breakfast I'm dying for,' she replied.

We went around seeing to the animals, filling buckets and haynets and forking out the muck into the wheelbarrow. In all it took around an hour to see the work done. Then, hand in hand we went back to the flat. We washed up in the kitchen sink and still hand in hand walked into the bedroom.

Because we had not seen much of each

other due to me working long hours, our love making was all too short and breakfast was soon on the agenda. After the meal, as it was a warm late summer day, we went for a walk down across the paddocks to the shady wood in the valley where we found a footpath that led up the other side. Emerging, we found we could look back at the stables and also see much more of the farm. I could even see Andy still baling the straw. We found a grassy mound under a big old oak tree and this time our love making was longer and not so frantic. Laying back afterwards, with the sunlight dappling the grass and bees, insects buzzing around, birds singing in the wood behind us and pheasants strolling haughtily along its edge, I was totally at peace. Tracy lay in the crook of my arm, my hand resting lightly over her breast and I loved her with an all-consuming passion. I think she felt the moment as she turned and kissed me and told me she loved me.

We must have dozed for a while and then it was time to stroll back for the lunchtime horse chores and to feed ourselves. She had got in some provisions and my Mum had provided some extra so we dined well. I moved the table out onto the landing at the top of the steps so we could sit outside. We talked about everything there was. I had finally weaned Tracy from her constant discussions about horses and we chatted happily. I discovered that her mother was English, from Sussex, her father was from Finland which explained the white blonde hair, the unusual accent and the surname Volanen.

I pointed out that her initials were TV – something fairly new to us, my folks having only recently purchased a set. So I told her she should be able to keep me entertained.

'I can probably think of a few ways,' she said leading me inside. The chairs on the landing were vacant for a while until we returned with a drink, ice chinking in the glasses. I helped again with the evening routine, a chill now in the air after the warmth of the day, along with the smell of dew and straw and horses. We walked again after fetching jackets from the flat, round the loop lane and back. It was as if we had known each other for ever: it would not have been possible to find a happier couple. We laughed and played the fool, tried to bring down bats with handfuls of gravel and huddled in mock terror when an old owl hooted nearby. Back in the flat, with the table and chairs returned inside, we made tea and had some supper listening to music on the radiogram. Then, cuddled together in Tracy's single bed, we slept entwined only to wake with pins and needles in arms that had been laid on and with her blonde hair across my face tickling me.

The horses were a bit late with their Sunday morning feed and I had that exquisite pleasure of laying in bed and watching Tracy dress. I did finally emerge and render assistance with a few things. We had breakfast, then Tracy had to exercise Moonshine and some of the others, riding one and leading another. She tried to get me to go but I chickened out of getting on a horse.

'You would love it if you tried it,' she coaxed me.

'No way,' I resisted. 'You only do it because you like something hot and throbbing between your legs.'

'What a good idea!' she laughed. 'Can you wait until I get back?'

'Only if you're quick,' I told her. The sun had returned so I moved everything out again and sat and waited for her return. She was soon back and off out again with another two. Clattering back into the yard, she called for me to put the kettle on and, with morning chores over, we sat over a cup of coffee ... eventually. It was a weekend to cherish. By the time Sue's Dad returned with her in the evening, Tracy and I were totally and completely committed to each other; we were enveloped in an all-consuming love that was almost frightening in its intensity. We both knew that we would spend our lives together and had even talked about a little farm. Tracy could run a livery stable and I could do the farming. I told her we would have to have a wooden veranda with an old rocking chair where I could sit chewing a piece of straw. Sue's Dad left and we all sat outside, the two girls in the chairs and me on the floor leaning against the rails. We asked Sue about her Mum and she said she was much improved.

'So, what have you two been up to?' Sue asked. 'Apart from the obvious.'

'What could she mean?' I said to Tracy. 'She can't possibly think that I have been taking advantage of you.'

'Put it this way,' Sue smiled, 'you're a damn fool if you haven't and I don't think those squeals I've heard coming from the bedroom were caused by you tickling her feet.'

'Damn, we've been rumbled!' Tracy laughed. 'I shan't be able to show my face again in polite society.'

'What about me?' I joined in. 'Dare I return to my family home after ... this?' We all fell about laughing and it was all in all a great finish to the weekend.

Soon after, I said goodbye to Sue and walked with Tracy to my motorbike, my haversack slung over my shoulder. Stopping by the bike I took her in my arms and we clung together as if I was going off to the Western Front or something.

'I hate to go,' I told her. 'I love you, Tracy.'

'I love you too,' she replied, kissing me again. 'See you soon, a.'

I rode out of the yard with my heart as light as a feather and the vision of her locked in my mental psyche. How could this be, I asked myself, at the start of this year I had no knowledge of girls? Now I'm madly in love, and making love, to a sensational girl who is crazy about me. Me, for God's sake! This cannot be true. I didn't get quite as far as pinching myself but it was a close-run thing.

Arriving home and going indoors my Mum and Dad asked if I had had an enjoyable time.

'The best weekend of my life,' I told them and the big stupid grin on my face told them the rest.

Chapter 18

The whole of the next week the weather stayed kind and we were able to cart in the straw bales. Andy finished baling on Monday afternoon so was free to help carting by Tuesday. The baler dropped the bales singly in rows so it was a matter of driving between them quite slowly. A man either side would fork the bales to two people loading. This was yet another knack, that of lifting a bale of straw weighing 30 or 40lb on a pitchfork and delivering it to the top of a load six bales high. A full day doing that and you knew you had been working; every muscle in your body ached. I was lucky because most of the time I was driving the tractor. If we were short-handed the driver doubled as a pitcher and that meant jumping on and off the tractor every few yards as well as pitching bales.

The general rule was that the two loaders, often a couple of the girls, would ride on top to the unloading point and help the driver unload.

I can't remember ever roping a load on; we relied on the skill of the loaders. We were bringing the last few loads back to the yard and I had Ruth and Percy on top of the load.

It had taken a bit of a shaking in the field and was leaning a bit when we got to the lane. All seemed well until we were about a hundred yards from the farm entrance. There was only one dwelling on the lane. A small cottage owned by a retired army major who had an immaculate garden full of roses and a mani-cured lawn. Of course it was right there that the load tipped off. Most of the bales, includ-ing Ruth and Percy, cleared the tidily clipped yew hedge and landed among the rose bushes and across the lawn. The two loaders were fine having had a soft landing among the bales but unfortunately some of the rose bushes didn't take too kindly to having heavy bales dropped on them from a fair old height.

The major was never very happy with us at the best of times. He often complained about the smell or mud on the road or noisy trac-tors and once, a whole lot of sheep we were moving, walked in his gate and played a merry dance on his lawn. When the bales arrived he was, to say the least, irate and all sorts of dire threats were bandied about. We took what was left of the load onto the yard and returned at once and cleared up the mess down to the last strand of straw. One or two of the rose bushes – oh, all right, four or five – were beyond aid and would have to be put down. I heard later that all were replaced by the Boss and a bottle of single malt seemed to smooth things over. The Boss did suggest to me that perhaps I might drive a bit slower with a load on but he did say it with a smile on his face.

Clearing the bales was really the last bit of the corn harvest. Tony gave me a rundown on what would be happening next.

'Now everything is clear,' he said. 'We'll get the stubbles cultivated and left for the weed seeds to germinate. Then we can plough and kill off all those weeds. Then it will be either left for plants or spuds next year or some of the wheat land will go to winter barley.'

'When do we start on the potatoes?' I asked him.

'It'll probably be around the second week in October,' he told me, 'depending on the weather.'

So for the next week or so it was all hands and all tractors to ripping up the stubbles. Cultivating with the Fergy was a fairly slow, second-gear job with the tractor working hard as the Boss liked to get the implement in as deep as was reasonably possible. Hardly a day went by without a visit from Tracy mostly on Moonshine. She would sometimes just trot down the headland and wave, other times especially on stubbles, she would come out in the field and ride alongside. We would shout to each other and Moonshine would toss her head and make a fuss because of the tractor but seemed to get used to it after a while.

My Dad told me he had bumped into the Boss by accident in the bank in town. During their conversation the Boss had said, 'I can always tell which field Graham is in. There is always a white horse on the headland or close by.' They had a laugh and Dad said there were some comments about young love. I got the feeling that they both thought it was a passing fancy, but both Tracy and I knew that we would be spending the rest of our lives together. We seemed to be growing closer with the passing of every week.

Later on in the week I heard about the harvest-home party. I was told this was held every year at the finish of the corn harvest. It was in the big barn and everyone to do with the farm was invited including wives, husbands, boy or girlfriends and, of course, the children. A week Saturday was the event, starting at 2.30 in the afternoon. I managed to have a word with Andy and asked him how he was getting on with his car.

'It's just about done,' he told me.

'Do you think it will be done for the harvest party on Saturday week?' I asked him.

'Be on the road this weekend,' he replied.

I then had to do some working out in my mind over the next few days. Most evenings I would make a quick call at the stables on the way home, sometimes, if arranged beforehand, I would stay for my tea. Usually

I would stop a few minutes then go home, have tea and come back.

After talking to Andy I called in and told Tracy and Sue about the party and insisted, as it was between their chore time, that they both come.

'I haven't got any tie up with the farm,' Sue protested. 'I'll be thrown out as a gate-crasher.'

'Trust me,' I told her. 'If things go according to plan you will have a partner to take you.'

'My, my. Is he tall dark and handsome?' Sue said perkily.

'No, he's short fat and old,' I told her, laughing. 'What do expect from me, miracles?'

Monday morning I again approached Andy. 'Any chance of a favour on party day next Saturday?' I asked.

'Will if I can,' he answered.

'I just wondered if you would mind picking up me and my girlfriend from the stables on the loop lane up Oldbarn Lane?' I asked him. 'I can get to her place on the bike but you know what girls are like. She won't want to arrive here all blown about sitting on the back.'

'This the blonde with the white horse that lives in whatever field you are in,' Andy grinned. 'She's a real cracker and no mistake. Yes, that's no problem. I'll pick you and her up at – what? – twenty past two be all right?'

'That will be great, Andy, thanks,' I smiled at him. 'There's one other thing. She's got a pal that works with her at the stables. Her name's Sue and I sort of had to ask her along as well. Do you think you could look after her for the party so that she doesn't feel left out?'

'Sure,' Andy replied. 'Be nice to have some company. Like I told you I don't get to meet many girls.'

'You will like Sue,' I said. 'She's good fun. I told her you were short, fat and old so you will be off to a good start when she sees you.'

I had to smile because Andy was, in fact, tall dark and I suppose most girls would have classed him as handsome. He was certainly a hell of a nice guy.

Outside work was halted for a while by the weather and another problem reared its head. The wheat we had combined last of all was heating up in the sacks and would have to be moved. We set to and shifted every bit of tackle out of the implement shed and swept the concrete floor clean.

Then we put a single row of straw bales across the front leaving one out at the end. The shed had tin sides that extended to the front so only the front was open. We draped sacks over the bales and then put a second layer of bales on the sacks to hold them in place. It was then the job of wheeling the sacks, one at a time, on a sack truck from the barn across to the shed, through the gap and tipping them out on the floor. We worked it so that there was empty floor left at one end in order that it could be turned with a shovel every day until it cooled and dried. It was a good start to the next few days, shovelling grain for an hour and a half. Once it was declared dry and safe it all had to be sacked up again and wheeled back to the barn where the sacks were weighed, tied up and stacked two high to await sale. The implement shed was then restored to its proper use and all the tackle put back inside. A case of where there's a will, etc.

I called in and told Tracy and Sue what was happening on the coming Saturday. I would get to the stables on the bike and then we would be picked up by the person who would escort Sue for the afternoon. I took Tracy aside and primed her about who was picking us up.

'You get all round the farm,' I told her. 'It's the guy that's been doing the baling. His name's Andy.'

'Oh I know,' she replied, light dawning. 'Gosh, he's a bit dishy. He gives me the eye every time I ride by.'

'Only because you encourage him,' I teased. 'Standing up in the stirrups and showing off your bum.'

'I do not,' she reared up, pouting and in a huff. 'There's only one man in my life and he's right here.' We went into a kiss that lasted until Sue threatened to throw a bucket of water over us.

Saturday morning just about the whole staff were involved in getting ready for the afternoon party. We used sacks of corn instead of trestles to hold up a collection of old doors and planks that formed the tables. Mrs Willis had a quantity of bright covers that we spread over them and we scattered grains of wheat over them for an authentic look. Bert had made some corn 'dollies' in a range of shapes and sizes and these were placed around the tables. Crates of beer and bottles of pop were stacked inside away from the door and bundles of balloons tied around for colour.

Outside in the yard a variety of side stalls were put together – tombola, skittles, several dart games and children's tractor and trailer rides – which we were all going to take turns at. We put a row of straw bales down the middle of a trailer and would use the lorry loading dock as a station for boarding and alighting. Mrs Willis had a small army of helpers including most of the farm women and they would get the plates of goodies out for 2.30. When all was ready, I double checked with Andy about picking us up and went off home to change.

Around 2.10 I rode into the stable yard and put the bike away in the barn. I went round and up to the flat after giving Moonshine's nose a rub. The girls were twittering around as if it was a coming-out ball instead of a farm harvest-home party, doing last-minute make up 'touch ups' and checking clothes. They both looked sensational. Tracy's hair was loose but she had somehow braided little bits of it and used the braids to fix it back. She was wearing the blue and white dress I had seen before. Sue had obviously spent a lot of time on her eyes using just the right amount of shadow to emphasise them. Her other assets needed no emphasising and she was wearing a green shirt, that was under some strain, tucked into a white pleated skirt and slingback sandals. Bloody hell, I thought, Andy's going to burst his boiler when he cops a load of her!

Just after 2.15 the Morris drove into the yard. I had been looking out for it and waved Andy over. He did a neat swing and stopped with the passenger door at the bottom of the steps, got out and came round as Tracy and me started down. Sue had remembered some last-minute switch to turn off and had popped back inside.

'Hi, Andy,' I greeted him. 'This is Tracy.' They shook hands and there was no doubt whatsoever that Andy was more than impressed.

'And this is Sue,' I added, as she came down the steps. Another handshake and I could see the colour rise in Sue's cheeks.

'We'll hop in the back,' I said, pulling Tracy to the rear and opening the door for her. Andy saw Sue into the front and came round to the driver's side. As he did so Sue turned in her seat.

'I thought you said you couldn't do miracles?' she said breathlessly. 'He's so ... wow!' She rolled her eyes as Andy got in and we set off.

Quite a few folks had already arrived when we drove in and parked up beyond the cattle yard where several cars were already standing.

I took Tracy's hand and led her to the barn where the buzz of conversation almost fell silent as we entered. Tracy had that effect on people.

Looking back, I could see Andy and Sue deep in conversation making their way behind us. The Boss was just inside with Mrs Willis. Tracy had met the Boss lots of times but had never met Mrs Willis. Greetings were exchanged and Mrs Willis shook hands with Tracy.

Tracy instantly won her over by saying how kind it was of Mr Willis to let her ride round the farm and said how much she enjoyed it. I left them to it and roamed around saying hi to everyone. Some of them I nearly didn't recognise in their good clothes but the caps gave them away.

The tables now groaned under plates of food of every description from chicken drum sticks to fancy iced cakes; the children (more seemed to arrive every minute) were tucking in like there was no tomorrow. I found a beer and helped myself to some pork pie and sausages on sticks. Tracy, would you believe, was now chatting to Anna and they were both laughing about something. A soft sexy voice spoke from close behind me.

'Did she fly in from Hollywood today?' it said.

'Hi, Katie,' I said, glancing over my shoulder. She looked scrumptious in a figure-hugging blouse and multi-patterned skirt, her hair hanging in those thick lustrous curls and held back with a sparkly alice band.

'Glory be,' I smiled. 'You look good enough to eat.'

'I seem to remember you making a start on that earlier this year.' She looked me straight in the eyes and I could see hers sparkling. In spite of me thinking I was over all that, I could feel myself colouring.

'Well, you did show me where to begin, if you recall,' I started to laugh. 'I couldn't bring myself to throw that bale out. It's still in the barn.'

She giggled and licked her lips in that so

sexy way of hers. She had a glass of something in her hand and looked at me over the top of it.

'Well, Graham,' she spoke softly. 'Any time you get hungry I'm always there.'

'Katie, you are a one-off. I'm only here because you got me through the first few days and then you and the rest sorted out my hang-ups. You gave me a taste of heaven and I shall love you always,' I told her.

'What the hell have you been drinking?' she laughed. 'Whatever it was, have some more.' We both dissolved into hoots of laughter and I gave her a quick kiss which caused a few catcalls from people watching and a lifted eyebrow from Tracy. I chatted to Katie for a while longer and then moved round to talk to some of the men from the farm. They were all mightily impressed with Tracy.

'I've sin 'er ride by a 'undred times,' Tom remarked. 'But niver thart she looked loike that.'

'I recon yew must a thart all o' yewr birthdays come at once,' Bert observed, 'when likes of she took up wid 'e.'

'She's a great girl,' I told them. 'As you say, Bert, I'm a lucky lad.'

Looking across the barn, I could see that Tracy had now got trapped by three of the local lads about my age, so I moved across and rescued her with the offer of getting her a drink and some food.

'Thanks for that,' she smiled. 'Things were getting a bit heavy. Why do young lads think that every girl they meet wants sex with them?'

'I always thought they did,' I joked, dodging another of those flat-handed swipes.

'What's with you and that farm woman?' she frowned at me. 'You were all over her like a rash. Just because she flashes her...' This time it was me who stopped her with a finger on her lips.

'I owe Katie a lot, I've told you why. There's nothing going on, she's just a very good pal,' I tried to explain.

'I've got to take a turn driving the tractor for the kids at three,' I said, changing the subject. 'Do you want to come and ride shot-gun? There has to be a grown-up with them, but I expect you will do.' This time the slap connected and caused general merriment.

'That be roight, missy,' a male voice called. 'Yew kip the bugger in order.' This followed by a female voice saying, 'be quiet, yew.'

We laughed together and went out of the barn hand in hand towards the loading dock. Part way across the yard I tugged her arm and nodded my head for her to look left. Andy had his arm round Sue's shoulders as they tried to throw hoops over pots of jam and things at Tombola. They were laughing together like old friends. I gave Tracy a thumbs up and she squeezed my arm.

Tony had the 2.30 to 3 shift and was away with a load when we got to the dock. Several kids were waiting for the next ride. They fell almost silent when Tracy and me arrived and gazed at her like she was the fairy god-mother or something. Tracy set to asking names and ages and chatting to them and in no time, they were her slaves, laughing and holding her hands.

Tony returned with his last trip, the child-ren being escorted by a fair-haired, attract-ive woman in her early twenties who Tony introduced as Jane.

Tracy got as many children on as could be safely seated and off we went amid shouts to watching Mums and Dads and lots of waving. We did three 10-minute trips, then handed over to Andy who had talked Sue into riding shotgun. Lots of the children, as there was no charge, were going on one trip after the other and we had to make sure that those who had been were not stopping those that hadn't. While the kids were changing over I asked Andy how things were going.

'Terrific!' he told me. 'She's a real nice girl and we seem to be hitting it off just right.' I punched him lightly on the shoulder.

'Great!' I couldn't help smiling. 'Hope it goes from strength to strength.' Meanwhile I had noticed Tracy and Sue were chatting twenty to the dozen with Sue very animated and excited.

After Andy had departed, with Sue reading the riot act to her unruly load, I compared notes with Tracy. She told me Sue was so excited with Andy.

'She's over the moon with him,' she went on. 'Like a cat that got the cream.'

'Bit soon for that, isn't it?' I said, moving fast to dodge another back-handed swipe.

'Sometimes you are just disgusting,' she scolded.

'Sorry.' I tried to look crestfallen. 'They should certainly wait for as long as we did.' This time I had to run to avoid getting well beaten up.

'You,' she said catching up, 'are impossible to hold a sensible conversation with.'

'Just joking,' I said, giving her a little kiss. 'After all, not all girls are the same are they? Some take their time about making sure they have got the right bloke. Others just hop into...' She saw it coming and took off after me again. I headed for the barn and the safety of numbers.

Grabbing another beer from the now dwindling stock I helped myself to some nibbles and took some to Tracy with a glass of lemonade. I held out my hand, palm towards her. 'I bring peace offerings,' I smiled at her. 'I'm sorry again, I shouldn't tease you. Can you ever forgive me?' I hung my head and tried to look as penitent as possible.

'Given time,' she mused thoughtfully, 'I

suppose it might just be possible. That's long enough, I forgive you.'

'Twit,' I laughed. 'You are worse than I am. Hang on here a mo, I want to find out about the mystery Jane.'

'Is this another excuse to go and chat up your farm tart again?' she asked frowning.

'Jealousy, Tracy darling, will make you fat,' I told her. Even so I could feel her eyes tracking me as I sought out Bert. I found him with a round-faced, cottage-loaf-shaped woman, whom he introduced as his wife Mary. She was a happy-go-lucky archetypal country woman with a ready smile and a dialect as broad as Bert's.

'So who's this Jane I've met with Tony?' I asked.

'Oh, she bin wid 'e nigh on a twelve month now,' Bert replied. 'She be a sister or summat at tha' 'ospital an very well thart of I bin told.'

'Well, he's kept her well under wraps as far as I'm concerned,' I said. I chatted on for a while and then saw that Tracy was in trouble again so headed back to her. The lads saw me coming and wandered off laughing among themselves.

'Bloody hell, woman of mine!' I said coming up to her. 'I can't leave you alone for five minutes without you trying to organise a gang bang.'

'You sod!' she flared trying hard not to

laugh. 'You get worse as the day goes by. How did you guess, anyway?'

'Guess what?' I said, before realising I had walked straight into it. The smile on her face worked straight on my heart and I loved her, God how I loved her!

We went back outside and Tracy wandered off while I stopped to talk to the Boss and Mrs Willis and thanked them for a super afternoon. I know Tracy's enjoyed it, I told them.

'What a lovely girl!' Mrs Willis remarked. 'Don't you ever get worried her riding round on that big horse?' she asked.

'You know,' I replied, 'I've never ever thought about it. Tracy is such a good rider.'

'That's the other girl from the stables with Andy, isn't it?' the Boss enquired. 'They seem to know each other well.'

'They met for the first time at two fifteen today,' I informed them.

'My goodness!' Mrs Willis exclaimed. 'They look like old friends. Andy is such a nice lad. I've known him since he was born. His mother and father have lived in the village all their lives. It's so nice to see him in good company.'

Looking around the yard it was not hard to pick out Tracy, her blonde locks like a beacon. She was bowling to win a pig and seemed to be doing rather well. I walked over and stood behind her as she bowled her last ball and finished up two points short of the winning number.

'If you had won it, it would have been in good company,' I said from behind her.

'OK,' she fell into my arms laughing. 'Let's call it quits.'

The afternoon gradually wound down with people drifting away. A lot of them had some livestock of their own to tend to. The farm girls had started to clear the tables and Tracy was looking at her watch thinking of the horses. Sue and Andy appeared from the barn and joined us.

'Ready to go?' Andy said. 'I'll go and get the car.' He walked off towards the top of the yard.

'Can you two cope with the chores at the stables?' Sue asked. 'Andy wants me to go for a drive and then to the pictures.'

'Course we can,' Tracy was quick to reply. 'It's about time he did something useful.' That directed at me.

Sue turned to me and gave me a kiss.

'Thanks, Graham,' she said. 'And that's not just for helping with the horses.'

'Well, well, who's Mr Popularity then?' Tracy chided. 'The lengths you go to just to get a kiss!'

'I better not do too much then.' I made eyes at Sue. 'Never know what I might get.'

The two of them looked at each other and

shook their heads as if to write me off as a hopeless case. Andy drew up with the car and we piled in waving to all and sundry and with much honking on the horn, drove off up the lane. He dropped Tracy and me back at the stables and after we had wished them a happy evening he drove off. Tracy went and changed and we set about bringing in horses that were out in the paddocks and doing the general feeding and watering. Once that was over we walked hand in hand to the flat.

'I could murder a cup of tea,' I said. 'I'll put the kettle on.' We sat for nearly an hour over tea and some biscuits and got to a time that both of us knew was right. Our love making had moved to a new height. It was no longer the frantic coupling of newly met youngsters but a long slow mix of emotions. We were able to talk and laugh, while joined as one. Be ourselves without any fear of giving offence to each other and very slowly reach out for that final wonderful union of hearts and minds. That mind blowing expression of complete and total love for each other that left us breathless and, oh so happy.

Late that evening Sue and Andy arrived back and it was obvious from their smiles and chatter that they had enjoyed the day and would want to see more of each other.

A wonderful end to a fantastic day.

Chapter 19

I called in to the stables mid-morning on Sunday and found Tracy with Mrs Williams. There had been no away trips with the horses lately because Mrs Williams had been in hospital for a while and was only now starting to fully recover. I waited by the bike until they had finished and she had departed, then went over to Tracy and said 'hi'.

'Hi you,' she greeted me. 'Looks like our boss here is well on the mend so I expect there will soon be time away again. How will I exist without you?'

This last bit was said as she moved into my arms for a cuddle. I was looking around over her shoulder.

'You on your own here?' I asked. 'Where's Sue?'

'Why?' she giggled. 'Are you going to push me down here in the yard and have your wicked way with me?'

'The thought had occurred to me,' I laughed back. She told me Sue had begged the day off and had vanished with Andy to the seaside.

'Now see what you have done,' Tracy moaned. 'I shall hardly see her now she's got

Andy in tow. Every minute it's Andy said this or Andy said that, she's driving me nuts. It's good to see her so happy though.'

We wandered down to the wood in the valley. The weather had changed from yesterday's sunshine and with the clouds threatening rain we returned to the flat doing the midday look round at horses that were out and seeing to ones that were in. It was around one o'clock.

'You know,' I said, 'Sue being away with Andy does have its compensations.' I took her in my arms and slowly walked her backwards through the bedroom door. Three o'clock we came out for some lunch, flushed and ecstatic, having arrived back from a prolonged visit to the outer galaxies. We made some sandwiches and cuddled up on the sofa. I had my arm round her neck holding a sandwich and we were taking alternate bites. At five o'clock we put some clothes on and did the usual, bringing in, feeding and watering. We had just finished when Sue and Andy arrived back happy and excited about their day out. What was much more important was the fact that they came with fish and chip suppers for all of us. We all sat around in the sitting room, girls on the sofa, and Andy and me at their feet on the floor. The meal was great and the view even better!

It was a happy evening. We laughed a lot and told jokes and teased each other until finally Andy and me kissed our girls and left for our homes.

If Andy felt as I did, he was floating on cloud nine.

Monday morning in the farmyard seemed a bit of an anticlimax somehow. We spent a couple of hours clearing up. Stacking away the doors and planks that had served as tables and putting back the sacks of grain. I gave the middle part of the barn a quick sweep out and picked up all the rubbish. The little sideshow tents belonged to someone else and had been cleared on Sunday. Once all was tidy it was back to the stubble cultivations. Later in the week I had my first try at ploughing. It was with one of the E27 Fordsons, the one with the hydraulic lift, and a Ransome 2-furrow plough. Tony spent a lot of time with me, helping to hitch the plough and then, in the field, showing me what was what. He told me that the plough had what were called 'semi-digger shares'. These had a short, fairly sharp twist to them which tended to shatter the furrow as it turned, thereby making subsequent cultivations quicker and easier on the way to getting a seed bed. A longer, slower twist on the share would stand the furrow up for over-wintering or fallowing.

'I thought a plough was just a plough,' I told him.

He laughed at that and told me complete books had been written about the art of good ploughing. He showed me how to open out a land after putting in marker sticks to get a straight furrow to start with. A plough will only turn furrows one way, so a land had to be marked out and ploughing had to be either side of it, gradually making it wider and wider. When it was too wide to drive properly round on the headland, another land would be opened and eventually the two brought together with a finishing furrow. I always found the job totally absorbing and time passed quickly whenever I came to do it in later years. So that was me set as the year rolled into October, ploughing every day, rain or shine. As long as the tractor could get along without spinning too much, I kept going, the smell of the freshly turned earth a delight and flocks of seagulls for company.

An almost daily visit from Tracy lifted me further (sorry about the pun), and she would stop at the end of the furrows to see how straight they were. Sometimes I got a little clap of her hands, more often a derisive wave indicating she thought it was rubbish. We would then laugh at each other and blow kisses and she would trot off. About a week into October, on a Saturday morning, I was ploughing the headland of a field when the Boss turned up and told me not to start another as he wanted to start potato harvesting on the Monday.

'You'll be out of here by tonight,' he said. 'Have tomorrow off and we can get a fresh start on Monday. The forecast is good.'

As he was speaking, Andy pulled into the same field with the discs and started working down the freshly turned furrows.

'Andy will be right up with you by tonight,' the Boss went on. 'Then he and Tony will get this drilled tomorrow. First thing Monday you could get this harrowed in as there won't be much spud carting to do until late morning.'

I kept a good lookout for Tracy and sure enough around mid-morning she turned up. Stopping the tractor I hopped off and went to her.

'I am honoured today,' she said. 'You actually mean you can stop work to talk to me?'

'Tracy, oh sweet and gorgeous one,' I smiled at her. 'Shut up and listen and don't be sarcastic. Is Sue working with you to-morrow because I know that Andy will be here all day?'

'Yes, oh master,' she said. 'I've shut up and listened. Sue was hoping Andy might be off but, as you say, he's working, she will be with me.'

'I've got the day off,' I said watching her face light up. 'Would Sue cope for the day if you came over to home for the day? My folks are visiting and won't be around.'

'Once I've beaten her enough she will agree,' Tracy replied, slapping a riding boot with her crop. 'I'd love to come. Sue's going to be well pissed off that Andy's working.'

'I'll pick you up about tenish,' I told her and blew a kiss on the way back to the tractor.

She blew one back, pulled Moonshine round and trotted off, standing in the stirrups and leaning forward. After a few strides, she looked over her shoulder and flashed a smile because she knew I would be looking at her bum. Proper little prick-tease, I thought, as I climbed on the tractor grinning. On the last run round the headland I walked over for a word with Andy.

'Pity you've got to work tomorrow,' I commiserated. 'Tracy said Sue was hoping you might be off.'

'Can't be helped, job's got to come first,' he replied. I told him of my plans for tomorrow and said that Tracy and me wouldn't be back at the stables until after 10.00 in the evening. His face brightened and I could almost see his mind working and guessed that the end of Sue's day would be rather romantic!

I collected Tracy as promised the next morning. Sue told me Andy had phoned about the evening so she was quite happy to look after things for the day. This was the first time Tracy had been to my place since coming to Sunday lunch. I had to give the grand tour including my room which I had remembered to tidy up before going to get her. She was impressed and I told her it was always like that but she knew I was lying. How do women do that?

It was a dry cool day, the leaves showing the first tints of autumn, the sky the palest of blue with pink-edged clouds drifting across like abandoned candy floss. The smell of wood smoke wafted on the light breeze and the sound of a tractor working in the distance, the only disturbance to the bird song. We went outside and wandered round the garden, our arms round each other, then down to the woods at the end of our little paddock. We strolled through to the edge and found an old elm tree that had canted over. I climbed into it and held down a hand to Tracy and we sat on the leaning trunk and looked out over the field. We had sat there for ten minutes or so talking quietly or just enjoying the peace when a fox emerged from the edge about forty yards from our hiding place. We both saw it at the same time and watched with delight as it came along the field edge towards us and actually sniffed around the base of the elm with us no more than six feet above it. It never detected our presence and trotted off on its rounds. We waited a few minutes then came down and hugged in pleasure at the spontaneity of the moment.

We strolled home and had some lunch and spent the afternoon chatting. During that time she asked if I would take her over to her parents' home one day, as she wanted them to meet me. I said there was no time like now, give them a call, we can be there in half an hour. She made the call and said that her folks would love us to come over.

It took just a few moments to tidy up and lock the house and we were off. Tracy guided me and we were soon cruising into the middle of a large village. Her folks lived in a fairly small bungalow tucked back from the village green. It had leaded windows in a diamond pattern and a neat garden surrounded by a well-clipped hedge. It would not have looked out of place on the front of a box of chocolates.

At the start of the year I would have been a nervous wreck, my hands sweating and dreading this meeting, but now thanks to Katie and the girls at work, I was actually looking forward to it. I parked the bike by the gate and we walked up to the front door which opened before we got there.

A tall man with a trimmed greying beard, glasses and very fair hair called a greeting. Tracy ran into his outspread arms and they kissed. She drew back as I arrived and said, 'Papa, this is Graham.' I shook hands, his grip firm and his hand cool and he ushered us inside. A dog was barking in a back room. We were in a small hallway, brightly decorated but with a distinct Scandinavian feel. Some of the ornaments on the wall and a few pictures were obviously from Finland. Mr Volanen stood aside so that we could enter the sitting room and Tracy moved to kiss the woman who had risen from her chair as we entered. Introductions were made again and I shook hands with Mrs Volanen. There was no doubt about where Tracy got her looks. The woman in front of me was about my height, blonde hair pulled back rather severely into a pony tail, same colour eyes as Tracy and strikingly attractive. She was wearing quite a simple cream blouse hanging outside a plain light blue skirt.

'How nice to meet you,' she said. 'Tracy used to talk on the phone about nothing but horses but now it's Graham this and Graham that all the time.' I looked at Tracy and burst out laughing and we had to explain that she had said exactly the same words about Sue only it was Andy this and Andy that. Mr Volanen left the room and I heard a door being opened, the patter of feet and a little West Highland terrier shot into the room and launched itself at Tracy who fielded it neatly in mid-air and cuddled it to her.

'This is Douglas,' she told me. I went over and made friends with it, giving it a stroke and tickle behind the ears. She put it down and it soon settled. We sat around chatting and they told me to call them Ralf and Amy. In no time we were like old friends. It turned out that Ralf was a precision engineer so he was most interested to hear that my Dad was also an engineer, as was my brother. They gave us a nice tea and from my point of view it was great to see that Tracy had a stable and loving home life, not that she was there very often. It really clinched the day when I told Amy that my Mum was from Sussex and that our house was named after the village of her birth. Amy knew it well and came from the area herself. In all it was a most enjoyable afternoon and evening and when we left at around 10.00, I had to promise to bring Tracy again soon.

'Perhaps we shall see more of her and you, Graham, now you have some transport,' Amy said. I shook hands with Ralf and gave Amy a kiss which went down well I think, patted Douglas and we went on our way.

Andy's car was parked at the bottom of the steps when we arrived back at the stables. I made plenty of noise with the bike and he came out on the landing and waved. Sue looked radiant and happy and I was delighted how things were going with their relationship. We made tea and chatted and I told Tracy how much I had enjoyed the evening. Now we had both met each other's parents. I was more than happy that our romance was progressing nicely as well.

Monday morning was like crowded market in the yard with women everywhere, a lot of them still holding their bikes. The female workforce had doubled to 16 with the addition of casual staff brought in for the potato harvest. Most of them, I found, were in some way related to our bunch of regulars, sisters or cousins or, in some cases, daughters. I heard a voice behind me saying, 'You'll be OK for a while, Graham, all these new girls about.'

'Morning, Katie,' I looked over my shoulder, 'you're always creeping up on me. Remember there's only one girl in my life at the moment.'

'That blonde,' Katie smiled. 'She's not fair on us poor mortals. What planet does she come from by the way?'

I laughed and told her I had met Tracy's parents yesterday and I could vouch for the fact that she was from Earth. I chatted for a moment and then went to get my tractor. I mounted the harrows and set off to the drilled field as the Boss had asked on Saturday. It only took a couple of hours and I returned to the yard, dropped the harrows, fitted the trailer and set off again for the potato field. It was a hive of activity. Tony had the other trailer on the second Fergy and was unloading empty fertiliser bags across the middle of the field. I found Bert and asked him how it all worked. He explained that for the duration of the potato harvest all the girls were on piecework. They were paid so much a sack full, that being about 1cwt. He had stepped across the field and divided the distance by 16. He then put up sticks to mark out 16 equal spaces or 'cants' as he called them. Each woman would pick between her sticks and a tally of full bags would be kept when they were carted away.

'Why start in the middle of the field?' I asked.

'Well, tha' spinner will chuck taters up int' edge if us starts at outside,' he explained. 'We can start int' middle an' work both sides for a few rounds, then we'll work one side out then do t'other. 'Tis a bit of a bugger to start as spinner do throw spuds over tha' ridges but 'tis only for two or three roun'.'

I went and saw Andy who had the spinner Bert was referring to, mounted on his Fordson. He was about to make a start and I wanted to see how it worked. There was a triangular blade about 2ft across at its widest, pitched downwards quite steeply to a replaceable flat tip that projected about an inch from the plate. Once the machine was dropped on the hydraulics at the end of a row and pulled forwards, the pitch on the plate would pull it down under the crop. The depth it would go was set by two rubber-tyred wheels running on top of the ground. The entire row, soil and potatoes would spill over the back of the plate where a rapidly spinning rotor threw the lot against a net that hung out to one side.

The soil would pass through the net but the potatoes were too big and would drop in a line at the base. That was the theory and in practice it worked quite well. The biggest problem was that not all the soil passed through the net and some of the potatoes got covered up.

The pickers would then have to scrabble about to find the buried ones. Tony had dropped a supply of sacks to each section and all was ready to start.

The experienced pickers used a cabbage bag split down both sides so that it was one long piece. They then gathered two of the short-end corners and attached string to each. This enabled them to tie it round their waist like a long apron, the other end dangling on the ground.

Assuming they were right-handed the dangling end was wrapped round their left forearm so that the apron formed a sort of bowl. They could then stay in a bent-over position, that left forearm almost touching the ground and flick the spuds into the apron with their right hand as fast as the eye could follow. When they did stand, there would be around 30lb of potatoes in the apron. A sack could be held in the right hand and the left forearm put inside and the grip released on the apron and the whole lot was safe in a flash. The apron rearranged in less than no time and the picking continued.

I was staggered at the pace the girls worked and they kept it up all day long and then went home to see to their children, housework, husbands and meals. Bert ran the whole operation walking around and resetting the sticks if the field edge tapered, making sure the pickers were not missing any of the crop by shuffling his boots around in the loose soil. Katie was in charge of the tally and walked alongside each trailer as it was loaded, ticking off the full sacks to each picker. Tony and me were the haulage team, ferrying the full sacks to the Dutch barn and tipping them out. Percy and Walter were the loading team, lifting the full sacks on to the trailer. It was up to the driver to arrange them on the trailer, so there was a lot of hopping on and off the tractor. Back at the barn it was a simple job to reverse in and tip the sacks off the back of the trailer. Once the heap had built up a bit, there was a petrol-driven elevator on wheels with a sort of holding tank at the bottom. The trailer could be reversed up to the tank and the sacks tipped in. The rubber conveyor would take the potatoes up to the level of the eaves. The elevator was quite light and could be wheeled about by one man easily, so it was not necessary to have a worker at the barn. Everything there was looked after by Tony and myself.

We were amazingly lucky with the weather. Soon after starting it turned very warm and we had an Indian summer. The younger girls were soon working in just bras and shorts. I can't recall any complaints from the men!

Most days Tracy would ride along the landway to one side of the field on one or other of the horses and the same again in the afternoon on Moonshine. She kept well clear of the spinner as it was noisy and dusty and the horses were not too happy with it. My evenings were free as the girls knocked off at 4.30 so I was seeing plenty of her. On one of those evenings during the first week of potato harvest she said she was having to go away with Mrs Williams on the Friday and would be gone around ten days. I had been expecting it to happen so just had to grin and bear it. I saw her on the Thursday evening. Andy had taken Sue off somewhere – actually I think the back seat of his car was seeing quite a bit of action. We were a bit low at the thought of our first parting. After all, we had known each other for all of five months, but to us it was a lifetime.

Our long, sweet lovemaking lasted nearly the whole evening and swept us to new heights of ecstasy, togetherness and fulfilment. We were just crazy about each other and even came to tears when it was time for me to go.

The next day, without her ride-bys, seemed empty and lonesome. I couldn't even contact her by phone, so I felt very down.

There were three fields to harvest, amounting to 62 acres and we were halfway through the last when the weather changed. It turned wet and cold, not wet enough to stop the job but enough to make working conditions unpleasant especially for the pickers. In all it took ten working days to finish the harvest, as the girls didn't work weekends.

I was being accused of being ratty by all and sundry, especially my folks.

'I'll be damn glad when Tracy gets back,' my Mum complained. 'Perhaps I'll be able to speak without you biting my tongue off!'

At work Katie had twigged I was feeling low and had noticed that Tracy had not been around.

'Has your beauty queen deserted you?' she asked. I told her Tracy was away with the horses but should be back soon after the weekend.

'You know,' she said, 'men and horses have one thing in common. They both can't do without their oats.'

'I guess you're right as usual,' I laughed. 'There does seem to be a gap in my life at the moment.'

'Yes,' Katie laughed back, 'and I know just where that gap is.' We had a laugh and I felt better. Katie always had that effect on me.

The Boss saw me on Friday and wanted me to heavy harrow the now empty potato fields and said that our girls would walk them on Monday and pick up any spuds that were missed. I was glad of the work as I didn't fancy moping around for the weekend without my girl. It was quite surprising how many potatoes were rolled to the top by the harrows. The girls will have good pickings here, I thought.

On Monday the girls walked to and fro in a line like beaters and cleared up. The fields were then fertilised, light harrowed and drilled with winter wheat. What had been fields full of potatoes two weeks ago were now smooth and sown with a new crop.

Back at the barn the top and face of the heap were covered with a layer of straw as riddling would not start until November. Strawing the top brought back memories of the start of the year, or should that be 'mammaries'. The vision of Katie still clear in my mind, I rode home hoping to see the big horse-box back in the stable yard but was disappointed.

Next day I had a new assignment. I had to drive the tractor and trailer for Bert and the girls who were going to cut cauliflowers. When the plants were first set out, alleyways were left every 15 yards or so with room to drive a tractor and trailer along. My job was to drive slowly along the alleyways with four girls on either side who were cutting the caulis and throwing them on to the trailer. For the girls it was a wet, cold job as the plants were now over knee high and the leaves seemed to hold cupfuls of water. It meant working in overtrousers or leggings, which was never very pleasant. My part in the operation was not very exciting as it involved creeping along at just below walking pace. A bit of shouted banter with the girls helped to pass the time but occasionally resulted in me having to take cover under a barrage of caulis. A pass across the field and back would produce a good load. A supply of boxes had already been brought to the field and stacked on the headland, inside the gate, so I would take the load to the boxes. There the girls would take the caulies off the trailer, cut the projecting top leaves flush with the crown and trim the stalk. They were then packed 12 to a box, the first six going in crowns up and the top layer crowns down. Bert and myself joined the girls in cutting and packing. The field was some way from the yard so Bert had fetched the fire drum and there were always some boxes that were part broken which we helped on their way to provide firewood. The boxes also provided our seats as we ate our breakfast and lunch. Sitting round the fire chatting, I again recalled memories of the start of my year when I would sit quiet and hope nobody spoke to me. What a difference now!

'I 'ear tha' blonde bombshell be away for a mite spell,' Anna said to me. 'Thart thy looked a bit peeky. Tha' be missin' tha' reglar meals, I 'spect.'

'Anna for Pete's sake!' Katie laughed, 'You're about as tactful as an elephant stampede!' I was already joining in the laughter, as Anna's turn of phrase was a constant delight.

'She might be back this afternoon,' I told them. 'I hope so because, as you say Anna, I'm starving for nourishment.' More laughter.

'What's tha' bettin' sod's law will make it tha' wrong week for tha' lass,' Anna was still going on. 'If 'tis, an' she be back, young Graham will 'av a face loik a wet weekend tomorrie.'

The general laughter was reaching the coughing and choking stage now, mine included. Even Katie, who found some of

Anna's crudities a bit much, was doubled up.

'If yew be right,' Bert gasped through his mirth, 'he'll 'ave to see Katie agin, she'll give un an' 'and.' Katie was still laughing but managed to roll her eyes at me.

Breaktime with the girls was always like this. Sometimes it was a job to get food eaten and tea drunk because of laughter, yet to see them walking about in their long, torn and shabby coats, their faces lined and weather-beaten, one would never have guessed at the wit and humour they were capable of.

Just before 4.30, knock off-time for the girls, the Boss arrived and dropped off Tony, who was going to help me load and cart the full boxes to the loading dock for Harry's run to London that night. There were three full trailer loads and it was nearly dark by the time we had the last back to the yard. Harry was loading so we put our last load straight on the lorry. All the best caulies were cut on this first run through and then, depending on the market demand, later cuttings would take the second best, and so on. Once all were cut, Tom would move in with his wire pens and the sheep would strip the field bare. I parked up the tractor and said good night to Tony and Harry and I'm sure my readers will be able to guess my first port of call on leaving the yard that evening.

Chapter 20

Riding round the loop lane it was too dark to see if the horse box was back. I could see the lights in the flat and my hopes were high as I turned in the drive way to the stable yard. My headlight at once picked up the reflectors on the rear of the box and I gave a little whoop of pleasure at seeing it there. I rode over to the bottom of the steps and before I had stopped, Tracy flew out of the flat door and down to meet me. I didn't have time to even get off the bike before her arms were round me and her lips were on mine. Eventually we pulled apart and I was able to put the bike on its stand before she was in my arms again. Sue called from the landing.

'There's tea in the pot.' A short pause, then 'but I expect it will be cold before you two manage to get up here.'

After a while we did make it up to the flat and the tea was still hot ... well warm. We sat at the table holding hands and drinking it and talking twenty to the dozen. It was so good to see her – it had seemed much longer than ten days. I phoned home and told my Mum that Tracy was back and that

I would be late. She said she would put my meal in a low oven for when I arrived. I didn't stay late, however, because it was obvious that Tracy was exhausted. She told me she had trouble sleeping in the horse box and the days had been long and hectic. I left around 9.30 with the promise that I would see her the next day. We hugged and kissed as I left.

'You smell of cabbages, darling,' she said.

'Cauliflowers, actually,' I told her.

'Oh, so sorry,' she laughed. 'Do you think as years go by I will be able to identify all the different things you smell of? I'm not even sure I want to know about some of them.'

'Just as long as you keep getting that close to sniff will be good enough for me,' I told her, laughing also.

With Tracy back things returned pretty much to normal. I had more ploughing to do and at the end of each day there were bags of sprouts to bring in to the dock for Harry. Katie told me that sprout picking was the most unpopular job of all. The plants were waist high and the girls had to bend down among them and every leaf had a pool of water in it. It was impossible to work fast enough to keep warm, as we did cabbage cutting, so hands got steadily colder and being constantly soaked didn't help.

It was so good to have the visits from Tracy on one of the horses nearly every day, and my eyes were constantly on the lookout for her. I realised now just how much I had missed her. Sitting together on the sofa at the flat, just talking, it became obvious that there was no way on earth that we were ever going to be able to live apart for long. I never actually proposed marriage to Tracy, we just accepted that it would happen. The big question was when. It was impossible as things were at that moment, I was just $17\frac{1}{2}$ and I wanted things to be right with our folks and not to go and do something silly. We talked around it and decided we could not do anything until after my birthday next year.

'Tell you what,' Tracy said cuddling up. 'Let's get engaged, not tell anyone, let it be just an "us" thing. We can make it official and broadcast it on the BBC whenever. I don't even want a ring, yet.'

'I'll go for that,' I smiled. 'Miss Volanen, you are now unofficially engaged and next year, my darling, sometime between June and Christmas, you will be my wife.' We were so happy it hurt and I went home that night feeling such adoration for her and so humble that of all people she had chosen me to love and to want to share her life with.

Autumn was well upon us now with leaves blowing around the yard and up and down the lane. It has always been one of my favourite times of year. I especially like those still misty mornings before the sun burns it off. Sounds seem magnified, the call of a crow or pheasant or a dog barking seemingly miles away. The smell of wet earth and the bursts of colour from holly berries. I walked miles with Tracy looking in wonder at cobwebs coated with frost decorating every clump of grass and hedge. Even things as cruel as barbed-wire fences were transformed into fairy-tale wonders, the wire white glistening and each post with a little fluffy cap perched on top. One such day when it was especially frosty and even the trees were white and glistening, we walked down through the wood to the grassy mound where we had made love in the Summer. Just as we got there the sun broke through and turned the area into a glistening wonderland. Tracy had the urge to run around the area naked in the frost. I had no objection as long as she didn't want me to! She emerged from behind the big oak totally nude and cavorted around like some wild, beautiful wood nymph, her blond hair loose and falling over her shoulders, until the cold forced her back into her clothes.

'You looked like the spirit of the woods,' I told her. 'Certainly made the day for that bloke walking his dog.'

Her hand went to her mouth.

'What blo...?' she saw my smile and laughed. 'I feel so happy I would not care if there had been people about. As far as I'm concerned there is just one and he's seen it all before.' She came into my arms and the kiss that followed left us both in tears with its intensity and love.

The farm moved on into the same winter routine that I had encountered in my early days. Most mornings I would give Tom a hand feeding the cattle, the hay bales feeling quite light now. I was able to carry two with no problem and could lift them into the cribs easily. The ploughing was pretty much up to speed and would be finished before Christmas if the weather held. Andy was the one finishing that off. It was strange, in a way, that even though it was not a huge farm, I often didn't know what the other men were doing. We each operated in accordance with what the Boss asked us to do and would see other operations going on that did not involve us. Then when things required a gang – like muck-spreading or harvesting – we would come together and work as a team.

One of those occasions arrived around mid-November when Percy, Walter, Tony and me formed a gang to go hedgecutting or 'edge brushin'' as they called it. An assortment of tools were loaded on the trailer plus some old sacks and a drum of diesel and we set off to the hedge to be cut. The rough grass and small light stuff at the base we cut first using what the men called a 'brish hook' but I also heard it called a 'bagging hook', a 'sickle' or a 'swop'. The bulk of the rest was cut with a handbill and the top where it was a job to reach, with a slasher, like a handbill on a long handle. There was a rush to get a bit cut so that a fire could be started before breakfast break.

The old sacks were given a good soaking in diesel and the dead wood and light stuff used to get a start. It was a pleasant job as long as it wasn't raining. The cold was not a problem, because the work was energetic enough to keep warm and often coats and jackets were discarded even with a layer of snow on the ground. I was surprised how quickly the work progressed. What had looked like a daunting task when we started soon diminished and it all looked very smart when we finished. I was told that a certain number of hedges were cut every year in a sort of rotation, which allowed cover for the wild birds in the ones that were left.

We didn't work overtime on this sort of job so I called in on Tracy after the first day's hedgecutting at my usual knock-off time. She ran up for the usual kiss and cuddle only to pull away quicker than usual.

'You smell of smoke and sweat,' she said.

'Actually, it's rather a turn-on. Pity Sue's around. You could keep just your jacket, shirt and jersey on and...' She looked all coy and made eyes at me.

'And what?' I teased, a big smile on my face. She came back into my arms and snuggled against the side of my face.

'And give me a real good seeing to because I want you like crazy,' she whispered huskily, poking her tongue in my ear.

'My God, woman you're sex mad!' I whispered back. 'Where can we go?' She pulled away and stood looking at me.

'Sue won't mind finishing off on her own,' she said. 'We've lived together long enough to know each other's moods.' She went over to a stable and I heard her talking to Sue, who appeared at the door and waved to me. Tracy came back and took my hand and we went towards the flat.

'Have fun,' Sue called and we both waved without turning round. By our usual standards it was lightning quick. Tracy had her wish, she pulled off all but my jacket, shirt and jersey and removed just her work trousers and we made mad crazy love that lasted all of three minutes. Laughing like idiots we put back on the few clothes and returned outside. Sue was coming from the barn with hay.

'Gosh, that was quick!' she called. 'That must be a record for you two.' She was unable to keep a straight face and had to burst out laughing and the three of us stood there doubled up, with tears rolling down our faces. It was a supremely happy moment, one to be cherished.

The hedgecutting continued into December with my thoughts starting to work on what to get Tracy for Christmas. There was a big job waiting before that, however. Most of the sacks of wheat and barley in the barn had now been sold and carted away by lorry. There was now space in the barn for more so the two stacks of wheat and the one of oats were to be thrashed before Christmas. Ted duly arrived, having come straight from another farm and with much shunting around and levelling, got the thrasher alongside the first stack. Andy and me crawled around on the roof of the stack removing the thatch and pulling out the hazel benders.

Jobs were assigned to a crew of 13 or 14 staff. The trusser that would tie up the thrashed straw was positioned, and Ted had all the belts in place including the main drive from the tractor to the drum, as the thrashing machine was always called. Once everyone was in place, the tractor was started up and the belt started to turn. A low whirr gradually built up to a medium-pitched whine that could be heard from a long way off, the note deepening slightly as

Tony started to feed the crop through. Andy, Ruth and me were on the corn stack taking turns to feed the sheaves to Katie, who was cutting the string and dropping the cut sheaves on the feeder table. This was a wooden tray as wide as a sheaf, polished by use, that sloped gently down to the mouth of the drum where the thrashing took place. It required a nice steady feed, so as Katie dropped the cut sheaf, Tony, as feeder, would spread it out on the table and allow it to fall in at an even rate. If he allowed a rather big lump to go through, the drum would give a sort of low thump and some-one was sure to hold up their arm with the other hand across the elbow, like a knife, meaning: has your arm gone through?

The thrashed corn poured out from outlets in the same way as on the combine. This end Bert looked after. Some boards had been put down so that he could wheel the sacks about on a sack barrow and a good layer of straw stopped the bottoms getting damp from the ground when he put them to one side.

Towards the other end all the chaff and little bits poured out and this was probably the worst job of all, keeping that area clear. It meant raking all this dusty stuff from under the machine, in all the noise, and bagging it up for ease of clearing later. The thrashed straw dropped straight into a trusser that turned it back into a sheaf, tied round the middle. Percy then pitched the straw sheaves to two or three women who were keeping Walter busy building the straw stack. It really was a hive of work with the thrashing drum as master and all its slaves toiling around it. Even in Winter it was hot work keeping up the pace which never let up for an instant. The whole area was shrouded in dust and we all looked like tinkers with black corners to our eyes and black rims to nostrils. I never gave a thought as to what its long-term effects might be.

The drum rolled into silence at 4.30 because the girls were knocking off and the job could not run without them. Everyone gave a sigh of relief that it was over until tomorrow. There was, however, the matter of a large area of full, 2¼cwt, sacks to be carted back to the barn and unloaded. It was nearly dark when we finished and, just for fun I called round to see Tracy. I kept the bike on low revs round the loop lane so as not to be heard and parked on the far side of the yard and walked to the flat. I was lucky and Tracy answered my knock. She was about to rush for her kiss when she saw the state I was in.

'Good God!' she cried. 'You're absolutely filthy and you smell.' Sue was behind, her hand to her mouth looking at me.

'But, Tracy darling,' I smiled at her. 'I

thought that was how you liked me. You said it turned you on. Shall we use your bed or Sue's?'

'You crazy fool!' she laughed. 'I'm not even going to let you in looking like that let alone anything else. What the hell have you been doing to get like that?' I told her about the thrashing and she said she had ridden that way but the horses got upset with the whine so she had gone in the other direction. We had a good laugh and I went home to a bath and my tea and came back later.

It took around two days to finish each stack so it was near to the end of the second week in December before we finished. There was quite a lot of clearing up work to do and straw sheaves to cart to the Dutch barn for next year's thatching.

I managed a present-buying trip to town at the weekend. I settled on a chunky knit sweater for Tracy plus a couple of records for the radiogram. 'I love you, yes I do', by Ella Mae Morse and, for a joke 'Mad about the boy', by Billy May. I picked up a box of bath goodies for Sue. I also had to get things for my and Tracy's folks and a few of my local relations. My brother, Barry, was also expected home so I had to find him something. I also got a small item for Katie. It was dead easy buying clothes for Tracy, as her wardrobe at the flat was nearly empty. Most of the things she wore were borrowed either from her Mum or from Sue. The ones from Sue were a bit baggy round the bust.

Arriving at the flat that evening, I saw that Andy's car was parked at the steps. Once inside the flat I suggested that, as we were all there, it would be a good time to plan Christmas. I had got holiday time due to me so I needed to use it before the year end. The girls had told me that they were both usually there for Christmas Day – not that both were required but one stayed as company for the other. Tracy's folks were going to Finland but she wouldn't go because of leaving Sue with it all to do on her own. There didn't necessarily have to be any one there between feeds as the stables were often left while the girls were riding together or, for example, when we were all at the Harvest Party. I suggested that Sue have Christmas Day off to do as she pleased. She could be free from after feeding, Christmas Eve. I would stay with Tracy and do the morning feeding with her then take her to my place. We could spend the day together there just popping back at lunchtime. In the evening I would come back with her and stay until the 30th when, perhaps, Sue could take over with Andy's help and do the New Year bit. The girls jumped at the idea.

'Mrs W will be pleased,' Tracy said. 'She usually has to come and do some time. This year she won't have to.' She cuddled up to me. 'And I'll be pleased because I'll have you here for nearly a week.'

'Might be an idea if I stayed over New Year,' Andy said. Tracy had told me that so far he hadn't stopped over but that the romance was still growing. Sue was blushing and a bit flustered but quickly made her mind up.

'That would be great,' she told him taking his hand. 'It'll be the bestest Christmas ever.'

They went off together after half an hour or so as they were going to a friend's engagement party and Sue said she would be very late back. Tracy was still excited at the thought of me staying for almost a week.

'You sure your Mum and Dad won't mind?' she asked me. 'I know you stayed a weekend, but a whole week!'

'Of course they'll mind but I'm too old now for them to order me about,' I told her. 'They'll be fine, don't worry.'

'Your Dad will think I'm a right tart,' she said, looking worried, 'but I'm sure your folks know how we feel about each other. I told your Mum I loved you like crazy.'

'Did you really?' I said, surprised. 'That was a nice thing to do. I bet she was impressed.'

'She said she already knew. She said she only had to see us together to know we were made for each other,' Tracy went on. 'I'm sure she will understand about the week.'

'Mum's not been too good lately,' I told her. 'She's seen the doc. He thinks she may have a kidney problem.'

'Perhaps we could go and see her tomorrow,' Tracy suggested, 'but right now I have things that I need you to do for *me*, lover of mine.'

She had hold of both my hands and was pulling me through the bedroom door. Of course, I was resisting like mad as I'm sure you can understand!

Chapter 21

On Monday morning I checked with the Boss and got the OK for the time off between Christmas and New Year. While I was talking to him, I told him in confidence about my plans for next year, that Tracy and me hoped to get married, perhaps in the late Autumn. What I really wanted from him was some indication of the possibility of a cottage. Most of the male staff lived in tied farm cottages with the exception of Andy, who lived at his folks' place and Percy who had a council house. The Boss told me that straight after Christmas he was having two new cottages built in the old orchard just past the farm. One was for Tony and the other he would sort out later. He also said that he knew of a bungalow in the village that was rented. The present occupiers were friends of Tony's. They were going to Australia in September, he thought, and if I did go ahead with my plans, he was pretty sure that there would be something for us.

It all sounded too good to be true and when I told Tracy the news that evening she was so happy. She danced around the flat and every time she passed me she gave me a kiss.

The weeks on the farm leading up to Christmas I spent acting as driver for the girls cutting the aptly named Christmas Cabbages. It was a wet, cold spell and the job as unpleasant as ever but better than the snow of my first week. I was able to keep up easily with the girls and still have time for the usual backchat.

'This must be about where you came in,' Katie observed, 'or was it after Christmas?'

'January 4th,' I told her. 'You remember the snow when we were cutting the January Kings, we got a bollocking from Anna for holding hands?'

'Oh yes,' she laughed. 'My God, what a difference a year makes! Look at you now. You must have put on a stone and I expect most of it's muscle.'

'It's certainly been quite a year,' I replied. 'One with some memories I will never forget. One memory in particular with your name written on it, Katie.'

She looked at me, those eyes as ever twinkling and a smile on her lips and, as we parted to get on with the work, she looked over her shoulder and said, 'Thank you, Graham.'

Christmas Day was on a Saturday and on the Wednesday before, on arriving home, I found that my brother had arrived looking tanned and fit as usual with tales of foreign parts, lots of which I had never heard of. He was amazed at the change in me.

'When I left, you were a skinny schoolboy,' he smiled, 'now you're a solid-looking working man, with a girlfriend I hear. Bit of a looker so Dad was telling me.'

'She is that!' I told him. 'You'll be meeting her before too long. Her name's Tracy.'

Barry told me he had taken his last leave in Australia and was full of stories about the place and its laid back life style. I rather got the impression that, given the chance, he would like to live there.

Friday, Christmas Eve, the Boss wanted a few bags of cabbage to go with some bags of sprouts he had kept back from earlier in the week. Harry was doing a late afternoon run to the markets. The Boss said once the cabbage were cut, we could all take the rest of the day off and he would pay for the day. I found a quiet moment to give Katie her present. She was taken aback and told me I shouldn't be spending my money on her.

'After all you have done for me this year it's the least I could do,' I told her. I suggested that it might be a good idea to open it when her husband wasn't around.

We quickly set about getting the bags of cabbages, taking only a few minutes for morning break. Everyone was keen to get home and to set about the final preparations for the next day. Late morning Tracy rode along the headland on a bay mare leading another horse and I grabbed a quick word to say I would be round about sixish.

Just after midday we were back in the yard, most of the rest of the staff drifting in from whatever they had been doing. The Boss came down from the house at around a quarter to one and wished us all a Merry Christmas and thanked us for all our efforts during the year. He then went round us individually and gave us our pay packets with a five pound note as a bonus, which for me was nearly a week's basic pay, so I was more than happy. Then with festive calls to each other we drifted away. I took time to go round each of the girls and give them a Christmas kiss. They knew what it was really for and each one gave me a hug in return. I wrapped my arms round Katie and gave her big hug and kiss and wished her and Alan and Timmy a happy time. I was surprised to see a wetness in her eyes as she thanked me and wished the same to me and 'the blonde goddess'.

I spent the afternoon at home chatting to Barry and my folks and having a drink or two. I had told Mum and Dad my plans and surprisingly enough they said they had half expected something along the lines I told them. My Mum packed up a whole feast for me to take with me for that evening and arranged that during the week, I had to bring Tracy for a meal at least once a day. She also said that she would get the spare bedroom ready for Tracy to stay over New Year. I really couldn't thank her enough for being so understanding.

'It's not all me,' she said. 'Your Dad suggested a lot of it.' So I went and thanked him also.

Sue was all set to leave when I arrived, Andy was taking her to her folks and they were each spending the next day with their folks at home and had things planned for the next few days. We saw them off and shut the door to the flat. I unloaded all the goodies that Mum had sent over.

'It's a feast!' Tracy cried. 'I'll never be able to get on a horse and if I did, its feet would go out sideways.' She then went on to prove that her respect for her horses' welfare had sadly diminished. Later we sat back full up and then thought of Christmas dinner the next day.

'I'll have to diet for the whole of January,' Tracy moaned. 'You won't love me if I'm overweight.'

'No I won't,' I agreed, smiling.

'You bugger!' she exclaimed. 'You are supposed to say you would love me anyway.'

'I will, Darling,' I told her, still smiling. 'Any way you like, just name the position.'

'You twist everything I say,' she said pouting. 'I could name half a dozen but I'm too full at the moment.'

We cleared away and chatted the rest of the evening, bathed together, and once again cuddled up in her single bed where the alarm roused us sublimely happy and content at 7.30 on Christmas Day. Our night before's plan of a cup of tea and then the feeding got held up and in the end there wasn't time for the tea and the feeding was a bit late. We rushed around and made up a bit of the time and managed to make it to my home by nine. The front door opened before we got there and Barry was wishing us a Merry Christmas. I introduced Tracy.

'Frankly, I'm surprised,' he said. 'I was told you were a stunner. My God you are miles better than that, you are quite simply gorgeous.'

'Oh no, not another one of them.' Tracy slapped her forehead. 'I thought this one,' indicating me, 'was bad enough. I always thought he had swallowed the Blarney Stone.'

We all laughed and it was obvious from the first minute that Tracy was accepted as part of the family. My Mum in particular was keen to enlist her help in the kitchen and soon took her off in that direction.

'Strewth!' Barry said, a result of spending some time in Australia. 'She is something else. Where on God's sweet earth did you find her, you lucky young sod?'

'It's more a case of she found me,' I replied. I outlined our first meeting.

'If I was you I'd never shoot another pheasant as long as I live,' Barry laughed. 'Anyone want a coffee? I'm looking for an excuse to go into the kitchen.' I said I'd have one and Dad agreed so Barry headed ... quickly ... towards the kitchen.

'She does seem to have an amazing effect,' Dad said, 'but I suppose looking like that she's got used to it.'

It was one hell of a long wait for the coffee and in the end I went in search of it to find Tracy, Barry and my Mum doubled up over some joke that Barry was telling, his arm round Tracy's shoulders.

'So, where's the coffee then?' I asked, smiling at their mirth.

'Oh, sorry,' Barry replied. 'I forgot all about it.' His arm was still across Tracy's shoulders – she looked at me and rolled her eyes quickly.

'Well, come on, it's pressie time,' I told him. We at last assembled by the tree and presents were distributed. Tracy had brought a bag and had placed her presents with the rest for handing out. The usual ripping of paper and shouts of thank you ensued. Tracy loved her sweater and the records and had a good chuckle at 'Mad about the boy'. She had bought me a leather jerkin for wearing at work, something I had promised myself I would get. I was delighted. She had even got something for Barry, as I had told her he would be home. It was a small leather-covered notebook and phone-list book and I could see he was made up with it. She had found a beautiful Beswick china horse, rearing on its hind legs, for my folks. In return they gave her a silver-backed dressing-table set. We were all happy and laughing when we then sat down for the usual ham and tongue breakfast.

Afterwards we talked and played games until it was time for us to pop off and see to the lunchtime feeding. Dad said he would take us in the car but it would mean him hanging about while we worked so in the end we went on the bike.

'Well, your brother comes on strong,' Tracy said when we got to the stables. 'I thought I was going to have to send him for a cold shower.'

'He's been locked up in a tin boat for God knows how long,' I excused him. 'Seeing the likes of you knocked him sideways, same as it did me.'

'Yes, I see about the boat,' she mused. 'But there must be plenty of girls in all the places he's been to. Lots of them better looking than me.'

'Plenty of girls, yes,' I replied. 'Better looking, never. You, my sweet, are a one-off, they don't come no better.'

She melted into my arms and for a moment I thought the lunchtime feeding was going to be late also but we did manage to sort ourselves out and get on with it.

We went back for Christmas dinner which was a great success and we left the table stuffed again. We all got together for the washing-up and clearing away and soon had it all squared.

The afternoon was a riot, with games of charades the most popular. Tracy proved to have no inhibitions and some of her mimes caused great hilarity and, in my Mum's case, the occasional blush. The time again passed all too quickly and we had to leave for the evening feed and would not return that day. We were seen off as if we were going on a huge journey. Tracy gave Mum and Dad a kiss each and thanked them for the great day. She had quite a job escaping from Barry but made it eventually.

The rest of the week flew by and being together so much brought home just how relaxed and happy we were in each other's company. Evening time we would sit around listening to music, then bath together and climb into her single bed, to wake in the morning with the covers all over the place, some on the floor and some wrapped round us. To see her face beside me or to look down on the blonde tangle laying on my chest. She would stir and slowly come awake and her first action was always to wrap herself around me for a long good morning kiss and to tell me she loved me.

We went back to my place each day at some time or other for a good meal. The rest of the time we looked after ourselves and were quite happy to stay in the flat and just be together; it was all we really needed. We would do the chores together then I would relax in the flat or wander around while she was riding. I had learnt how to harness and unharness a horse, so every time she returned I helped her change over and so cut down on the 'turn round' times.

The end of the week arrived and Andy and Sue were back by 9.30 on the 30th having also had a wonderful Christmas and they were now looking forward to spending some days ... and nights together.

Tracy packed what she needed for a three-day stay (she didn't seem to have much) in my haversack and the bag we had brought the food over in. She could carry that easily on the bike. We wished Andy and Sue a Happy New Year and left them to it. If they enjoy the time half as much as I have, I thought, they will be more than happy.

I showed Tracy to the spare room at home that Mum had prepared for her. It was at the end of a short passageway past my room.

We had three more wonderful days together at my place. On the 31st we went for a drive down to the coast. My Dad had a Wolseley 6/80 that had a bench-type seat in the front so seated the five of us easily. Even though it was cold windy and overcast, Tracy insisted on a walk on the beach so we carried on like a couple of kids running along the surf line dodging the incoming waves. Her zest for life was so infectious that I just had to join in with whatever she wanted to do. She stood for a moment at the edge of the water, looking at the horizon, her hair streaming behind her in the wind, her clothes moulded to her breasts by its force, looking like some Valkyrie goddess about to take over the world. We got back in the car, cold and breathless but lifted by the experience and cuddled in the corner to get warm.

We stopped at a nice hotel on the coast for lunch and then drove on into Sussex to give Mum a treat. Later we stopped at a pub for drinks and sandwiches. I always had a secret smile on entering a crowded place like a pub bar with Tracy. The noise and chatter would fade for a moment or two as she walked in and the looks on the faces of the male section were a delight. They ranged from admiration to naked lust. She never seemed to notice as she always maintained that her looks were nothing out of the ordinary.

We stayed up and watched the New Year in and toasted good luck to each other and then had another drink or two before staggering off to our beds.

The next two days we unwound by walking and watching television in the evenings as that was the only time it was on.

On the 2nd I took Tracy back to the flat at just after nine in the evening. Andy was still there but ready to leave. Their happy faces said it all and when Sue went off to say goodbye to him we began to wonder if she was ever coming back.

Next day it was all back to normal and in two days' time I would complete my first year at Manor Farm. The mood in the yard was quite happy with a lot of chat going on about the holiday period. Katie found me and thanked me for her present. She was wearing it, a jade-coloured silk scarf that I had suggested, in a note that I sent with it, would look great as a bandanna for work. It looked as good as I thought it would, the green setting off those dark ringlets.

Tracy's Mum and Dad returned from Finland and we paid them a visit and had a sort of late Christmas. They had enjoyed their stay and were pleased that Tracy had been looked after and had enjoyed herself. Around the end of the month our two lots of parents got together for the first time, which was a bit of a milestone. My folks asked me about them and suggested they should meet. I gave Dad their address and phone number and he contacted them and invited them over for the day the next Sunday, Barry was still home so we could all meet up for the day. It was a huge success with my Dad making arrangements with Ralf to show him over the 'works' and the three engineers chatting machines and technical stuff. The two Mums had Sussex in common and it turned out they both knew people there so they were going at it twenty to the dozen. I caught Tracy's eye and we had developed almost a sixth sense in knowing what the other one was thinking. She excused herself and went out and a few minutes later I followed her. We put coats on and went for a stroll.

'That's another hurdle cleared,' I said. 'The folks are getting on well.'

'It's brilliant,' Tracy agreed. 'When are you going to ask my Dad if he'll let you marry me?'

'I thought just after your 21st in May,' I told her. 'Then we can make the engagement official and I can get you a ring. Then your vet can fit it through your nose and I can put a chain on it.'

'Rotten sod,' she laughed, 'as if I would stray. You are stuck with me now, man of mine, so you had better get good and used to it.'

We strolled arm in arm to the bottom of the garden and along to the 'fox tree' as

Tracy called it and arrived as a watery sun broke free of the clouds for a while before disappearing again in the overcast. The wood smelt of decaying leaves and there was a dampness everywhere.

The field had been ploughed since we were here last and the freshly turned earth shone in the weak light, polished by the passing of the plough share. Tracy was in a skittish mood brought on by the success of our parents meeting. She leaned back against the tree and pulled me close her lips seeking mine and her tongue probing deep in my mouth. There was a minute or two of seeking and finding, fumbling and adjusting and then her little cries were mingling with the harsh calls of the crows out in the field. We clung together in our climax, her head thrown back, her eyes reflecting her love. She looked so beautiful I felt the tears stinging my eyes and I loved her with all my heart. We drew apart at last and did up our coats and things and started to return home, our arms round each other and a spring in our step.

After the 'ice breaker' in January our folks got on well especially after discovering that they were all fond of Whist and met up on almost a regular basis for a game. Barry had to go back to sea and we all went down to Thames Haven to see him off and he managed to wangle a trip round the ship, the size of which was totally amazing. The size of the engines had both of us gawking and even in dock I found the heat and noise distressing. How Barry put up with it while under way I could not imagine. I told him in confidence of our wedding plans and asked if there was a possibility he could get back in the Autumn to be best man. He told me that it should be no problem as he could fly home and rejoin the ship at the next port of call. Another hurdle jumped.

The year progressed. I was quite the old hand now and could go off and do most of the farm work with no instruction. The only new job that came my way was the spring drilling which I loved. There was something so very satisfying about planting the seed and then coming by in a couple of weeks and seeing it up and growing.

The headland was always drilled first. We went five times round the field and the last time round left a clear wheelmark to start and stop by when sowing the rest. The operator on the drill would look for the mark and just before it went under the drill, he would drop the coulters which also started the drill sowing. Exactly the reverse happened at the other end when, as the coulters crossed the mark, he would lift them out and stop the sowing. I always thought that turning on the sown headland would disturb the seed, but it never seemed to have any detrimental effect. It was a maximum-concentration job on the tractor keeping the rows straight, because one's skill would show up all the time the crop was in the field. Any wavers would be commented on and any gaps were ridiculed as poor workmanship. I talked to Tracy about organising a 'do' for her 21st birthday but she would have none of it. All she wanted was a quiet day perhaps with both lots of parents and maybe Sue and Andy could come in the evening. I tried to talk her into a party but she was adamant that was not what she wanted. She explained that she hadn't got a wide circle of friends, because it was difficult living where she did to get and see anyone and the horses took up so much time. In the end I gave in and agreed that a quiet day it would be. I did, however, know exactly what I wanted to get her and on my next trip to town I called into the main jewellers and looked at their stock. There was nothing there that was anything like what I had in mind so I started going round the smaller shops and at last got lucky. It was exactly what I was after.

A gold, heart-shaped locket on a gold chain with an engraving of a horse's head on the front with a delicate flower pattern surround. I wanted some words engraved inside, on the back of the lid, and the shop agreed to get that done. I paid for it and arranged to collect in two weeks' time. When I went back for it there was more jewellery shopping to do. I had borrowed a bit of extra cash from Dad and set out to buy a ring. After a long search going from shop window to shop window and back again, I finally settled on a gold band with three diamonds offset from the line of the band. It didn't look too flashy, which I knew Tracy would hate. Sue had helped out again with size. All was now set for the visit to the future in-laws and Mr Volanen's permission for me to marry his daughter.

Chapter 22

Something took us all by surprise at the beginning of May – Andy and Sue announced their engagement. She hadn't even told Tracy it was going to happen. They put on a good party at the pub in the village. Even the Boss and Mrs Willis were there along with a good number of the farm staff. It was a great evening with a lot of 'toasting' going on.

'You're a dark horse,' I said to Sue. 'Not even a word to Tracy and then all this.'

'Andy wanted it to be a complete secret so that we could be sure nothing was said until we made the announcement,' she told me.

Andy came over as we were chatting and held out his hand. 'This is all down to you and I want to thank you for it,' he said. I shook his hand and he went on, 'Would you do one more thing for me? Would you be best man at the wedding next Spring?'

'Andy, nothing would give me greater pleasure, old mate, I'll look forward to it,' I told him, chuffed to bits that it had all worked out so well.

Tracy had been listening, a big smile on her face and after Sue and Andy had circulated away, she sidled up to me and said: 'I suppose you are going to add match-making to your list of talents, are you?'

'Well, it's nothing really.' I tried to keep a straight face. 'You know, great personality, super lover, ace tractor driver. A bit of match-making comes easy to me.'

'Well,' she looked pensive, 'personality yes, ace tractor driver yes, super lover ... well that really needs a bit more practice. Perhaps ... later.'

We couldn't hold on any longer and burst out laughing, adding to the all round merriment of the occasion. Andy and Sue had to stay to the end as it was their party so we were able to slip away back to the flat where I did manage to get some more practice!

Later in the month Tracy got her wish and we had the quiet celebration of her 21st at my folks' place. Her Mum and Dad spent the day and exactly as she had wished, Andy and Sue came for the evening.

The bright spot of the day was when she opened the parcel containing the locket. She threw herself into my arms and hugged me for all she was worth. She made me put it on for her and quickly found a mirror to see how it looked.

'Graham, it's just so beautiful, I'll never be able to thank you enough,' she said, tears in her eyes.

'Darling,' I told her, 'it looks twice as beautiful now you are wearing it. The engraving says it all.'

The only worry at that time was my Mum's health which was giving more cause for concern. She had stopped work and was having help in the house from a lady in the village who actually did the cooking for Tracy's day. The doctor and hospital were convinced it was a liver problem and she was on medication to try and correct it.

The first weekend in June we arranged to spend Sunday afternoon at Tracy's folks and in spite of my new-found confidence I admit to being nervous about asking Ralf for her hand in marriage. We arrived to be given an excited greeting by Douglas and a more restrained but warm welcome by Tracy's folks. It was a warm sunny day so deckchairs were brought out and we sat in the garden having tea and talking. We had chatted for a while when Tracy got her Mum indoors on some kitchen thing and left the way open for me.

'Ralf, there's something I'd like to ask you,' I began, still nervous.

'Fire away,' he said. I thought it best not to beat about the bush so dived straight in.

'Tracy and me have been together for a year now and we are very much in love. I would like to ask your permission to marry her later on this year.' I was going to go on and say that, yes, I might be a bit on the young side but ... Ralf forestalled me.

'I could not possibly say no,' he said, smiling. 'I have never seen a young couple so obviously made for each other. I know you are young but you have a wise head on your shoulders and a solid background. You have my blessing because I know you will love and respect my daughter and will do your very best to make her happy. Now go and fetch them both. She must have her Mother trapped somewhere.'

I found them in the kitchen, Tracy pretending she suddenly needed a recipe for apple pie, and told them Ralf wanted them. When we all returned he was pouring drink into glasses which he handed round, then said: 'Let's drink to our daughter and her husband to be, our future son-in-law. The happy couple.'

Tracy gave a squeal of delight and rushed to kiss her Dad and then her Mum and finally to me. It was a wonderful moment, one I will remember all my life.

I gave her the ring there and then and her delight was complete – we explained about the unofficial engagement and her folks thought it was very touching. I suggested a party but Tracy again would not agree and was happy to just let people know as and when.

Later that month it was my turn for a

birthday, my 18th. Tracy gave me an Irvine jacket like fighter pilots used to wear. It was great for riding the motorbike. I got a red and white spotted scarf so that I could let a bit of it stream in the wind. All I needed was the Red Baron to shoot at. I certainly looked the part, or thought I did! I was now also old enough to drive a car and, although I had never had a lesson, I figured all the time I spent driving tractors was practice enough, so put in for my test. I spent the next week or so studying the Highway Code booklet and went for the test, with the family car, at the end of July and passed. I would have liked to have got a small car of my own but we were saving every penny for the wedding. That we hoped would be towards the end of October, after all or most of the harvest was over, depending on the weather.

August arrived and the pea harvest was looming so I grabbed a Sunday afternoon off to spend at the stables. After the evening feeding I walked with Tracy down to the wood. We walked to the clearing and 'our mound', as it had become, and sat for a while listening to the birds and watching the rabbits and squirrels. Suddenly she turned to me and said: 'Graham darling, have you thought about babies?' Her words threw me for a moment and I looked at her in surprise.

'Er no, I haven't thought about it ... them,'

I replied, flustered. 'You're not pregnant are you?'

'No, you know I'm not,' she said, 'but we ought to know each other's ideas on a family, surely?'

'Well,' I mused having recovered my thoughts. 'I always thought three would be a nice size. What about you?'

'Yes, I agree.' She smiled at me. 'Three would be just right. Oh darling how wonderful! Our own little cottage and three young children to watch growing up!' She kissed my cheek and hugged me sideways on.

'I can't believe this is all happening,' she said, her eyes moist. 'I'm just the luckiest, happiest, most in love girl in all the world.'

The other topic we talked about was the question of a honeymoon. I rather favoured the Italian lakes but Tracy was more conservative and said she would rather stay in the UK. We talked over it and round it and then agreed to leave it for a while and talk about it later.

She told me she would be away again with the horses shortly as both girls had been away since Christmas and it was her turn. It was good timing as she would be away during the pea harvest when I would be working all hours and so would not see much of her anyway. We had a good Sunday together and then, as expected, in the middle of the week she went away.

We started in on the peas straight after the next weekend. It turned out to be a difficult time because of the rain. The peas couldn't wait so we had to work through. This meant towing the lorries in and out of the fields, which made the job a lot longer.

Tracy returned and took the opportunity to go off with her Mum sorting out wedding and bridesmaids' dresses, flowers and all the bits and pieces that go to make up a wedding day. She had two young cousins that lived not too far away that were going to be bridesmaids and Sue, of course, as chief. She seemed happier than ever and was spending a bit of money on clothes – something I had not known her do before. Her whole mood and outlook was lighter as if some problem had been resolved or a trouble lifted from her.

The wedding was to be in the village where her folks lived so we booked an appointment with the vicar to arrange a date and to get the banns called. At last we had a definite date to aim for, October 15th, just around eight weeks away. Before, it had seemed like a dream but now with the date booked, it was all falling into place. We were both getting excited and nervous at the same time but above it all we were getting more and more in love. One last piece fell into place out of the blue, the honeymoon. My Dad told me that a friend of his owed him a favour. This chap had a motor cruiser moored in a marina on the River Avon at Tewkesbury and would be happy for us to have it for ten days. We would only have to pay for fuel and any mooring charges and could cruise the Avon and the Severn or the Sharpness Canal if we wished. It sounded too good to be true. When I told Tracy she was thrilled – it was just what she wanted. It would be just us with no crowds and no dressing up. We could eat at riverside pubs or see to ourselves as we wished. So it was all arranged, Dad brought the keys home and a little map to show exactly where the boat was and said that his friend had contacted the marina to let them know we would be taking it out.

Just about everything was in place now. I had done my bit, arranging suit hire for me and Barry and I had organised, with Sue's help, a rather special wedding gift for Tracy. I also had gifts for Sue and the bridesmaids.

August gave way to September and the corn harvest began. The weather did not improve and harvesting became a stop start job totally different from my first year.

It was during one of those damp spells that, as I left home to go to work, I said cheerio to my Mum and thought how unwell she looked. She smiled and seemed bright enough but I was worried about her. I was tractor-hoeing a field of cabbage plants over towards Hills Lea. The day had warmed up and the sun was trying to dry things up a bit. There was no one working near by so I sat and had my lunch on the bank beside the field, hoping that Tracy might make her almost daily visit while I was stopped, but she didn't turn up. I set back into work and went across the field and was on the way back when she did arrive, on Moonshine, and stopped at the end of the rows I was working on. Tractor-hoeing takes a lot of concentration or plants can be ripped out but I soon noticed her and waved. She stood in the stirrups and waved back and then turned Moonshine and trotted off to the corner, gave another long wave and turned up the landway back towards the stables. It was not often she would stop because she didn't want the Boss, if he came along, to think she was stopping me working. It was enough, anyway. The sight of her on that horse was enough to make my day.

I always saved a half cup of tea in my flask for a quick stop at around four in the afternoon and I was just thinking about having it when I saw the Boss pull up in his car at the corner. During the summer months he often drove round the farm in his car rather than the Land-Rover. The field I was in had a landway on either side. I was trying to watch what I was doing and look to see what the Boss was up to at the same time. He got out of the car and a quick look told me that Tony was with him and someone else. They all started to walk to the point I would arrive at shortly. As I got nearer, I suddenly realised that the third person was my Dad. What on earth is he doing here, I thought? Then it hit me. Mum. There must be a problem, but Dad would be with her if there was a problem. My thoughts progressed and my heart sank. I got to the end of the rows and the Boss made the 'turn off' sign with his hand so I stopped the tractor engine, hopped off and went over to them. I could tell from their faces it was bad news and steeled myself, wondering how I would get on without Mum. She had always supported me and been there when needed.

'Graham, I'm so sorry, there's no easy way to say this,' my Dad said, his eyes moist. 'There was an accident on the Oldbarn Lane and Tracy is no longer with us, she's dead. She was taken straight to hospital but was pronounced dead on arrival.' ... My world imploded, collapsed and vanished.

My mind slipped into neutral and stayed there. I was incapable of speech, thought or movement and, had it not been for a hand grabbing my arm, I would have fallen. I felt myself guided to the car and helped inside. I looked out of the window and saw nothing. My mind was a void. There were questions I should be asking but nothing was working. We drove back to the yard and I was transferred to Dad's car and taken home. I got my legs working enough to get indoors and sat at the dining table. My Mum put an arm round my shoulders but was too upset herself to speak.

A cup of tea appeared in front of me and I automatically took a sip. I cleared my throat and in a voice I didn't recognise, asked.

'What happened?' My Dad came over and sat opposite me.

'I don't know the exact details,' he said, his voice hoarse with emotion. 'There were two vehicles involved, a car and a lorry. It seems the car hit the lorry and bounced off into the horse. She didn't stand a chance.'

'What about Moonshine?' I managed to get out. Dad's look told me all I needed to know. I got up and told them I'd like to be on my own for a while and went up to my room, shut the door and sat on the edge of the bed. The sobs started from deep in my gut and were then wrenched out of my throat. It felt as if I was being kicked to death. I rolled over onto the bed and tried to curl up but it was no use; tears poured from me and I gasped for air. I have no idea how long I cried for my love but when I finally managed to half sit up it was getting dark. There was a tap on the door and my Dad came in to see if I wanted anything to eat or drink. I asked him to leave it until morning.

My bed was under the window with just enough room to walk down beside it. I rolled over and sat on it with my arms on the windowsill so I could look down the garden. I felt totally drained of all emotion except grief. I could not imagine how I could go on existing in the world without Tracy by my side. I rested the side of my head on my arms and this brought the corner of the room into sight. Just visible in the gathering darkness was my shotgun. In the top left-hand drawer of the bedroom furniture were at least three boxes of cartridges – I would only need one. I got unsteadily to my feet and walked over to the weapon. It felt cold to my touch, the all too familiar smell of gun oil coming from it as I picked it up. I went to the cartridge drawer and as I did so, in that final flare of light before darkness falls, I caught sight of a photo of Tracy that I had had enlarged and framed. It stood right above where I was heading for and stopped me in my tracks. I looked at her beautiful face and at once knew she would not want me to do this. She valued life and lived it to the full. There was no way she would respect me for taking my own. Almost guiltily I replaced the shotgun in the corner and moved back to where I had been before.

Darkness had now taken over the garden apart from a small piece of lawn illuminated by the lights from the house. I sat and just gazed into the blackness, my mind still not properly functioning. I rested my head on my arms again and must have dozed for a while. When I stirred the moon had risen and every now and again would cast its silvery light across the area before hiding behind the clouds. It had just made one such appearance when a fox, nose down, trotted across the lawn heading for the woods lower down. I bet that's the same one Tracy and me saw from the fox tree, I thought. They are very territorial. I felt the tears start to splash on my hands and the fox became distorted and seemed to swim off the ground as my eyes clouded. Mercifully, the moon faded again and total darkness descended across the garden. I sat and let the grief take over and again cried myself into a fitful doze to wake cold and shaking, still sitting by the window. It was early hours so I laid on the bed and pulled a cover over me and must have slept again because I was woken by the birds singing and daylight in the room. I got up and went downstairs. Mum and Dad were up and produced the usual cup of tea. My throat was dry and the tea tasted like nectar. I managed to eat some breakfast and very slowly my mind started to function. I went off to shave, bath and change my clothes, then to sit in the sitting room. There were a number of thoughts in my head and a lot of them I couldn't add up. Trying to think was impossible, my brain was not functioning correctly. The phone kept ringing and my Dad was kept busy fielding the calls. I kept hearing him say 'thank you' and 'no, he's not really ready to come to the phone just yet'. I asked Dad to find out where Tracy's body had been taken to and what police station had handled the accident call.

In the afternoon, I went out and walked to try and clear the fuzziness from my mind and it was during this walk that it finally clicked back into work and when it did, there were timings that didn't add up and I stopped short in amazement. I know I shouldn't have but I walked on to the fox tree and leaned against it, the bark rough and gnarled under my touch. I sobbed quietly to myself for a while and then seemed to be getting a grip on things and returned home. I phoned the stables but got no reply, so I called Sue's parents. Her Mum answered and, after saying how sorry she was, told me that Sue was there but she thought she would be too upset to speak to me. I asked her to ask Sue if I could come and see her tomorrow as there were some things I needed to know. She was only gone a moment and told me that would be fine.

I went to my room very early and sat trying

to assemble my thoughts into some sort of order, but failed most of the time. I worked out exactly what I needed to do the next day. My Dad had found out the things I had asked him about, so I had somewhere to start. I felt a complete wreck so turned in and dropped to an exhausted sleep. The morning found me more stable and able to muster my thoughts.

I told my folks I was going out on the bike and not to wait lunch for me. I rode into town to the police station and asked the desk chap if I could speak to the officer in charge of Miss Volanen's accident. He asked who I was and then told me I needed to speak to Sgt Ian Bell who was out on duty but would be back in an hour's time. I told him I would return before then and went off and found the funeral directors. I was dreading this but it had to be done. They also asked who I was and then after a ten-minute wait they showed me into their chapel of rest. Tracy looked as stunning as she always did. She had a graze on her forehead and one cheek but otherwise... I laid my hand on her face and knew in an instant that she wasn't there. The spirit and soul that had been Tracy had left. All that remained was the shell, the covering she had worn to walk among us. I left after only a few minutes, dry-eyed, and went for a cup of tea. Later I returned to the police station and waited for the return of

Sgt Bell. He eventually turned up and introduced himself. He was a tall man around 45, starting to go grey at the temples and I thought I detected a slight Scots accent. He took me into a side office and asked how he could help. The desk officer had outlined who I was and what it was about and he had some files with him.

'Can you tell me exactly what happened in the accident?' I asked. He opened a file and his notebook.

'We have been able to establish pretty well exactly what transpired from witness statements,' he told me. 'Miss Volanen was riding the grey horse towards the stables where I understand she resided with another girl. She was approaching the bend before the entrance to the unnamed lane that loops round past the stables. A delivery lorry approached from behind her and, inadvisably, as it turned out, pulled out to pass her. A car coming the other way, perhaps rather too quickly, rounded the bend and found the lane blocked by the lorry and Miss Volanen. He braked and the lane being wet and a bit muddy just there, down between the banks, caused the car to slide. It was in collision with the near side front of the lorry which threw it into the horse being ridden by Miss Volanen. The horse reared up as it was struck and Miss Volanen was thrown backwards onto the lane. The horse then went right over and because of the bank on one side and the lorry on the other, it landed on top of her.'

He opened another file and looked through it.

'This is the post-mortem report,' he said. 'Are you sure you want me to tell you this?'

'Can you just outline it for me?' I asked him.

'Right, from the report it would appear that Miss Volanen struck the lane with the back of her head, fracturing her skull and that this blow would have rendered her unconscious and would possibly have been fatal. The horse then landed on her, causing multiple injuries of which at least four would have been fatal. It is probably merciful that she was knocked unconscious as soon as she fell.'

'Thank you.' I was struggling to hold it together. 'Can you give me the exact timing of the accident?' He consulted his notebook and another file.

'Right, the first emergency call was received at control timed at twelve fifty,' he read. I felt goose pimples spreading up my back.

'The police and ambulance were on scene at five past one and transported the casualty to hospital where Miss Volanen was declared dead on arrival at ... two fifteen.' He stopped and looked up.

'Are you all right, lad?' he asked. 'You're as white as a sheet. Would you like a glass of water?'

'I'm ... OK, thanks,' I managed to say, my mind spinning wildly.

'Is there anything else you would like to know?' he asked.

'Yes, it's Moonshine, the horse.' I was fighting to keep my voice level and maintain my senses. 'Have you got any information?'

He rifled through the files and after opening a couple, found what he was looking for.

'Right, yes, the horse was obviously badly hurt and was unable to stand. It had managed to get itself off Miss Volanen but was in a very distressed condition. The local vet, Mr Bowen, was contacted by his office as a result of our call, timed at one zero seven. It was lucky that he was at a local farm and was on the accident scene at one twenty. He carried out a very quick examination and diagnosed that the animal's right leg was broken in several places and was dislocated from the shoulder. He therefore terminated its life by injection at one twenty-five.'

He put the paper he had been reading from back in the file and picked up the others, patting them into a neat pile. He cleared his throat.

'Can I just say how sorry I am,' he said quietly. 'In this job you get to attend at quite a number of accidents. This was one of the worst and most difficult to deal with from the point of view of the emergency teams involved. The young age of the casualty and the fact that she was quite obviously a beautiful girl, plus the horse, plus the fact that nothing that occurred was her fault, made it all the harder.'

'Thanks for all your time and trouble,' I said, standing up. 'Will there be prosecutions for the drivers involved?'

'I'm sorry, but I can't comment on that. It's not up to the local police; a decision will be made elsewhere,' he replied. We shook hands and I left the station much more dazed than when I went in.

I sat sidesaddle on the bike in the car park and tried to make sense of what had occurred. I had seen positive police records to show that Tracy had been declared dead on arrival at the hospital at 2.15 and that Moonshine was put to sleep at 1.25. Yet she had ridden along the edge of the field, on Moonshine, at 2.15, give or take a few minutes.

I started the bike and set off towards the farm. I rode along the landway and propped the bike at the end of the hedge at the top side of the field.

The field lay on the side of a gentle valley and sloped down from the hedge where I now stood and where I had sat and eaten my lunch. There was a landway on both sides and I guessed that Tracy would have ridden in on the one on my left hand as I drove up towards the hedge. There was a tree on that end of the hedge and another about two-thirds of the way along and it was in front of that tree she had turned to face me and waved. I could remember her and Moonshine being silhouetted against the foliage. She had then turned and ridden to the right hand landway, waved again and rode off. Because of the slope in the field it was not possible to see along either landway on the far side of the hedge. I knew that if Tracy rode along a field she always kept right to the very edge. With that in mind I walked slowly the width of the field, looking from the edge out a couple of yards. I then walked back again close to the plants so as to cover the whole headland. There was not a hoofprint anywhere.

I looked at the left-hand landway and found plenty of prints but none leading off to the edge of the field. The right-hand landway also had lots of prints but none coming off the field. I had to look but, you know, I wasn't really expecting to find any. How could there have been any? The horse and rider, when I saw them, were no longer tied to this earth. They were free spirits able to roam the cosmos as they wished. I sat on the grass under the tree where I had eaten my lunch and put my head in my hands. Visions came to me of Tracy and Moonshine galloping up star-lit valleys, her blonde hair streaming behind her, giving the little whoops of pleasure that she was prone to.

Quite suddenly my mood lightened – it was all right. I would miss her like crazy and I would love her all my life. But I was enormously comforted in the knowledge that somehow, somewhere in a life and substance that I could not even hope to understand, she and her wonderful horse lived on. I must have sat there for an hour and then remembered I had another call to make. Sue.

Chapter 23

I stood for a moment at the corner of the field and looked back along the headland, my mind still not really able to take in what had happened. At last I tore myself away and rode to see Sue. Mrs Weston, Sue's Mum, answered the door and ushered me in, all the time saying what a tragedy it was and how sorry she was, for which I thanked her. She showed me into their neat and tidy sitting room where Sue stood up as I entered. She came over and put her arms round me and sobbed on my shoulder. Her Mum went off to make tea and I got Sue to dry her eyes and sit down.

'What's happening at the stables?' I asked, hoping to get her to think of something else.

'Mrs W came straight over when I phoned and told her what had happened,' Sue explained. 'She's staying at the flat. I'll probably go back there tomorrow. Then I suppose she will have to find someone else.'

'She must be pretty upset losing Tracy and Moonshine,' I said. Sue looked at me oddly. Her Mum brought in a pot of tea and a couple of fine china cups along with a small plate of assorted biscuits and left us alone.

Sue remained quiet as if pondering on something. She passed me the plate of biscuits and I remembered I'd missed lunch so took a couple. She drew a deep breath, almost a sigh and said at last.

'Moonshine belonged to Tracy. I was a bit surprised she hadn't told you, but thinking about it, I know why she didn't.' She poured out the tea and passed me a cup.

'Do you feel up to telling me about it, Sue?' I asked. She thought again for a moment and then replied.

'Yes, I think you should know. It might explain a few things. Tracy was like you, she was eager to leave school. Because of her looks she was pestered all the time by boys. She had been mad on horses from a small child so it was natural she would want to work with them.' Sue stopped for a sip of tea, then went on:

'She took three equestrian courses at the local Agricultural College and managed to get a job with a stables close to her parents' place. The owner was a chap called Charlie Turner. She had just turned sixteen. It all worked out well for her. She was a quick learner and Charlie taught her a lot and gave her more and more responsibility which she loved.' Sue's Mum appeared and took away the tea pot for refilling. Sue collected her thoughts and continued:

'Tracy kept on doing courses with Charlie's

355

blessing and, with all the knowledge she had acquired, became a top girl at the stables. She had a favourite horse there called Molly, I believe, that looked like it was going to foal overnight. Tracy said she would stay with her and make sure all was well. Molly started pushing late evening but by midnight had got nowhere so Tracy thought she better check her, you know, internally. Right at that moment there was a power cut but there was a bright full moon that was shining straight in the stable. Tracy used the moonlight to check Molly and found that the foal had a leg back, so after a good old struggle, she got it pushed back and the leg forward. Molly then went ahead and Tracy delivered the foal around four in the morning, all the time working by moonlight. When Charlie and the others arrived in the morning, Molly was standing quietly and the foal and Tracy were snuggled up in the corner fast asleep. Because of the power cut and that, Tracy asked Charlie if it could be called Moonshine.'

'So that's where the name came from!' I exclaimed. The full pot of tea arrived and Mrs Weston asked if I wanted anything to eat which I declined with thanks. Sue stirred the pot and refilled our cups and I pinched another biscuit. We had a drink and Sue thought some more.

'Three days later the mare, Molly, suffered a massive heart attack and dropped dead.

There was a panic search for a foster mare but one couldn't be found anywhere. Everyone thought the foal would never survive but Tracy wouldn't give up on it. She bottle-fed it every two hours, warming up milk and supplement the vet provided on a primus stove in the tack room. She slept in the stable with it for over a month until it was advanced enough to drink out of a bucket. By this time Tracy was just about out on her feet. I don't have to tell you the foal survived until,' tears welled in her eyes, 'the day before yesterday.' She broke off and sobbed quietly. I poured yet more tea while she wiped her eyes and blew her nose.

'You OK, love?' I asked. 'Drink some tea and have a break.' I patted her hands and put my hand on her shoulder.

'I'm all right,' she said, 'it's just so awful I...'

'I know.' I tried to find words to comfort her but couldn't. She gradually regained control and looked more at ease.

'So how did Tracy come to own Moonshine?' I asked. She looked troubled as if not quite sure of her ground and then said.

'I'm sure Tracy would have told you and it's best you know. When Moonshine was six months old, Charlie dropped a bombshell and said he was going to sell up. Tracy asked him straight away if she could buy Moonshine. The price he wanted was a good way above what Tracy could afford. She asked him to give her some time to raise the funds, which he agreed to. Tracy sold all her jewellery and lots of other stuff and borrowed from everyone she could, including her Mum and Dad.

'She gave Charlie all she had got but it was still short of what he wanted so she asked him for more time and asked if she could pay him off out of her wages for as long as it took. Charlie agreed, because he knew how much she wanted that foal and he felt sorry for her. He wrote her out a bill of sale because he knew he could trust her. Tracy has been trying to pay back all the money she borrowed ever since she came to Mrs W's, as well as keeping up her deal with Charlie. That's why she didn't have any clothes or bits and pieces. Just about everything she wore she borrowed from me.'

'How did she meet Mrs W?' I asked.

'When she took Moonshine away from Charlie's, after the sale, she had to put her in livery even though she was just about broke. It was there she met Mrs W, who had just bought the stables at Oldbarn. I used to work at the livery and Mrs W sort of recruited us both to come and work at Oldbarn.

'Tracy worked out a deal with Mrs W so that she could keep Moonshine there and have so much deducted from her pay for feed and stuff.

'That made it more difficult to pay back

the money she owed. There was a time I thought she would starve to death.' Sue checked and muttered, 'Sorry.' I waved it aside. 'The reason she didn't tell you is because she knew what you were like and was sure you would want to help her, you know, financially. She didn't want you to think she had taken up with you because you are, well, sort of well set up.'

'I wish,' I laughed. 'I had to borrow off my Dad to buy Tracy's engagement ring.'

'You know what I mean, though,' Sue said quietly.

'It must have been a struggle for her to buy me Christmas and birthday gifts,' I said.

'Well, it was a bit,' Sue replied 'but she would have walked over hot coals for you, Graham. She loved you like nothing else, even more than Moonshine and you have just heard how much she loved that horse.'

'I know, Sue,' I managed to say, struggling for control.

'Now you can see why she was in such a state when the Willie Williams problem started,' Sue said. 'Mrs W had been so good to her. She didn't want to be the one to break up their marriage. You were her knight in shining armour that day, I can tell you.'

'Yes, I see now,' I mused. 'I thought she was overreacting a bit but now I know the things you have just told me ... well, it's understandable.'

We were both silent for a while, busy with our own thoughts. Sue finished her tea and turned to me again and said:

'Tracy contacted Charlie just to let him know she was getting married and would be moving a short way. He was brilliant and cancelled the rest of the debt, saying it was his wedding present to her. Her Mum and Dad had already been paid back, so for the first time for ages she was able to spend a bit on herself and buy some clothes and things.'

'I thought she seemed lighter and less worried,' I told Sue. 'That was obviously the reason.'

'Yes, it was a great relief to her, I can tell you. She didn't want to get married with any secrets between the two of you,' Sue replied.

'Sue, can you tell me about the day of the accident?' I asked. 'I have been to the police station and got the full report from them. I would just like to know why Tracy was where she was and what her plans were for the day.' Sue looked at me a bit confused as if wondering why I wanted to know. She then explained.

'Well, the farrier was due at three in the afternoon. She was going to ride Moonshine round to see you lunchtime, then come back here and grab a bite to eat. She would then see to the farrier and ride out on Bobo and lead Trixie. She had got Moonie

360

all tacked up around midday when the farrier phoned – you know the phone has got an outside bell – to ask if he could come at one. Tracy couldn't not go on Moonie because she was all tacked up and restless to be off, so she decided to go a short way and be back for one. Then she would ride Boots round to see you and one or other of us would see to the other two.' I nodded.

'It's crazy how things happen,' I said. 'If the farrier had stuck to his original time, Tracy would not have been on the lane at that time.'

'Yes, I know,' she replied. 'I thought the same thing.'

'Well, I had better be going,' I said, getting to my feet. 'Thanks for telling me about Moonshine and everything. It's made a lot of things clear to me now.'

'I'm certain Tracy would have told you in her own good time.' She came over and hugged me. 'I'm so sorry for you. You are going to miss her so much ... we all will.'

'Yes,' I agreed. 'It's never going to be the same without her.'

I said goodbye to her and Mrs Weston and went on my way. It was getting on in the afternoon but I had one more call I had to make.

I parked the bike and walked up the short path to Ralf and Amy's front door. My knock produced an outrage of barking from Douglas and when Ralf opened the door, the dog had a brief sniff at me and went looking for Tracy. It knew that, if I arrived, Tracy would be there too. After a struggle, it was persuaded to return inside. Ralf stood aside for me to enter.

'Graham,' he said, 'how good of you to call. You must be as devastated as we both are. Come in, please.' He showed me into their sitting room where just a short time ago, I had asked for his daughter's hand. Amy got up as I entered and started to cry before she reached me. I put my arms round her and held her while she sobbed for her only child. Tracy had told me there had been serious complications when she was born and her Mum was unable to have any more children. Ralf went off to make tea. My God, I thought if I drink much more tea I shall drown in it, what a way to go! Amy at last regained control and apologised.

'Please,' I said, 'it's best to cry. I've done enough over the last twenty four hours.'

'It's so terrible for you,' Amy sniffed. 'Your whole life to spend together and now it's all gone.' Ralf returned with the tea and we sat and talked mostly about Tracy. I told them I had been talking to Sue and learned about Moonshine.

'Ah, so, Tracy never told you she owned Moonshine,' Ralf said. 'I can guess why.'

'Sue's already solved that little riddle,' I told them. We talked for half an hour or so and then I said I had better be getting home as I had been out all day. I kissed Amy and said I would see her soon, and Ralf showed me out. In the hall he put his hand on my arm and said:

'I would like for you to have these.' He opened his hand and showed me Tracy's engagement ring and the gold locket I had given her for her 21st birthday.

'I'm sorry about the locket,' he said. 'The door is missing and the police said they were unable to find it. They were a bit mystified as to how it got damaged.'

'Thank you, Ralf,' I croaked, unable to control the tears that were running down my cheeks. 'I'll cherish these always.' He put his arm round my shoulders and neither of us could say more than 'goodbye'.

I rode home, my mind still not able to cope with a few things, but a lot of blanks filled in. My Mum and Dad had been worried about my long absence but soon understood when I told them where I had been.

Next day there was a lot of unwinding to be done and all sorts of cancellations to be made. I sent a cable to the shipping line that Barry worked for and they were able to get a message to him. He phoned a day later and was almost unable to speak, as I was. He had really taken a shine to Tracy and was looking forward to his duty as best man.

Nine days later it was Tracy's funeral. I remained quite composed because I knew we were not laying Tracy to rest, just her earthly image. I was able to read a eulogy I had written about the all-too-short time I had known her. I said I thought she was the most beautiful girl I had ever seen, with her warm and ready smile. I spoke of her love of the countryside and its animals, especially Moonshine. I spoke of the love that we had shared, how it had blossomed into an almost spiritual thing that was beyond our understanding. I told the congregation that our love would live on, that I would never forget her and I thanked God for the privilege of having her in my life if only for such a short while. The day passed with tears and memories as those days do and finally finished.

On returning home I went for a walk alone and made the effort of trying to put my life back together. There was a huge void that I doubted would ever be filled, but I knew that Tracy would want me to rebuild and to live what was left of my life and to try and be happy again. The next day I returned to work. This was tough because everyone wanted to say how sorry they were and there were tears from a lot of the girls, especially Katie. I was glad when I was once again alone with the tractor and my thoughts.

A week or so later there was an inquest. I decided not to go as I had no wish to see the persons responsible for Tracy's death. A verdict of accidental death was recorded. Both drivers were prosecuted and found guilty of careless driving and were fined. I don't suppose they had the faintest idea of the shattering grief they had caused.

The harvest continued as if nothing had happened and at last we got the fine spell and wrapped it up in the first week of October. The 15th passed as just another day and I tried to keep as busy as possible but admit to some tears as I tried to sleep that night. Later in the year, Tony married Jane in a quiet service in Surrey where her folks lived and where she had been born.

The following Spring I was honoured to be best man at the wedding of Sue and Andy. It was a wondrous happy occasion and the bride looked beautiful. Now I am even more honoured to be godfather to their three children. I worked at Manor Farm for another five years until, out of the blue, Dad said he had received an exceptional offer for his business and was selling up. He had decided to buy a farm and wanted me to go into partnership with him and run it for him, but that's another story.

I never mentioned to anyone about Tracy's visit to me in the field that fateful day. After all, who would believe me? I considered it should be our secret. Now as I approach 70 years of age, I consider the story should be told. If I raise my eyes from my writing desk, hanging on my study wall in front of me, is a painting. It was done by a wonderful artist who specialises in painting a likeness from a photograph. It was done in the Summer before Tracy and I were due to get married. It was to have been my wedding gift to her.

Hanging over one corner of the painting is a locket. On the chain is also a ring with three diamonds. The locket is complete with its little door, because, you see, when I searched that headland for hoofprints, I didn't find any, but I did find something. When I sat on the grass under the tree and put my head in my hands, there by my feet was the locket door, the horse's head engraving on the front, and inside the words I had asked to be put there, *'My Darling. I will love you for eternity'*. The jeweller I purchased it from refitted it for me.

The painting is of a white horse, all tacked up, ears pricked ready to go. It's just waiting for its rider who is also its saviour and its owner. There is a little brass plate on the bottom that I polish now and again. It reads: *'Yours for ever. MOONSHINE'*.

The publishers hope that this book has given you enjoyable reading. Large Print Books are especially designed to be as easy to see and hold as possible. If you wish a complete list of our books please ask at your local library or write directly to:

Magna Large Print Books
Magna House, Long Preston,
Skipton, North Yorkshire.
BD23 4ND

This Large Print Book, for people
who cannot read normal print,
is published under the auspices of

THE ULVERSCROFT FOUNDATION